THE JINGLER'S LUCK

THE JINGLER'S LUCK

The Sixth Thomas the Falconer Mystery

John Pilkington

severn House

This first world edition published in Great Britain 2006 by
SEVERN HOUSE PUBLISHERS LTD of
9–15 High Street, Sutton, Surrey SM1 1DF.
This first world edition published in the USA 2006 by
SEVERN HOUSE PUBLISHERS INC of
595 Madison Avenue, New York, N.Y. 10022.

British Library Cataloguing in Publication Data

Pilkington, John, 1948-
    The jingler's luck. - (A Thomas the falconer mystery)
    1.   Thomas the Falconer (Fictitious character) - Fiction
    2.   Great Britain - History - Elizabeth, 1558-1603 - Fiction
    3.   Detective and mystery stories
    I.   Title
    823.9'14 [F]

ISBN-13: 978-0-7278-6373-7
ISBN-10: 0-7278-6373-8

All Severn House titles are printed on acid-free paper.

Typeset by Palimpsest Book Production Ltd.,
Polmont, Stirlingshire, Scotland.
Printed and bound in Great Britain by
MPG Books Ltd., Bodmin, Cornwall.

To David, who knows more about rivers
than I ever will.

Prologue

The ice was coming.

Lowdy Garth could feel it in his bones as he walked slowly along Deptford Strand in the grey dawn. He paused by the water's edge, muffled in his heavy woollen jerkin and seaman's toque, and looked across the river to the marshy wastes of the Isle of Dogs. Gulls wheeled above his head, their screams ringing in the still air. He nodded to himself: the river would freeze soon, not only above the Bridge, but maybe below it, too. Already, to Lowdy's eyes, the water looked slow and heavy. The last two days had been colder than he could recall in years. His breath steamed out before him, and to his surprise he shivered.

His thoughts drifted, recalling other times when the Thames had iced over. He could go back thirty years: to the great Frost Fair of 1564, when the young Queen Elizabeth had danced on the ice, surrounded by admiring courtiers . . . he half-smiled to himself. The very sun had seemed to come out, wherever she went . . . he fancied he had seen it reflect off her jewels. His rheumy eyes narrowed as he groped for vaguer memories . . . old King Henry riding along the ice with his frail queen Jane Seymour, all the way from the city down to Greenwich. When was that – fifty years ago? No . . . nearer sixty. Lowdy shook his head. He was but a small boy, back then. Now he was an old man – of no more use than the flotsam that lay along the shoreline, washed down-river from London. He drew a long breath, and turned to resume his eastward trudge, past the water-gate towards Deptford.

It wouldn't do, all this dwelling on the past. But in spite of himself, he gazed ahead at the familiar masts of the

1

Golden Hind, beached beside the mouth of Deptford Creek. There was no denying it: Drake's famous vessel, her timbers hacked and chipped at by souvenir-hunters, had become a forlorn sight. For years she had lain in dry dock, near to the Queen's great palace of Placentia, whose towers loomed in the distance. Lowdy recalled the spring of 1581, a few months after the old privateer's triumphant return from his voyage around the world. He remembered the great crowd watching as Drake was knighted on board ship by Her Majesty. That day the riverside had rung with cheers, as he arose Sir Francis, the greatest seaman in Europe. Who could have guessed at the times which lay ahead: war with Spain . . . the great Armada . . . and now?

Now the Queen too was past her sixty years, like Lowdy was, and even the most deluded optimist on the Privy Council had finally accepted that she would never marry, let alone produce an heir. It was said the new breed of young courtiers flattered her shamelessly, calling her Gloriana and Astraea – ageless and beautiful; then mocked her the moment her back was turned. Already their loyalties were shifting towards James of Scotland as England's likely king – yet Elizabeth herself stubbornly refused to name an heir. And why should she, Lowdy grunted to himself. The moment the Queen's life was spent they would cast her aside, like one of the dead dogs he sometimes came across, washed up on the strand . . .

He stopped. There was something floating in the shallows . . . he watched as a small wave nudged it ashore – then he stiffened. Thoughts of dead dogs, even of dead cattle, faded at once. Lowdy Garth knew a corpse when he saw one.

He walked forward, his heavy boots crunching on the gravel. To his right, smoke was beginning to rise from the chimneys of the waterfront cottages. He glanced about, saw that no one was yet outdoors. Grimly, he approached the water-logged body.

In a lifetime spent by the waterside, and on the seas too,

Lowdy had seen many terrible things. He had fought for Sir John Hawkins, the wicked old slave-trader. He had known murderous brawls in the sailors' taverns of Limehouse and Wapping; he had survived yellow fever in the tropics, and plague in London. Yet there were sights that could still unsettle him, and this was to be one of them.

The corpse was that of a young woman, dressed in a good taffeta gown, cut low at the neck. Her blonde hair was unbound, floating like weeds in the water. Then, as the body rolled, Lowdy drew breath sharply. For the face which turned towards him was unrecognizable. It was horribly scarred, from the cheeks to the neck: the skin blotched red and purple, puckered as if ravaged by some nameless disease. The glassy eyes stared past him into nothingness.

He looked towards the waterfront, hearing distant sounds of the village rising: the bark of a dog, a door slamming, a shouted greeting. From the royal shipyards came the thud of a heavy timber being dropped. He turned his gaze back towards the dead woman. Now he caught the glint of silver. One of her hands floated free; there were rings upon the fingers.

Lowdy hesitated a moment, then stepped into the icy shallows, reached down and gripped the woman's heavy skirts. Gently he drew the body from the water, feet first, and dragged it up on to the strand. He stopped, breathing heavily, staring down at the terrible face. What had caused such cruel disfigurement, he did not know. On closer inspection, the marks resembled burns. He frowned, and tried to look beyond the scar tissue. He saw the fine bone structure, the well-shaped nose, the large eyes . . . whoever she was, he decided, she had once been an attractive woman.

There came a shout. Lowdy glanced round, saw two boys trotting towards him with fishing poles on their shoulders. He raised a hand, then saw that one was Richard Rycroft, the constable's son. As the pair drew closer, he called out.

'Fetch your father, boy! There's a poor soul drowned . . .'

The boys stopped, staring at the shape at Lowdy's feet. Young Richard dropped his pole and ran back towards the village.

The other boy came forward, eyes wide with excitement. Lowdy turned back to gaze down at the dead woman. By the look of her she had been in the water all night, perhaps longer . . . he sighed. Could her dreadful appearance have some bearing on her death? He had known of young girls taking their own lives for less: jumping from the Bridge into the arms of old Father Thames . . .

'Lord save us, Lowdy . . . what happened to 'er face?'

The boy with the fishing pole was looking down in horror. But Lowdy made no reply. He dropped to his knee on the shingle beside the young woman, peering at her throat. He frowned; he had seen bruising like that before . . . gingerly, he reached out and touched the woman's cheek, then drew his hand back at once. Above him, the boy gasped. Both of them saw the head fall loosely aside, like a doll's. But the sight meant more to Lowdy Garth than it did to the youngster. Whoever she was, he realized, she had been strangled, her neck broken.

Lowdy stood up stiffly. From the village he heard shouts, but he was unable to take his eyes off the young woman. What in heaven's name could such a poor, freakish creature have done, he wondered, to get herself murdered?

Overhead the gulls gathered, shrieking. Angrily Lowdy waved his arms to scatter them. But there followed the harsh cries of crows – a small flock of them, flying out from the trees beyond Deptford Green. Already, the winged creatures seemed to smell carrion. Lowdy threw out his arms again. The boy, sensing his mood, dropped his fishing pole and ran at the birds, shouting and sending them flapping away. Then he came back to where Lowdy stood. There the boy and the old man stayed, as if keeping silent vigil over the body of the young woman who had no name, and no face.

*　　*　　*

4

At the same moment, a few miles upriver, a group of watermen sat in their boats below the Old Swan Stairs, gazing at the sight they had dreaded for the past week: sheets of ice spreading outwards from the piers of London Bridge . . .

One

The ground was iron-hard, and the grass crackled under Thomas the falconer's feet as he walked down from the Ridgway towards the manor.

He wore thick breeches and his heavy winter jerkin. Used to the outdoors as he was, the chill barely troubled him. For her part, the big falcon sitting hooded on his gauntlet seemed oblivious to the cold. She was a wily old haggard that Thomas had been hard pressed to train at the lure, these past months. But as a hunter, she surpassed any of those presently in his master's possession. He had yet to find a name that would do her justice.

He took her back to the mews, settling her on her perch and noting with approval that all the birds seemed content. Ned Hawes, his helper, had done his work well. No longer did Thomas fret about leaving the boy in charge. He turned to glance downhill towards the great house. Smoke rose from the Petbury chimneys, thin columns of blue-grey in the still morning air. From the kitchen yard, the wood-cutter's axe rang out. It was turning into a hard winter, the Downland folk said – and worse was to come. There would be snow by Christmas . . .

Thomas was thoughtful. Surely Sir Robert would be home by then? His master had been in London for a month, and had sent no word. It was unlike him – and as a result, gossip was rife throughout the estate. According to Thomas's daughter Eleanor, maid to Lady Margaret, the mistress was fretful. Still dwelling on the matter, he was about to go to his cottage when he was hailed by a servant, calling from the garden archway. It seemed his breakfast would have to wait.

A few minutes later he was conducted to Sir Robert's morning chamber, where his master often received him to give instruction. But today Lady Margaret was seated behind her husband's carved oak table, which was scattered with papers. Though the mistress of Petbury normally did the household accounts, the sight of her in Sir Robert's private room was rare. At her side sat Martin, the white-headed old steward, muffled in his heavy black gown, though a good fire crackled in the hearth. Thomas came forward and made his bow.

Lady Margaret, in a blue morning gown and narrow ruff, nodded absently. Martin coughed, and gestured to a jug that stood before the fire.

'There's mulled ale, falconer . . . will you act as footman and pour us each a mug?'

Thomas went to take up the pot. He filled two pewter cups with the steaming brew and offered one to Lady Margaret, who waved a hand in refusal. He and Martin were left to drink alone. After a moment, having waited in vain for his mistress to speak, Martin frowned and cleared phlegm from his throat.

'Sir Robert . . .' He cleared his throat again. 'As you are aware, falconer, Sir Robert journeyed to London for the Queen's Accession Day Tilts . . . November seventeenth, that is. He was honoured to be called . . . indeed, since he went hawking with Her Majesty last year at Cowdray he seems to have found favour with her, if somewhat later in life than most . . .'

Lady Margaret shifted impatiently. These days, the thoughts of her ageing steward tended to wander somewhat. When Martin paused and turned an enquiring gaze towards her, his mistress spoke. 'Thomas, I know we may be plain with you. Sir Robert was supposed to return home by Advent Sunday – almost two weeks ago. And here we are in mid-December . . .' she shrugged. 'Yet, if he could hear the news that reached us last night, from Stanbury,' she continued, 'I am certain he would wish to hurry back at once.' She smiled slightly. 'Our daughter Ann has borne a child – a fine healthy boy. Sir Robert and I are now grandparents.'

Thomas returned her smile. 'That's wondrous news, my Lady . . .'

Lady Margaret inclined her head. 'So . . . as you see, word should be taken to Sir Robert with all speed.'

It was then that Thomas realized he had not been summoned merely to be told the good news. 'My Lady,' he began, 'surely any servant, well-mounted, could carry such a message . . .'

'Indeed, falconer . . .' Martin coughed, and threw a sidelong glance at his mistress. 'The matter is, I . . . we think it wise to send a man of discretion. It is possible Sir Robert is in some difficulty or other . . .' He broke off, somewhat awkwardly, whereupon Lady Margaret spoke up.

'He was to be the guest of our good friend Sir Marcus Brooke, at his house on the strand. Yet it seems he is no longer there.'

There was a silence, before Martin broke in.

'My Lady, we do not know that for certain,' he countered. 'We only know he has been absent . . . it may be that the Queen has him dancing daily attendance on her, as she does all her courtiers. At Richmond, say, or Whitehall . . .'

'I realize that,' Lady Margaret replied. 'Yet to have no word, in all this time . . .' She drew herself to her full height, which was always impressive, and looked Thomas directly in the eye. 'I do not thrust this commission upon you,' she said quietly. 'I know you have your work – but then Ned is a capable deputy. I do but ask you, as a favour to me, to travel to London, find my husband by any means you can and tell him the good news. I'm sure that when he hears it, he will be grateful for your seeking him out.'

Thomas sighed inwardly, but he did not hesitate. 'Of course, my Lady,' he answered. 'I will leave today.'

And Lady Margaret's smile was such that he could only return it and make his bow. He would have more than enough time on the long journey, he knew, to rail at her for sending him to London in the middle of winter. Since there seemed nothing more to say, he turned to go. But as he opened the door, he heard the scrape of a stool on the flagged floor. Martin was shuffling round the table towards him.

'I will give you full directions, falconer,' he muttered, which caused Thomas to glance from the old steward back to Lady Margaret. Only then did he see how distressed she was. But Martin was upon him, urging him outside with an impatient frown. The two of them went out into the passage. Not until they had walked the length of the house, to emerge from a side door into the gardens, did the steward speak.

'This is for your ears alone,' he said. His face was grim, the lines of care deeper than ever. Thomas kept his silence, waiting for the old man to address him. When at last he did so, it was in a voice of some distaste.

'I fear . . . nay, I hear rumours, of a certain lady.'

Thomas raised his eyebrows.

'Only rumours, I repeat,' the old steward continued hastily. 'Yet . . .' In agitation he gripped Thomas's arm, causing him to look down in surprise. The two of them had never been close friends – indeed, they had often been at loggerheads. What united them, Thomas well knew, was their devotion to Lady Margaret – which over the years, though neither of them would have admitted it, had somehow grown stronger than the loyalty they bore towards Sir Robert.

He met the old man's watery eyes. 'You think this one is more serious than the others?'

After a moment, Martin nodded. 'You and I both know something of the world, falconer,' he said, 'and we know Sir Robert. It's an open secret that he has taken his pleasures elsewhere at times . . . particularly in recent years.' He shook his head. 'My Lady has borne it with the stoicism which we know is but a shield for the hurt she suffers. But then, each dalliance has been brief and of little consequence . . . always he returns to her, and becomes the devoted husband once again.'

He paused. 'But what I hear of Lady Imogen Semple fills me with dread.'

The name meant nothing to Thomas. He waited.

'A widow,' the steward said, frowning. 'Yet still in her prime . . . as sharp-witted and as beautiful, as she is vain and covetous. It would be hard for any man to resist her charms, should she have designs upon him . . .' he faltered.

'And from what I have been able to discover, she has designs upon my master.'

Thomas was frowning too. 'Are the reports reliable?'

'I fear so,' Martin replied, 'and there is worse.' He shivered, and thrust his hands into the wide sleeves on his gown. 'Falconer – Thomas, this is more than a matter of your finding Sir Robert and telling him of his new grandchild. I believe you will need all your wits, and your powers of persuasion, to make him see the error of his ways. For I hear from Sir Marcus's lawyer, Doctor Perkins, that our master is thinking of purchasing a town house. A figure of four thousand pounds has been mentioned . . .'

Thomas blinked. 'A tidy sum, even for Sir Robert,' he murmured, but Martin shook his head impatiently.

'That isn't all! I have kept the letter from my Lady, for fear it would distress her – yet it cannot remain a secret for long. According to Perkins, Sir Robert is spending lavishly – I may even say recklessly. On clothes and jewels, on a new Neapolitan horse and heaven knows what else – the bulk of his money showered upon the Lady Imogen! I begin to think he has taken leave of his senses!'

Thomas returned the old man's gaze. 'It's not unknown for men of his age to behave in such a manner,' he said. 'As if they burn to recapture their younger days, before they grow too old to play at barley-brake.'

'Indeed . . .' Martin shook his head helplessly. 'The matter appals me. The consequences for his position, let alone for his family, could be very grave indeed.'

Thomas gazed across the frosty lawn towards the paddock. In the distance, grooms were exercising the Petbury horses. 'What aims do you think this Lady Imogen might have?' he asked. 'Sir Robert is a well-known knight of this shire, from a family of ancient lineage, with wife and children . . . what could she hope for, save that he treat her as a kept woman? He is seldom in London, in any case . . .'

'Until now,' Martin finished. 'And he shows no sign of coming home.' His frown deepened. 'As for her designs, I cannot fathom them. But her reputation is such that I am full of foreboding.' He fixed Thomas with his watery blue eyes.

11

'My hopes, as well as my Lady's, rest on you, Thomas. There's none from Petbury that Sir Robert trusts more – none, indeed, that he would listen to as he will you.' He hesitated. 'Who is more resourceful than you? And who else but you would dare confront him in such a matter?'

Thomas drew a long breath. 'You lay a heavy charge upon me, master steward.'

'I do,' Martin agreed. He looked away briefly, then added: 'Mayhap I should have said this long ago: I too trust no one more than you, to bring our master to his senses and get him home.'

There the matter was, laid out in its simplicity. After a brief silence, Thomas clapped the old man on the shoulder, then walked off to find Ned, and give him what instructions he could. His thoughts were whirling: Eleanor too, he must see – and lastly Nell, Petbury's celebrated cook – who also happened to be his wife. He grimaced, knowing how she would take it: with their duties, they saw little enough of each other as it was. Now he had but a short time to make his farewells – and no idea of how long he would be gone.

Two days later, after a punishing ride across two counties, Thomas walked his black gelding, one of the best in the Petbury stable, through the village of St Giles. On all sides, chimneys smoked, dogs barked and folk in their winter clothes pressed about him. Through a tangled maze of streets he rode downhill, towards the ribbon of large houses that lay along the strand, fronting the river all the way to Westminster. And it was here, passing down a narrow way to the water-side, that he received his first shock since leaving West Berkshire: for the Thames had disappeared. The great lead-grey, sluggish stream that he knew, lay hidden under a vast expanse of ice that reached from shore to shore.

On his journey, he had passed frozen ponds and leaped over frozen streams, but never had he seen anything like this. He drew his mount to a halt and sat gazing at the wondrous sight, the mingled breath of horse and rider puffing out in clouds. Stretching out before him, where there should have been water, was a great field of dull white. And where there should have been barges and wherries, and the grand vessels of noblemen, there were people: moving in all directions, singly and in groups. From all sides came the shouts of children: some skating, others pulling sleighs. Further off . . . Thomas rubbed his eyes, as if unsure of what he saw, but there was no mistaking it: a coach, drawn by a full team of horses, was crossing towards Lambeth. Could the ice really be of such thickness?

Scanning the teeming vista he now made out other riders, while away to his left a jumble of booths and tents stood upon the ice, with a small crowd about them. It was almost a fair . . . then he remembered: Frost Fairs, they called them. Beyond the tents, in the distance, the great bulk of the Bridge loomed like a rampart. But now, no boats would shoot the rushing waters between the arches. In their place Thomas fancied he could see boys sliding down the icy slopes to the Pool of London below . . . which was a further shock. He had heard, in hard winters, of the slow-moving Thames freezing above the Bridge, the wide piers acting as a dam; he did not know the waters below it could freeze too. Did the ice reach all the way out to sea?

Then, it was mighty cold . . . as if to remind him of it, his tired horse stamped a hoof and shook its head. He glanced at the sky: already the afternoon was waning. He reached forward and patted the animal's neck. Their needs were the same: a good supper and a warm bed. He tugged at the rein, and turned the gelding's head away from the frozen river, towards the mansion of Sir Marcus Brooke, between Somerset House and the Savoy.

At the gate he was challenged, and gave his name and station. But the bearded servant in Sir Marcus's livery stared at him blank-faced.

'Sir Robert? He's gone from here, more than a week since.'

Thomas returned the man's stare. 'Then I ask leave to speak with Sir Marcus . . . I've news from my mistress.'

'Sir Marcus is in the city on business,' the other answered. 'And Lady Alice is unwell. Give me your message and I'll convey it.'

Thomas hesitated. 'Do you know the whereabouts of my master?'

The man shook his head. 'There's naught for you here, friend. You must seek news of him elsewhere.'

Thomas was silent, as he stood holding the horse's rein. The big gelding shifted its feet, prompting the servant to flinch. 'Do you wish to give me a message or not?' he asked sharply.

Thomas eyed him. 'Your master and mine are old friends,' he said. 'I guess Sir Marcus would think poorly of the way I've been received here, after such a long ride.'

The man frowned. 'What would you have me say? Your master was here for the Tilts, almost a month since, and for a while thereafter. Now the Court's moved down to Greenwich – mayhap you should look for him there.'

After a moment Thomas nodded. 'I will . . .' A thought struck him. 'Do you know if Sir Robert took his manservant with him? His name's Simon . . .'

The man's frown cleared. 'Old Simon?' To Thomas's surprise, he gave a snort. 'He's cast out of your master's service – did you not know it?' When Thomas showed his surprise, the fellow laughed. 'You country folk,' he said, shaking his head. 'You scarce know what day it is!'

Thomas was weary and saddle-sore, and his patience was ebbing away. He made as if to step forward, which took the grin off the other's face at once.

'Cast Simon out?' Thomas echoed. 'He wouldn't do such – the man's been Sir Robert's devoted body-servant all his life.'

The fellow's frown was back. 'Is't so?' He pointed over Thomas's shoulder. 'Then you'd best go and comb the nearest alehouses: the Dagger, the Mitre – any of 'em. For the last I heard, Simon was bewailing his lot to any other drunkard who'd listen to him. And if you want my free opinion, 'twill be but a short step from there to begging in the streets, like the watermen. Our London winter has no mercy for those who cannot work!'

Then with a hard look, the man turned on his heel and strode up the path towards the big house, which was barely visible in the gathering dusk. With a heavy heart, Thomas caught up the gelding's rein and led it away.

To his relief, he did not have to search far – either for a night's lodging, or for the unfortunate Simon. At the third tavern he looked in, he found both.

The inn was the Bel Savage; a rambling warren of a place on Ludgate Hill, just across the Fleet Bridge. Having entrusted the gelding to an ostler, Thomas stepped from the yard into the taproom to be greeted by the heat of a blazing fire. The smell of beer assailed him along with the noise of a lively crowd, though it was yet early in the evening. Pushing his way inside, he peered through the haze of tobacco smoke . . . and stopped. There in a corner sat the forlorn figure of Simon, Sir Robert Vicary's old manservant. He was nursing a mug as if it were his last . . . which, had Thomas not found him, he thought later, might well have been the case.

Without preamble he shouldered his way forward, found a stool and plonked it down, prompting the old man to look up in alarm. His hand shook, so that he almost spilled his drink.

'Thomas!'

'Simon.' Thomas's gaze was stern, and quickly the other lowered his eyes. 'What do you want of me?' he asked in a sullen voice. 'I'm in no mood for company. I've lost my place – and today someone stole my purse. I've lost every-thing!'

A drawer appeared and Thomas called for a mug, then stayed the man as he turned to Simon. 'When did you last take a proper meal?' he asked. When the other merely mumbled a reply, Thomas faced the drawer again. 'We'll have a good supper for two,' he said. 'Whatever you've got.'

The man nodded and gestured towards a doorway. 'There are tables in the parlour, master.'

As he moved away, Simon tilted his mug and drained it. 'You may play the good Samaritan if you choose, falconer,' he muttered. 'I didn't ask for your charity.'

Thomas looked him up and down. 'What in heaven's name's happened to you?'

Simon opened his mouth, as if on the point of spilling the tide of woe which, Thomas guessed, had already bored other drinkers enough to move off and leave him. But seeing the falconer's sharp eyes upon him, he shortened his tale.

'I've done nothing wrong! Rather you should ask what's become of our master . . .' He looked away, growing maudlin. 'Ever since he was a boy, I've served him . . . washed and dressed him, wiped his backside – and this is how I'm repaid!'

Thomas said nothing, but his expression softened, prompting the old servant to stiffen. 'He didn't send you to seek me out, did he?' he asked hopefully. When Thomas shook his head, he lapsed back into gloomy silence.

Thomas leaned forward. 'Would Sir Robert's behaviour have aught to do with a Lady Semple?' he asked.

Simon jerked as if he had been struck, and banged his mug down on the nearest table. Heads turned towards him.

'You know of her? That she-wolf . . . that Salome – she is a witch!' His outburst prompted groans from the nearby drinkers. As one, they turned their backs to the madman.

Thomas sighed. 'Witch or no, from what I hear she has bewitched our master right enough.' He rose to his feet. 'Come, let's go to our supper. Then you can tell me the whole sorry tale.'

A half-hour later, Thomas watched Simon clean the last morsel of food from his trencher, then empty a mug of weak beer down his throat. He had begun to look a little more like the man he knew: a familiar figure back at Petbury, fussing over Sir Robert's linen, or the altering of a new doublet. At last the old manservant wiped his mouth, sat back and met Thomas's gaze. 'Well – I've told you all,' he said with a sigh. 'But what may be done about the matter, I know not.'

It had indeed been a sorry tale, though barely worse than Thomas expected. The challenge he faced would have been difficult enough under any circumstances: how to free a besotted, middle-aged man from the clutches of a younger woman, who for some reason, had decided to ensnare him. When the man also happened to be a knight of the shires and Thomas's master, the task looked almost impossible.

'She stalked him like a huntress,' Simon said for the third time. 'From the first day of the Tilts, she had him in view . . . next thing they're riding out together, then dancing at Whitehall Palace, with the Queen and her Court. Soon after that, Sir Robert failed to return to Sir Marcus's house of a night-time . . .' He shook his grizzled head. 'I hear the Lady Imogen's skilled in the arts of the bed-chamber. Lives in comfort at her late husband's house, in Hart Street by the Tower—'

Thomas showed his impatience. 'You have said,' he broke in. 'Yet I still don't see why Sir Robert dismissed you.'

'Dismissed me?' Simon repeated, and gave a yawn. 'In truth he did not dismiss me . . . rather, he flew into a rage one afternoon and told me to get out – that was more than a week ago.' A look of bewilderment crossed his face. 'All I did was question his taste in a new suit of flame-coloured satin . . .'

Thomas frowned. 'So when he went from Sir Marcus's house, he left you behind?'

Simon nodded. 'Said he wouldn't need me at Sayes Court, and I should get myself home – yet he failed to give me money for it. Did he think I could walk all the way to Berkshire in mid-winter – a man of my years?' He looked close to tears. 'I who have served him faithfully, ministered to his every need—'

But Thomas broke in sharply. 'Sayes Court? I thought you said Sir Robert stays at Lady Semple's house, near the Tower—'

'Nay, nay – I never said such,' Simon answered testily, while Thomas struggled to retain his patience. The old man's mind was fuddled, both with drink and weariness. Clumsily Simon picked up his mug, peered into it and saw that it was empty.

'Simon – listen to me!' Thomas gripped his arm. 'Where is Sayes Court? Had you told me of it sooner, I could have gone there at once!'

Startled, Simon met his gaze. 'You don't know?' he muttered. 'Sayes Court is at Deptford, close to Greenwich Palace. It's the home of Giles Baldwin, the Clerk of the

Green Cloth . . . he's a whitestave – a man of the Royal Household, and a new friend of Sir Robert's. They talked of hawks, at the Tilts . . .'

Thomas let go of the man's sleeve, and sat back. In the taproom, someone was tuning a lute.

He sighed: at least he had found out where Sir Robert was, and quickly. But his brow soon furrowed again. For that, he guessed, was the easiest part. The hard part was yet to begin.

Two

In the morning Thomas roused Simon from the cramped chamber they had shared at the Bel Savage, gave him a breakfast, then steered him outdoors into the noisy street. Ludgate was open, and carts clattered over the Fleet Bridge towards the city. Behind Old Bailey, the walls loomed above the rooftops.

Simon wore his winter cloak, and carried his few possessions in a pack. As he stood shivering in the freezing air, Thomas fumbled for his purse. 'Find a carrier bound for Reading or Newbury,' he said. 'Any will be glad to take you, for a fee. From there you can hire a mule to get you up to Chaddleworth . . .' He stopped, for the old man was shaking his head.

'No, Thomas,' he muttered. 'I'm beholden to you for coming to my aid. But I did some hard thinking this morning, before you were up.' Simon's mouth was set, and his face wore a stubborn look.

'I'll not go back to Petbury,' he said. 'When you see Sir Robert you may tell him I've gone to my sister's at Wantage. She and her husband will give me a roof . . . there I shall stay, until such time as our master comes to his senses and sees fit to recall me to his service. He'll not find a better body-servant than me, should he search all England!'

After a moment Thomas nodded. 'Indeed he will not,' he smiled. He opened the purse and drew out a few coins. 'Will you take this for your journey, with my blessing?'

Simon took the money and nodded his thanks. 'When you see Sir Robert, tell him . . .' He looked away. 'Tell him I remain his loyal and devoted servant.' Then he walked off, head bowed, towards Holborn and the West Road beyond. Thomas watched him go, then went back to the inn yard.

*　　*　　*

A short time later, leading the gelding, he entered the city, passed before St Paul's and made his way towards the river. He had been thoughtful since leaving his lodging, but soon he grew alert; for there was danger in the very air of London, of a kind he had not sensed before. He could almost smell it, though he was hard pressed to fathom its cause. His thoughts went back to his last visit here, which had been in the summer of the great Armada – six years ago. There had been danger then, too: fears of invasion, no less. He recalled the ditches dug south of the city, and the wary soldiers eyeing him, suspicious of all strangers. But this was different . . . it seemed as if London folk were ill-at-ease with one another, fearing their own fellows. Perhaps it was merely the cold that made them hurry along the icy streets, seldom pausing to greet each other. But only when he turned into Thames Street, the long thoroughfare that ran eastwards all the way to the Tower, did he begin to understand, for the street was crowded with watermen, thrown out of work by the freezing of the river. Hard of eye and loud of voice, these normally proud, self-reliant fellows, who earned their living ferrying Londoners about on the water, were now reduced to begging – and not surprisingly, they were angry.

They milled about restlessly in twos, threes and larger groups, muttering and stamping their feet against the cold. Some had rough cloaks thrown over their jerkins, others had only mantles of sacking. All had begging bowls, which they thrust out at passers-by, demanding charity as if by right. Those that refused were railed at, even abused, prompting all but the bravest to hurry on their way. Those that produced a coin were thanked profusely, but to Thomas's eye the gratitude was sardonic and tinged with bitterness. He recalled the words of the surly gate-keeper, the day before: the London winter was indeed merciless.

He gave what he could spare, but was soon reduced to shaking his head helplessly, so great were the boatmen's numbers. Finally he passed into Fishmonger Row, expecting the crowds to thicken. But the stalls were all but empty; even the market folk, he realized, were victims of the ice. Glancing down an alley towards the river, he saw boats drawn up by the dozen along the wharves, idle and forlorn.

Quickening his pace, eager to be free of the noisome, smoky city, Thomas was about to lead the horse up to the Bridge gate. Then as the great expanse of frozen water came into sight, he stopped. As before, the ice teemed with folk, crossing to and fro . . . and for the first time since entering London he relaxed. What need had he of bridges? He would ride across, like everyone else.

He led the gelding down by Fish Wharf, with the Old Swan Stairs at his right, seeking a way on to the river. Soon he found a slope, dug crudely into the bank and lined with stones, leading down to the narrow strip of gravel beside the ice. The next moment he had swung himself into the saddle and was easing the horse on to the Thames.

At first the animal was nervous, but responding to Thomas's encouraging commands it began to walk steadily forward, parallel to the Bridge. Soon they were halfway across the river, and Thomas was looking warily downwards. Though the ice appeared to be several feet thick and hard as stone, he could only guess at how deep the water was beneath. So it was with a small sigh of relief that he gained the Southwark shore and urged his mount up another slope, on to which someone had helpfully thrown a few spadefuls of gravel. Then he was riding through Bankside, the old pleasure ground with its streets of rough taverns, brothels and bowling alleys, to the orchards and open fields beyond. Soon he had left the river and turned on to the Old Kent Highway. To his right, low on the horizon, a blood-red sun showed through the mist.

There was little traffic on the road, and he made good progress. After a few minutes he gave the horse full rein, and cantered through open countryside. Though he was not certain of the way, he had made some enquiries at the inn the night before, and knew Deptford lay a few miles east. Beyond Redriff, he had been told, the river bent south into a great horseshoe. He would see the spire of St Nicholas's church, and beyond, the towers of Placentia: the vast palace of Greenwich where the Queen had been born, and spent a large part of her year. Many court officials lived in the neighbourhood – including Giles Baldwin, at Sayes Court; the largest house in the area. Thomas's face grew sombre as his thoughts turned again to the task ahead. He was still dwelling on the matter when the river came into view again, beyond the fields to his left. As he slowed the horse to a walk, a big, three-gabled house appeared beyond a line of trees. Further off he saw the church spire, and the rooftops of Deptford. A moment later he had turned down a lane leading up to the grey-stone manor, and was drawing rein in a cobbled courtyard.

Dogs barked from the rear of the house. As Thomas dismounted a groom emerged, looking askance at the tall man who was so well-mounted, yet dressed in plain fustian. When he asked Thomas his business, he appeared startled by the answer.

'Sir Robert's man?' he muttered. 'Then I fear you've had a wasted journey.'

Thomas's face fell. 'Is he not here, then?' he asked, with a glance towards the leaded windows.

The fellow shrugged. 'He's master Giles's guest – or was. We've seen little of him lately. His chamber's not been slept in for the past two nights . . .' He stopped. 'You'd best go inside and present yourself to the steward.'

Thomas sighed. Leaving the gelding in the man's care, he went into the house.

The steward's name was Nicholas Capper, and for some reason, he took a dislike to Thomas from the outset.

He was a portly, florid-faced man with flabby cheeks and a reddish beard, dressed in a well-padded suit of walnut-brown. His private chamber was on the ground floor beside the kitchens, from whence came sounds of great activity. He looked Thomas up and down, fingering the chain of office about his neck, from which several keys hung.

'Sir Robert's not here,' he said. 'Nor has he said aught to me of any servant expected from Berkshire. How do I know you're who you claim to be?'

Patiently, Thomas gave his name and station again.

'His falconer . . .?' Capper hesitated. 'Then there may be work for you . . . my master has two birds, and no time to exercise them now the Queen is come. He attends upon her every day.'

Thomas nodded. 'I'll be glad to look at them . . .'

The other gave him a bland look. 'I don't doubt it,' he snapped. 'But if you were hoping for a bed here in the house, there's none to be had. The master's hired extra servants – he's a busy man with the Christmas Revels nigh. You must make do with the stables.'

Thomas shrugged. 'It matters little to me where I sleep . . . and in any case, I do not expect to remain here long. When Sir Robert hears the news I bring, I believe he'll want to hurry home at once.'

For a moment the steward made no reply; then an odd smile appeared on his lips. 'You seem very certain of that,' he observed.

'I know my master,' Thomas said.

'Do you?' Capper's smile faded. 'I wouldn't be quite so sure of my ground, if I were you.'

Thomas met the man's eye, but the next moment he was brushed aside, as Capper turned abruptly to the doorway. 'You may take your meals with the other servants,' he said over his shoulder. 'Otherwise, I do not expect to see you in the house again. And remember – you are within the Verge, here at Sayes Court. Any bad behaviour close to Her Majesty's residence would amount to treason!'

Having delivered his parting shot, the steward left him to his own devices. Thomas drew a breath and went out through the kitchens, seeking the falcons. Perhaps, he reflected, they would afford him more of a welcome.

Sayes Court faced east, towards the village. The outbuildings were to the right of the house, on the side nearest the river. Thomas found the stables, and saw that the gelding was being well cared for. The two grooms, at least, were civil enough to him. The one he had already met conducted him out of the yard to the small mews of wattle, open at the front, where master Baldwin's falcons sat on their tall perches.

They had been fed and watered, but Thomas saw at once how restless they were. The big female lifted her wings, blinking and eyeing him suspiciously. The tercel, little more than half her size, merely looked up, then went back to pecking at the scraps of meat at its feet.

He nodded: he would let them digest their food before taking them out; there were hoods, jesses and gauntlets hanging on pegs nearby. He turned, sniffing the cold wind that blew from the east, fancying it carried a whiff of salt . . . Having nothing better to do, he walked through a paddock and found a gate opening on to a path that led down to the river. Soon he was walking into Deptford.

The morning was drawing on, and despite the cold, folk were about the cottages that straggled along the waterfront. As he neared the shore he passed a large yard, from whence came a din of carpenters' hammers, and paused to look. At first glance he failed to make out the source of the noise, since there seemed to be a wall of timber blocking his view . . . then he looked up, and saw what it was: the hull of a great ship, half-built, propped on heavy beams. Though as yet without masts or rigging, it was an impressive sight. Filled with admiration for the skill of the shipwrights, Thomas stared, and did not hear the footsteps approaching from behind. When he did turn, somewhat sharply, he found himself face to face with a thin, lank-haired fellow in a moth-eaten black cloak and woollen hat, who bowed to him with a mocking grin.

'A stranger – and paying close attention to Her Majesty's Shipyard, eh? You should have a care, friend, lest someone take you for a spy!'

Thomas blinked. 'I'm no spy.'

'Are you not?' The fellow's grin vanished. He glanced about furtively, as if expecting trouble. So exaggerated was his demeanour, that Thomas felt inclined to laugh. 'To my mind, you look a little like a spy yourself,' he said.

The man's eyes widened. 'Say you so? Is it my dress which suggests such, or my manner?'

Thomas looked the other up and down; then a notion sprang to mind, though it seemed far-fetched. 'It couldn't be that you're one of the theatre folk, could it?' he asked.

The man's face fell. But he seemed to recover quickly, and made Thomas another ironic bow. 'Lorel Cox,' he announced. 'Of the Lord Chamberlain's Company of Players.'

With a smile Thomas gave his own name, and that of his master.

'Sir Robert Vicary?' Lorel Cox frowned. 'I've heard the name . . . he's been at Court lately, has he not?' He gestured towards the distant bulk of Greenwich Palace.

Thomas's gaze followed the outstretched arm. 'Very likely . . . I've not clapped eyes on him for a month.' He faced the other man. 'Might I ask how you know this?'

Cox raised his brows. 'I'm there most nights! Her Majesty often has players to entertain her, especially throughout the winter Revels. We are honoured to be chosen – but then, we're the best!'

Thomas was relaxing in the man's company. 'So you're lodging here, in the village?'

The other gave a nod, then glanced about. 'I am – unlike the rest of my company, who have been given rooms at the palace . . .' He lowered his voice. 'The fact is, I'm in character!'

Thomas stared.

'I play an intelligencer – a spy, in a new work we're presenting,' Cox told him. 'It's an important role – the biggest part I've had. The very plot hinges upon it, hence . . .' He spread his cloak, then with an exaggerated air drew it tightly about him. 'I reside in Deptford, a hive of intrigue if ever there was! Folk from many countries dwell here – some of them illegally. They slip upriver by night – while by the same token, others wait here to make their escape down-river. Me, I watch, listen and learn – to fill out my role, do you see?'

Thomas nodded gravely. 'You're clearly a man who takes great pains in his work.'

Cox smiled with a child-like pleasure. 'In truth, I always fancied I had the makings of a spy . . . do I not live by my wits?'

Thomas glanced up at the sky. 'It must be near midday,'

he murmured. 'Do you know of an inn somewhere—'

'The Sea-Hog!' Cox was nodding. 'I often take a mug there myself . . .' He waved a hand towards the houses that faced the shoreline. 'Will you join me?'

Thomas signalled his assent, and falling in step with the player, walked the few yards to the strand. Then as they stepped on to the loose shingle, he looked at the river for the first time, and stopped suddenly.

'By heaven . . . it's solid ice, as it is in London. I had not noticed.'

Cox shrugged. 'Nature has her moods, as do we all,' he said, and shivered a little. 'A bad time if you're unlucky enough to be a fisherman – or a sailor. Now, may we get indoors and warm ourselves? This cloak's more decorative than practical.'

Thomas turned his eyes from the great, furrowed ice sheet, which was even wider than the one he had crossed that morning, and followed Lorel Cox to the inn.

The Sea-Hog – named, Thomas soon learned, from the black porpoises that sometimes swam this far upriver – was unlike other taverns he had known. Its interior looked familiar enough: soot-blackened beams, a sea-coal fire, tables, a row of barrels and a door to the rear. But as he moved inside, grateful for the warmth from the chimney, he realized it was the company that was unusual. His keen eyes swept the room, taking in the oddly-assorted collection of drinkers, a few of whom met his gaze. Some indeed seemed to hail from other lands: Frenchmen, Dutch, and yet others whose country he could only guess at. On several occasions eyes were averted, and backs turned . . . he sensed secrets, as he felt threats, of a kind he knew well enough. He was miles from London, in a little Kentish river-port, yet he might have been inside a city tavern of the worst sort, where a man feels re-assured only by the dagger at his belt. Among the Sea-Hog's customers, he saw, were men for hire, and who cared little what it was they were hired to do.

Lorel Cox, however, was known here; and since Thomas was in his company, there seemed no immediate threat. They found a couple of stools and sat down with their backs to the window. As the drawer appeared Cox called for mulled ale, then turned to Thomas.

'You look wary, master – what was your name again?' He was reminded, and went on: 'Thomas . . . of course. Sir Robert Vicary's man. Are you here to attend on him?'

Thomas nodded, and mentioned he was carrying tidings for his master, about the birth of a grandchild.

'Indeed?' The player stared in surprise. 'So, he has a family?'

Thomas frowned. 'Why do you ask?'

Cox shrugged. 'Because when I last set eyes on him at the palace, he was paying close attention to a certain lady.'

Thomas stiffened. 'Lady Semple?'

The man hesitated. At that moment the drawer brought two steaming mugs, and with obvious relief Cox made a show of taking his up. 'Ah! I'm sorely in need of a warmer . . . drink, my friend, before it cools.'

Thomas lifted his mug but watched the other man, who was skilfully avoiding his eyes. 'Let me spare your blushes, master player,' he said. 'I know something of Lady Semple, as I do of my master's friendship with her.'

'Friendship?' Cox met his gaze at last, then looked away. 'Women such as she have no friends. Only such as they may make use of for some purpose . . .' He took a drink, then lowered his mug. 'I hope your master knows what he does.'

Thomas said nothing. He had begun to realize that Lorel Cox, with his Court connections – even if humble – was a promising source of information. 'Why not tell me more of this Lady Imogen?' he suggested.

But a wary look came over Cox's face. 'Why do you wish it?'

Thomas shrugged. 'If Sir Robert's dallying with a courtesan, mayhap it'll give me some leverage, next time I ask him for a favour.'

Cox stared at him. 'You're no blackmailer, master Thomas. And like other falconers I've met, you're a poor liar.' He grinned, and wagged a finger. 'Never try acting when you're with a professional.'

Thomas held the man's gaze, which this time did not waver. Then he relaxed, and took a pull from his mug. The warm ale, well spiced, was better than he expected. 'I will not, master Lorel. And I ask pardon for my poor estimation of you.'

Cox too, relaxed. 'You have it, and welcome.' He took up his mug again – then froze, staring ahead. Thomas caught his expression and looked across the room. At first he saw nothing untoward: men sat talking, drinking and smoking their long pipes . . . then he too stiffened. For a fellow in a hat and pinked leather jerkin had stood up from a bench near the fire, and was giving him a very hard stare indeed.

'Looks like we've caused offence, somehow,' Cox muttered. 'There's some who think actors are fair game for a bout . . .' He gulped, and turned quickly to Thomas. 'Not an enemy of yours, is he? I've no weapon upon me . . .'

To his dismay, Thomas ignored him. He and the rough-looking man continued staring at each other as if there were no one else in the room. Other drinkers began to notice, and looked warily at them both.

Lorel Cox swallowed loudly. 'If you wish my advice, master Thomas,' he said under his breath, 'it's most unwise to lock horns with someone you don't know in a place like this!'

But Thomas stood up slowly. 'I do know him,' he said.

Cox swallowed again, and his voice rose half an octave. 'Then I'd be most grateful if you would allow me ten seconds to get myself outside, before you take a step towards that fellow,' he began – but he was too late. For Thomas had moved forward, even as the other man moved towards him. A silence fell, every pair of eyes upon the two as they approached one another. Then each broke into a smile; and the tension snapped.

'Ben Mallam . . .' Thomas was shaking his head. 'Are you dealing in sea-hogs now, instead of horses?'

'Jesu, falconer . . .' The jingler drew close, then put out his arms and clasped Thomas in a warm embrace, which was returned. The drawer and his customers relaxed, and voices rose again.

Thomas and the other parted, and both men broke into laughter. 'We never did meet at the horse fair in Wantage,' Ben Mallam said. 'Or anywhere else, come to that. How long has it been – five years?'

'Six, by my reckoning,' Thomas said, gazing into the other's face. His thoughts flew back to Armada year . . . to the last sight he had had of Ben Mallam, sitting astride a good Spanish jennet in a little Surrey village, waving his farewell. Other memories flooded in: he and Ben being set upon at Banstead Horse Fair, fighting for their lives . . . Ben charming a country woman into buying one of his broken-down nags . . . now . . .?

Now he saw the care-lines, deeper than he remembered, and caught sight of a wisp of grey hair poking from beneath the battered old hat. He saw also the frayed sleeves of the doublet, and the scuffed leather patches on the man's jerkin.

'So . . . how have the years treated you?' he asked, realizing that Mallam was judging him in his turn, looking him over with the same shrewd stare he employed when judging horses. After a moment the jingler smiled again, if somewhat sadly.

'Not as well as you, I would guess,' Ben answered. He sniffed, and his grin faded. 'In fact, some might say I've had the devil on my back for the past two years . . .' He looked towards the window, where Lorel Cox sat watching both men with obvious relief, and favoured Thomas with a lopsided grin.

'Would you or your friend like to buy me a mug?'

Three

Thomas and Ben Mallam sat by the window of the Sea-Hog and talked for the best part of two hours. Over several mugs and a good dinner, and after Lorel Cox was long gone, Thomas took in the jingler's news. Seldom, he reflected, had he heard such a tale of ill fortune.

'I was doing well, around the time you and I last saw each other,' Ben told him. 'And for years after that. Then it all turned sour . . . mayhap it was the plague that started it. A bad couple of years; I couldn't move around so easily . . . folk didn't look kindly upon travellers, especially a jingler with a string of horses to sell, from heaven knows where. I was turned away from villages – threatened, too. Then, I bought a Barbary – a real bargain; only it chose to die before I could get it to the fair! I'd naught to sell, so I borrowed – then I got robbed by a couple of roaring boys, in an alley . . . I swear to you, Thomas, after that I grew desperate. For it seemed to me my wits were starting to fail. Like a fool I let a slaughterman have my last pair of nags, and you know what? The cove never even paid me! Before I knew it I was up to my neck in debts . . . lodging with a drunken cutler in St Giles, behind with my rent, the old fool threatening to throw me on the streets. I knew then, that I was but a step away from begging. I even thought of taking the fugitives' road, out to the Isle of Dogs . . . live among the lowest; thieves and murderers. At least my creditors wouldn't seek me out. But believe it, there was worse to come.'

Thomas listened, giving a sympathetic nod from time to time, letting the man unburden himself. The afternoon wore on, folk came and went, but neither of them noticed.

'Nay . . .' Mallam shook his head. 'That wasn't the worst. The worst was when the Tom-tit caught up with me.' He gave a short laugh. 'Peter Sly, that is. They call him Tom-tit because he's a little man – but you know looks can deceive. He's a bad fellow, iron through and through – even the other jinglers give him a wide berth. I'd crossed him once, in a deal over a Galloway mare . . . though I believed it was all patched up and forgotten. But then . . . last summer it was. I'm wandering round West Smithfield, feeling sorry for myself, when Sly comes up with a couple of fellows at his back, collars me and demands payment. 'Course, he knew I hadn't got a farthing . . . he was feeling wicked, that's all it was. To cut the tale short, I fetched up in a ditch with a broken arm.' He raised his left arm until the pain made him wince, and lowered it again.

'From there, Thomas, it's a downhill gallop. A barber-surgeon set the arm, and made a poor job of it. Now I can barely climb into a saddle . . . and what hope is there for a jingler, who lives by the buying and selling of horseflesh?'

He took a deep breath, and for the first time ever, Thomas saw fear in the man's eyes.

'I tell you plain,' Ben said, 'I need a powerful change of luck – and quick. Or there'll be precious little left of Ben Mallam!'

Having finished his story, he was slumped against the wall, drowsy with drink and the first good meal he had had in days. Thomas watched him, then turned to gaze through the window, across the strand to the river. On the far side, which looked like wasteland, lights twinkled. He sighed, thinking he should go and exercise master Baldwin's falcons, as he was expected to do. But he would not let Ben Mallam go away penniless. As he was about to speak, the jingler opened his eyes.

'You still here?' he muttered. 'I thought you'd have grown tired of my company. Not that I'd blame you . . .'

Thomas interrupted. 'What do you do in Deptford?' he asked. 'Not much here in the way of horseflesh, is there?'

Ben shook his head. 'I told you, I haven't had a jade to sell in months . . . nor yet the funds to buy one with.' He picked up his mug, saw there was a drop left, and drained it.

'Nay . . . the fact is, I've had one piece of luck. Called in the only favour I had left – there's a ships' chandler on the strand here, Simon Lovett. Friend of a friend . . . he and his wife have no children, and an empty attic. He said I could pass the winter there, then I must get myself gone.'

Thomas nodded, then caught an odd, fleeting look in the other's eye. And at once, he understood. 'Was it the chandler, or was it his wife, you talked into giving you a roof?' he asked bluntly.

Ben blinked. 'Jesu, Thomas – you always did have a low opinion of me.'

Thomas gave him a wry look. 'So it's the wife. I only hope you're discreet: these are hard times to be on the streets.'

The other smiled. And there at last was the old Ben Mallam Thomas had once known. It would take more than a stretch of bad fortune, he reflected, to defeat him; then suddenly he thought of the dinner he had just paid for.

'I may be down, but it's only my arm that's ruined, master Thomas,' Ben told him. 'The rest of me works well enough.'

'Including your stomach,' Thomas observed dryly.

Ben met his eye. 'I'm obliged to you for that. You were always a man who would share what he had.' He sat up and stretched himself, wincing as he did so. The tale of the arm at least was genuine, Thomas guessed. Though as for the rest of it . . . he had remembered a lot of things, in the past few hours. One was that he had never been entirely sure how far he could trust Ben Mallam.

He stood up. 'I've hawks to see to,' he said.

Mallam nodded, and got stiffly to his feet. 'Was there ever another reason for your being anywhere?' he asked. When Thomas merely stared at him, he gave a short laugh. 'I jest, my old friend. Make no mistake: running into you again has been the best thing that's happened in a long while. Will you come in again tonight, and let me stand you a mug or two in my turn?'

Thomas raised his brows. 'Do you expect to lay your

hands on money by evening?' he asked, then saw the glint in Ben's eye.

'Master Lovett's a hard worker,' he said. 'In his shop until past six of the clock every day, leaving poor Alice alone . . . small wonder she feels the need of company. And she's a generous woman.'

Thomas shook his head. 'You've no shame,' he murmured.

'Can't afford it, Thomas,' Ben replied, and followed him to the door.

Though there was barely enough daylight left, Thomas took both of Giles Baldwin's falcons out on the gauntlet and flew them in an open field away from the house, close to the Kent Highway. His mind was busy as he watched the birds soar and swoop in the cold air. Uppermost in his thoughts was not Ben Mallam, but the meeting he was yet to have with Sir Robert – when his master finally made an appearance. The thought of kicking his heels for days at Sayes Court, where it seemed he was less than welcome, filled Thomas with gloom. He was even contemplating riding to London and seeking the house of Lady Imogen Semple, in hopes of finding Sir Robert there; though what reception he might receive, he did not know. As dusk fell he called the birds down, hooded them and walked back to the mews, relieved that they had responded well to his commands, and not carried off as he feared. By the time he settled both falcons on their perches, he felt they had accepted him as their keeper, if only a temporary one.

But an hour later, having been given a supper by the kitchen maids, he was sitting beside the open fire when he received news that lifted his spirits: Sir Robert had returned, and being told of his arrival, would see him after supper.

He was conducted to the main hall, a well-appointed room hung with portraits and Turkey carpets. A great fire blazed at one end, and servants stood in attendance about the long table. Seated beside Nicholas Capper the steward was a middle-aged man whom Thomas assumed to be Giles Baldwin: grey-bearded and dignified, in the ruff and formal black gown that the Queen's higher servants and councillors always wore. On Baldwin's other side was Sir Robert. Thomas came forward to make his bow . . . then as he drew close, found it hard not to show his alarm. For the change in his master's appearance was a shock.

In a matter of weeks, Sir Robert seemed to have aged. Though he was in his late fifties, he had always been an active man, the greying of his hair the only sign of encroaching years. Now, Thomas struggled to hide his dismay. The knight's face was drawn, almost haggard, while the dark areas beneath the eyes spoke of a lack of sleep. By contrast, his beard was trimmed in a style worn by men twenty years younger, the moustaches twisted to protrude at either side. Thomas's immediate thought was that something unwholesome had happened to the man he had served all his working life. His spirits sank; and yet he must play his part, and show nothing but delight in seeing his master again.

'Thomas!' Sir Robert waved him forward. Now Thomas noticed the sleeves of golden silk, and the ornate embroidery of the jewelled and padded doublet. Here were the first signs of Sir Robert's spending spree that Martin had spoken of.

'I'm most happy to see you well, sir,' he began. 'I'm sent by my Lady Margaret, with news . . .' Then he broke off, for an impatient frown creased his master's brow.

'Yes, yes – the grandchild.' Sir Robert nodded briefly. 'I was told of it last night.'

Thomas blinked. 'Then the news has overtaken me . . .'

Sir Robert lifted a silver goblet and drank. 'Indeed,' he murmured, wiping his mouth with his hand. 'I fear you've had a wasted journey – not to mention a cold one.'

Thomas let his eyes stray to the erect figure of master Giles, who was gazing at him. Sir Robert shifted in his chair, aware that some introduction was necessary.

'You know that our gracious host is the Clerk of the Green Cloth – that is, the Controller of the Queen's Household,' he said. Turning towards Baldwin he waved a hand to indicate Thomas. 'My falconer, sir; sent by my wife to check up on me.'

Baldwin said nothing, but to Thomas's eyes he seemed to dislike Sir Robert's tone. When Thomas made his bow the man smiled without irony, and nodded a greeting. 'Falconer – I'm told you have already made yourself useful, and exercised my birds.'

'I was glad to do so, sir,' Thomas answered. 'They are a fine pair, and have been well-kept.'

Baldwin acknowledged the compliment. 'You may have noticed the haggard is restless. She is troubled in the left eye – are your doctoring skills sufficient to the task?'

Thomas nodded. 'If it's a lash, it may be soothed with burnt alum and sugar. If something worse, I can try the stalk of fennel—'

'Enough!'

Thomas broke off, and faced his master. For Sir Robert, it seemed, resented the discourse. 'Your pardon, master Baldwin . . .' He forced a smile. 'Thomas will talk of hawks until you are weary of it . . . even if he is the best falconer in Berkshire.' He threw Thomas a look which carried not only irritation, but a warning too. 'He and I will speak later of affairs at home – and no doubt he will cure your bird too. With your approval . . .?'

Baldwin met his gaze, then nodded and turned to face Thomas.

'Till tomorrow, falconer,' he said. 'No doubt you would be glad of a good night's sleep . . .' He looked at Capper, who had sat silently throughout the conversation. Thomas saw him bristle, as if he expected to be told to do something he disliked.

'Has this man been well bestowed?' he asked.

Immediately the steward nodded. 'He dines with the kitchen servants . . . as for a bed, he said he was content with the stable . . .'

Baldwin frowned. 'In this cold?'

Capper cleared his throat. 'He, er, said he was content,' he repeated.

'Well, I am not.' Baldwin looked round and gestured to a manservant, who hurried forward at once. 'Sir Robert's falconer will have a good pallet in the men's chamber, so long as he remains here,' he said. 'And give him whatever aid he requires, in tending my birds . . .' He turned to Sir Robert. 'If that meets with *your* approval, sir?'

There was a tense moment. Watching both men, Thomas saw that relations between his master and Giles Baldwin were not nearly as warm as he had assumed them to be. Precisely what their nature was, he could not guess; again he wondered why it was that Sir Robert had left the house of his old friend Sir Marcus, and moved down here. Especially since the Lady Imogen lived in the city . . . but his master was speaking, and he was careful to give him his full attention.

'You are generous as always, sir,' Sir Robert murmured, inclining his head towards Baldwin. To Thomas he said shortly: 'Wait upon me tomorrow, when I rise – we'll talk then.'

Thomas bowed, and with relief turned and left the hall.

But the hour was not yet late, and in any case he was too restless for sleep. His time was his own until the morning, and now he thought of Ben Mallam and his offer to buy him a mug. The thought cheered him; and soon he was stepping out into the dark, guided by a waning moon, and picking his way along the path down to Deptford Strand.

The Sea-Hog by night was more crowded, and its air of suppressed menace more intense than in daytime. The fire, and the few tallow candles, threw deep shadows into every corner, which, Thomas thought, no doubt suited some of its inhabitants. He pushed his way in, looking around for Ben Mallam. The drawer came forward, recognizing him from earlier in the day. But when Thomas asked if he had seen Ben, the man shook his head. Thomas sighed and called for watered brandy, realizing he should have known better than to expect the jingler to keep an appointment. Taking his mug, he looked round for a vacant stool, then felt a hand upon his shoulder. He turned sharply, to find Lorel Cox the player grinning at him, still wearing his moth-eaten cloak.

'Thomas! Shall we continue our conversation, so cruelly cut short when you encountered your old friend?'

Thomas gave a wry smile. 'Are you not called to play at the palace tonight?'

Cox shook his head. 'There's no performance. The Queen entertains ambassadors . . .' He gestured to a bench near the fire, and Thomas followed. The bench was full, but seeing Thomas's tall frame bearing down upon them, men made way for him. Cox squeezed in beside him, his eyes sweeping the room. Lowering his voice, he addressed Thomas in conspiratorial fashion.

'The constable's here tonight, which is why some folk have made themselves scarce. That's him in the hat.'

Thomas followed his eyes, and saw a dark-bearded man in black clothes and a tall, crowned hat with a buckle on it. Indeed, it was hard to miss him, since the fellow's Puritan-style garb stuck out so incongruously. Then a notion struck Thomas, causing him to frown. He was about to dismiss it, when he saw the gleam in Lorel Cox's eye, which may have been only the firelight's reflection . . .

'He wouldn't be another of your fellow players, would he?' he asked. 'What did you call it – in character?'

Cox blinked. 'You truly think that?' When Thomas shrugged, he gave a snort of laughter. 'By heaven, your fancies fly away with you! His name's William Rycroft, and he is the constable of Deptford . . .' He threw his head back and laughed loudly. 'Anyone less suited to a life upon the Stage, I could scarce imagine!'

Thomas sighed, and took a pull of his brandy. 'It's hard to know who's what, in this place,' he said.

Cox wiped his eyes. 'You're a treasure, master Thomas,' he said, and started laughing again . . . which was a mistake. For in his carelessness, he spilled at least half the contents of his mug across the knees of the man next to him. There was a cry of outrage as the fellow sprang to his feet. Even as Thomas's head snapped round, a silence fell.

'Jesu – your pardon, sir . . . my clumsiness confounds me . . .' Cox too was on his feet, stammering, attempting to wipe the man's breeches with his tattered cloak. But the other was having none of it – and the gravity of the situation was soon apparent. For the victim was a brawny fellow, likely a shipwright who hefted timbers about for a living. In a moment he had taken Lorel Cox's arm in an iron grip. Cox gulped and squirmed, while Thomas's heart sank. From all sides of the room rose a sound like the humming of angry bees, giving way to hard words. Violence was about to be unleashed, and like it or not, he would be caught up in it.

The first blow, delivered by the burly hot-head, landed squarely on Cox's jaw and sent him to the floor, where he sprawled senseless on the carpet of mouldy rushes. But in falling he upset another fellow on the bench, who got up in turn, growling, and started towards the assailant. Not to be outdone, others threw aside their mugs and scrambled up, fists already whirling.

As the men sprang forward Thomas ducked aside, then stooped to drag the luckless Cox out of the way. He did not look up when he heard the second blow, since it mattered little on whom it had landed. He knew that in no time the room would be a mass of flailing fists and falling bodies. There were shouts and cries of pain, followed by the clatter of mugs and cannikins flying in all directions. Bracing himself, keeping his head low, he pulled Cox by the arms, away from the fireside towards the farthest corner by the row of barrels. It was his guess that most of the brawlers would steer clear of upsetting the ale.

A stool flew past his head, and broke against the wall. He dropped to one knee beside the unconscious figure, frowning. Blood showed about Cox's mouth. Likely he had lost a couple of teeth, Thomas thought, and slapped the man's cheek, which brought no response. The player was out cold.

There was a lot of shouting now, but a gradual lessening of the thuds, cracks and grunts which had marked the earlier stages of the fight. Two or three voices were calling for order. Thomas glanced round, thinking how fortunate he had been not to find himself set upon, as companions of men who spill drinks over other men are wont to be. But at once he stiffened, realizing that far from being out of danger, he was now the focus of attention.

Several men were on the floor nursing hurts of one kind

or another, while others had retreated from the fray to become spectators, or made themselves scarce altogether. The drawer was one of those trying to calm things down, as well as calling attention to the damage. The other voice, Thomas now saw, was that of Rycroft the constable. As Thomas watched, the man seized two fellows by the ears and cracked their heads together. The report caused a collective groan from the remainder of the company, most of whom fell back, doubtless thinking it best to let matters subside.

But it was not over. For bearing down upon Thomas was the instigator of the affair: the heavy-set fellow, now bruised and bloodied but still defiant. And it seemed that nobody dared challenge his right to take revenge.

'Get up, long-shanks!' he shouted at Thomas. 'Your friend's been paid for soaking me – now it's your turn!'

Wordlessly, Thomas stood up to his full height, which made some men blink – but not the challenger; he merely raised his fists and lurched forward.

Thomas dodged the first swing, but the other caught him on a stinging blow on the cheek. Ignoring the pain he brought his guard up, meeting the man's eyes, seeking to predict his next move. But the fellow was weakened by his exertions, and puffing like a plough-horse; when he swung his right arm, Thomas was ready. He caught the fellow's wrist, pulled him off-balance and bent his arm back sharply, causing him to twist round with a howl. The next moment Thomas had kicked the man's legs from under him, sending him crashing face-down on to the floor. There he lay, hissing with pain, while Thomas stood over him, keeping the tension in his arm. The man's feet thrashed at the floor, but he was help-less.

Thomas looked up, seeing movement. 'Master Constable,' he said, as William Rycroft came towards him. 'Do you wish to take charge, or should I break this fellow's arm?'

Rycroft stopped, and met his eye. 'I'd prefer it if you didn't do that,' he answered mildly. 'Master Jukes is my wife's brother.'

Thomas blinked. 'Your pardon,' he said. At his feet the brawny man continued to struggle, grunting with frustration.

Finally Thomas let go of him and stood back, whereupon his assailant scrambled to his knees, glaring at him.

'You'll wait,' he breathed. But the constable stooped, and to Thomas's surprise seized the startled Jukes and yanked him to his feet with considerable force.

'I've warned you often enough, Dick,' he said, even as Jukes shook himself free of his grasp. 'Next time it'll be the magistrate who deals with you!'

But the bruiser said nothing; merely threw a last, smouldering look at Thomas, then turned and shoved his way outside. One or two others followed him, allowing a blast of cold air through the doorway that, to Thomas's mind, was quite welcome.

There came a groan from a few feet away; Cox was regaining consciousness. But at that moment a figure in a hat appeared through the doorway, and hailed Thomas across the room.

'Jesu – what have you been about? Looks like I've missed all the entertainment . . .'

Thomas threw Ben Mallam a look of disgust, and rubbing his bruised cheek, turned to attend to the hapless player.

Four

It was Ben Mallam's idea to take Cox to the house of Simon Lovett, the ships' chandler, where he lodged. It was close by, he said, and mistress Alice was skilled at tending minor wounds. How he came by that information, Thomas did not bother to ask.

They left the inn, Cox groaning between them, and stepped out into the freezing night air. The player had recovered enough to find his voice, and was bewailing his lot in eloquent fashion. Before they had gone twenty yards along the strand, Thomas had had enough.

''Twas your own carelessness brought about the fray, master Lorel,' he said. 'And given the company that frequent that place, you're lucky to have lost no more than a tooth.'

'Lucky?' Cox was massaging his swollen jaw. 'I've three hundred lines of speech in my next part, and I must declaim them before my sovereign Queen . . .' He winced. 'I should seek a surgeon . . .'

'Mistress Alice will put you right,' Ben Mallam told him. 'There's a poultice she makes from herbs and such, that has near miraculous powers. She cured a lame hound with it once.'

He slowed his pace abruptly, causing the other two to check theirs. They were walking westward, with the river to their right. On the left was a large garden, open to the strand, cluttered with what looked like stacks of timber. A lantern was swinging in the breeze, and from a few yards away came the thud of a hammer, followed by a sound Thomas least expected: someone was singing a lively song in a high tenor voice. He stopped, and in the dim light saw Ben break into a smile.

41

'Sir Ralph, still at his great task!' the jingler exclaimed. 'Does he never tire?' He turned to Thomas. 'You must meet this fellow – there's none like him in all England!'

Thomas frowned. 'I thought we were taking our friend to mistress Lovett's . . .'

But Ben was already opening the little wooden gate. 'Ho there – Sir Ralph!' he called out. 'How goes the ark?'

The singing stopped, then a cracked voice answered. 'Who asks? There are no places left, if that's what you seek!'

Ben was stepping into the garden, which on closer inspection would have been better described as a boatyard. Thomas now made out the silhouette of a half-built vessel of some kind, which took up almost the entire space. He turned to Cox, who met his gaze with a wry look.

'You've not heard of Sir Ralph Monkaster, then,' he mumbled, still holding his jaw. 'Deptford's very own Noah?'

Thomas blinked. 'You mean when Ben said "ark", he meant—'

'Exactly that,' Cox finished. He glanced at the yard, and sighed. 'My wound can wait . . . come, 'tis an opportunity not to be missed.'

His curiosity aroused, Thomas followed the player into the garden, stepping between logs and rough-hewn beams. In the lantern's yellow gleam Ben Mallam stood beside a stooped figure, muffled in thick clothes against the cold. As they drew close, the man turned quickly, peering at the newcomers with sharp little eyes. Thrusting his face closer, he recognized Lorel Cox.

'Ah – the player.'

Cox nodded, but the man had already snapped his head towards Thomas. 'You, I do not know . . .'

Thomas made his bow, gave his name and station and the name of his master. But when he added that he was a guest of Giles Baldwin at Sayes Court, Sir Ralph scowled at once.

'They think I'm a madman!' he cried. 'All of them – yet do they not know their scriptures? The words God spake unto Noah: *The end of all flesh is come before me, for the earth is filled with violence through them; and behold, I will destroy them with the earth . . .*'

He broke off abruptly, for Thomas was nodding. '*Make thee an ark of gopher wood,*' he finished. As Sir Ralph's eyes widened, he smiled and added: 'From the sixth book of Genesis, if my memory serves.'

But Sir Ralph did not smile; merely gave Thomas a piercing look. 'If you know so much, why do you delay?' he demanded. 'There's little time left before the deluge – when all who walk upon the earth will perish!'

Thomas glanced at Mallam, who stood behind Sir Ralph wearing his lopsided grin. At his side he sensed that Cox, despite his swollen jaw, was suppressing a smile. To them this man was a figure of fun, despite his title, which fact merely saddened Thomas. For want of something to say he turned towards the half-built ship, now that he knew what it was.

'How long have you toiled to construct it, sir?' he asked.

Sir Ralph hesitated, as if unsure whether Thomas mocked him or not. Then abruptly his mood changed, and he gestured excitedly to his ark. 'Five years!' he answered. 'Ever since I made my calculations, and discovered the secret that has eluded everyone – even the greatest scientific minds of the age!' He lowered his voice suddenly. 'Do you want to know what it is?'

After a moment Thomas nodded – which to his surprise prompted a squeaky laugh from Sir Ralph Monkaster. 'Well – you shall not learn it from me! Many have sought me out, and gone away disappointed! Only the chosen shall be given their places, when the day comes . . .' His brow creased suddenly, and he swung his gaze towards the other two. 'And you shall not be among them – you rogues, who come only to deride me! Away with you – begone!'

'Pray don't fret yourself, Sir Ralph . . .' Cox was moving away. 'Your work is too important to be interrupted.'

Thomas caught Ben Mallam's eye, signalling his own desire to leave. But Ben could not resist a last dig at the ark-builder. 'Folk hereabouts often wonder how you'll find room for all the beasts, when the deluge breaks,' he said in a cheerful tone. 'Two by two, I mean. Remember, when it comes to choosing horses I'm your man . . .'

'Get you gone!' Sir Ralph raised his hand, which still held a carpenter's mallet. 'You think I don't know how you mock me? You're little better than a horse-thief!'

Ben raised his hands and backed away in mock fright. 'Nay, sir – you wrong me! I'm a concerned citizen, who—'

'Citizen?' Sir Ralph snorted. 'A fugitive, more like – as are half the inhabitants of this god-forsaken hamlet . . .' He glanced at Thomas as if about to include him in the dismissal, before deciding against it. Instead he drew himself to his full height, which was still several inches below Thomas's. 'If you will heed my advice, falconer,' he said with dignity, 'you should remove yourself from Deptford at the first opportunity. It's an unwholesome place . . .' He lowered his voice. 'Even murder is done here – only yards from my door!'

He pointed towards the strand. For a moment there was silence, broken only by the wind, which seemed to be rising. The lantern rocked, and Sir Ralph shivered. Then without further word he turned and began moving along the hull of his ark, tapping with his mallet as if checking for something. As he did so he resumed his song. Thomas watched him for a moment: a rather sad, bent figure, stooping in the lantern's beam. Then without looking at Ben Mallam, he made his way back to the shore.

Having accompanied Ben and Lorel Cox to master Lovett's house, he had intended to return at once to Sayes Court. But Sir Ralph's words still rang in his head; and try as he might, he could not forget them. A half hour later he was still sitting in mistress Alice's kitchen, having been made welcome and accepted a warm cup of watered brandy. It was an odd company that sat about the well-scrubbed table: Cox the player, holding a poultice against his swollen jaw; Mallam, fully at ease, spinning tales of other affrays he had witnessed in his eventful career; and the Lovetts.

Mistress Alice was somewhat as Thomas had expected: a comely, fair-haired woman in her thirties, with a drowsy manner and a wandering eye. Her smile was wide, and to Thomas's unease it often seemed to be directed at him. She and Mallam seldom looked at each other; when they did, the nature of their relations was as clear to Thomas as it would have been to anyone of average perception – save her husband. And one reason for that, at least, was obvious: Simon Lovett was half-blind. A big, rough-bearded man, he was handsome enough save for one jarring feature: a livid scar running down the left side of his face from eyebrow to jawline, and an eye that was cloudy as skimmed milk, staring at nothing. As a young man he had sailed with the great Sir Francis himself, until wounds received in a fight with the Spanish had put an end to his career as a seaman. Back home in Deptford, he had married and sunk his share of captured prize-money into a chandler's shop, where he could live out his days in some degree of comfort. And yet, there was a restlessness about the man; he struck Thomas as one who, if angered, would be a dangerous opponent. He sighed inwardly, knowing from experience that Ben Mallam was the sort who often courted danger without paying it any mind, until its consequences broke upon him. This liaison with mistress Alice under her husband's nose was typical of the jingler: seldom had Thomas known a man who stretched his luck as Ben did. And here he was, setting down his empty mug with a grin after giving a summary of the recent encounter with Sir Ralph Monkaster. Only then did Thomas notice that Simon Lovett was not amused.

'Now, master Ben, it's easy to mock the man.' Lovett was staring down at the table. 'But there's no malice in him – and what harm does he do? Let him build his ark – 'twill likely take him the rest of his days, which is no bad thing, seeing as the vessel will never float.'

Thomas raised his eyebrows. 'Will it not?'

Lovett looked up at him and shook his head. 'The man's no shipwright, master Thomas. It's madness that guides his hand, not skill. At one time he had a company of fellows working for him, until they saw the futility of the task and left him to it. By then his money had begun to run out, in any case . . . now there's only old Lowdy Garth helps him from time to time. He's too gentle a soul to tell Sir Ralph the truth.'

There was a silence, then Lorel Cox spoke up. 'Yet, can any man truly be certain there is no second deluge coming? Men of science have often predicted such: mayhap one day, when we're up to our necks, we'll find Sir Ralph was right all along.'

Ben Mallam snorted. 'Sounds to me as if Dick Jukes knocked your wits out along with your tooth,' he said. 'Monkaster's as cracked as the tenor bell of St Dunstan's church . . .' He turned to Thomas for support. 'Tell him so, my friend.'

But Thomas did not answer, for he was still thinking of Sir Ralph's parting words. Now at last he voiced his question.

'What did he mean,' he asked, 'about murder being done a matter of yards from his door?'

Alice Lovett stiffened; it was her husband who answered. ''Twas almost a week ago,' he said grimly. 'A young woman washed up on the tide . . . it's not so uncommon here. She was thrown in to make it look like a drowning, old Lowdy says. He found the body, and saw the marks upon the neck . . .' He looked away. 'What's less common is the way someone took such pains to make sure she couldn't be identified.' He met Thomas's gaze with his good eye, and added, 'Her face had been burned away.'

There was a silence. Thomas glanced round at the other men, and saw that the incident was not news to them. After a moment, he said: 'What's happened to the body?'

At that, Ben Mallam threw up his hands. 'Jesu, Thomas . . . the look in your eye says it plain!' With an exasperated air, he turned to the others. 'You have not been on the Berkshire Downs, else you would know the reputation of Thomas Finbow – as famed for the uncovering of buried truths as he is for his falconry! Could ye not have kept silent on the matter?'

Simon Lovett glanced at Thomas, and his brows knitted. 'Is it so? Then you should seek out Will Rycroft, our constable, and offer your aid. He'd be mighty glad to put a name to the girl and see her turned over to her family. He's got the body stored in a casket filled with ice.'

Thomas stared, torn between his unwillingness to become embroiled in this affair and his fierce curiosity. 'I might consider it,' he said, 'save that I have no idea how long I must remain here.'

Cox stood up, yawning. 'If my advice means aught to you, Thomas, I'd keep well out of the matter,' he said. 'Now I'm for my bed . . .' He bowed graciously to mistress Lovett. 'My fair hostess, your kindness is matched only by your healing skills . . . permit me to thank you properly in my own way, upon another occasion . . .' – then, realizing how that sounded, he looked at once to her husband. 'That is – I mean to thank you both, master, for your hospitality . . .' He reddened, prompting both Thomas and Ben to get to their feet in turn.

'I too thank you both,' Thomas said. 'I will think on the matter, before I sleep . . .' he paused. 'Where might I find the old man you spoke of – Lowdy . . .?'

'Lowdy Garth.' It was Alice who answered. 'He has a hut by the Creek. Though most mornings you'll find him walking the shoreline, looking for whatever the tide's washed in. Even though it's ice now, he still walks.' She smiled suddenly. 'He brought me a little box of rosewood, once . . .'

Thomas returned her smile briefly, and took his leave.

The next day, a Friday, dawned bright and sunny; yet for Thomas it was filled with foreboding. All morning, he waited at Sayes Court for his master to rise from his bed. Finally, when his frustration threatened to boil over, he went outside to the falcons' mews to busy himself. He inspected the haggard more closely than the day before, and found, as master Giles had said, a redness in her eye that could be treated. He returned to the kitchens to ask for alum and sugar, when the face of Nicholas Capper, whom he had managed to avoid since the previous night, appeared in the doorway.

'Falconer!' the steward beckoned to Thomas as if he were a scullion. 'Your master is up, and calling for you.'

Thomas nodded, and under Capper's stare, went out into the passage. A servant directed him to Sir Robert's chamber, and in a moment he had climbed the stairs to the first floor and was knocking at the door. Hearing a shout from within, he entered to find Sir Robert dressing himself.

If the knight had slept well, there seemed little improvement in his demeanour since the night before. With a grunt he gestured Thomas forward. 'Help me with these damned breeches, will you?' he muttered. 'There's more points to them than a stag's antlers.'

Keeping his own irritation under control, Thomas helped his master lace the garish red breeches to the doublet – a different one from yesterday, he noticed. Glancing about the large room he saw the profusion of clothes, most of which were indeed new. He seized the moment.

'I confess myself surprised to learn how you had dispensed with your body-servant, sir,' he said mildly. When Sir Robert made no reply, he added: 'I found Simon in poor circumstances, near Ludgate . . . he had been robbed. I gave him money for his journey home—'

'You did what?' Sir Robert rounded on him. 'Well, I trust you won't look to me to recompense you! The old fool's impertinence was his own undoing – let him cool his heels back at Petbury.'

Thereupon Thomas conveyed Simon's message: that he would not go to Petbury, but would wait at his sister's home for Sir Robert's call. At that, the other exploded.

'D'you mark the cheek of the fellow?' he cried. 'A lifetime's service, a good wage and a roof, and he thinks he can treat me in such fashion – well, he'll have a long wait! He can stay in Wantage until he rots!'

Thomas said nothing, though inwardly he was in turmoil. This was clearly not the time to air the matters he had been charged with by Martin and Lady Margaret, yet he had no idea when he might get another opportunity. It distressed him even more than yesterday to see his master behaving in a manner so unlike him. While he struggled to find the words, Sir Robert strode to the great curtained bed, still in his stockinged feet, and began flinging aside the covers.

'By the Christ,' he said, 'I've lost a gold ear-ring somewhere. I had it last night . . .'

Thomas swallowed and spoke up. 'Sir Robert, I beg you to hear me. I'm sorely troubled . . .'

'You too?' Sir Robert barely looked up. 'What is it now?'

Thomas stood his ground. 'I should rather say, sir, that we are all troubled. Lady Margaret, master Martin, and—' But he broke off as Sir Robert turned and glared at him.

'So, I was right! This news of my daughter's child was but a lame excuse – my Lady sends you to do her bidding, as she has always done, and call me home!' With a savage movement he tore the sheet off the bed and threw it to the floor. 'You and she always were thick as thieves!'

Thomas's spirits sank. 'Sir Robert, you must know that the whole of Petbury yearns for your return – especially in time for Christmas. We wish you naught but good . . .'

'Do you?' Sir Robert snapped. Then seeing the look on the other's face, he faltered. 'Nay – I believe you do, Thomas . . .' His gaze dropped. 'Perhaps you, and you only, might understand . . .' He took a breath, and met Thomas's eye again. 'It's . . . it's as if I am part of a different world, up here. Of course I'm pleased to hear of the birth of my grandson – but the child will wait. I have business here – new friends at Court . . . I'm expected at Greenwich Palace, for the season's festivities.'

Thomas managed a nod. 'So you will not be home for Yuletide . . .?'

'Nor likely for Twelfth Night,' Sir Robert replied. 'The Queen . . .' he hesitated. 'The Queen, Thomas, is . . .' he fumbled for suitable words. Sir Robert had always been considered a true country knight – fit for his dogs and his hawks, but not for the glittering Court; a mere bumpkin among the wits and gallants, the nobles and scheming officials that populated it. Thomas did not like to think what such people said about his master behind his back.

'She is a jewel,' Sir Robert said at last. 'The centre-piece of a great setting of lesser jewels, that radiate from her . . . I know not how better to put it. Once a man has been accepted among such company, he . . . his desire is but to remain, and to serve her – to shine.' Suddenly, Sir Robert's expression changed. He took a step forward, as if to confide in Thomas.

49

'You're a man who's seen the world beyond Petbury,' he said softly. 'You have stood at my side, among some of the greatest in the land. Why, you were with me when I was the favoured guest of the Earl and Countess of Reigate . . .'

Unable to stop himself, Thomas blurted it out. 'Aye, Sir Robert – and I recall how the Earl ended up!'

There was a silence. He bit his lip, meeting his master's eye. There was little need to remind Sir Robert of their sojourn some years back at Barrowhill, the seat of the corrupt, pleasure-loving Earl. The man had ended his days locked in his prospect tower: a living statue who neither saw, heard nor spoke, while his disgraced widow was a recluse.

Now, for a moment, there was a look in Sir Robert's eye that caught Thomas by surprise; of mingled surprise, alarm, even something akin to guilt. Then abruptly it vanished, and the knight sprang backwards as if he had been struck.

'How dare you!' he shouted, the colour rising to his face. 'How dare you presume to speak to me in such a manner!'

'Your pardon, sir,' Thomas said at once; then realizing the situation was beyond saving, he decided to throw aside all caution and deliver his piece.

'Sir – you may do what you will with me,' he said. 'But I only speak what all your servants, your friends and your family fear to voice: that you are not yourself. That you have strayed into company that is unfamiliar to you . . .' He took a breath. 'And that you have fallen under the influence of a . . .' He saw Sir Robert's jaw drop, but ploughed on. 'Of a certain lady, who appears—'

'You rogue! You whoreson javel!' Sir Robert's look was one of disbelief. 'You . . . you're my falconer! And you make bold to lecture me on my behaviour? I've a mind to cast you from my service this instant!'

His master was almost frothing. With an emptiness in his heart Thomas met the man's eye, and saw nothing but rage: worse, it was the rage of a man who suspects he is in the wrong, and cannot bear to admit it. And such anger, of course, he directed at Thomas, who had presumed to show him the error of his ways.

'Get out!' Sir Robert cried, pointing towards the door. 'Out of my sight – I no longer want you near me! Get yourself gone, back to Petbury and your hot-tempered wife, who's as bold and as insolent as you are! Tell her she too is cast out – the pair of you are no longer in my service! Leave your cottage and leave my lands, and turn the falcons over to the boy – he at least is loyal, and knows his place!'

Then, as Thomas stood rigid, the knight strode to the door and flung it open. 'You heard me!' he shouted. 'I never want to see your lanky frame again!'

Thomas's heart thudded. From the passage outside he heard voices, which were soon stifled. His master's words had been heard, and would be repeated throughout Sayes Court within minutes. Thomas's world had just collapsed, yet for some reason, he felt oddly calm. The thought came to him, bizarrely, that at least he would be spared the indignity of seeing the smirk on Nicholas Capper's face when he heard the news.

Without looking at Sir Robert he made his bow, and walked past him. The moment he was outside, the door was slammed shut behind him. Then he was walking without seeing, down the stairs, along stone-flagged corridors and finally out into the open air. The sunlight stabbed at his eyes, yet his thoughts remained shrouded in blackness.

Five

Having no desire to remain at Sayes Court a moment longer, Thomas went to the stable and made ready to saddle the gelding. At least he would ride back to Berkshire in style, he told himself, though the thought gave little comfort. Then he remembered that he must fetch his belongings from the servants' chamber. With a heavy heart, he was retracing his steps towards the house when someone called to him. He looked up to see one of the kitchen wenches walking towards him with something wrapped in a scrap of cloth.

'You asked for alum and sugar, falconer,' the girl said, and held out the little bundle. 'The cook sent this – there's precious little alum, but it should serve.'

Thomas sighed. 'I thank you,' he said. 'But I fear you must pass it to someone else. I leave here within the hour.'

The girl looked surprised. 'Then who will tend master Giles's sick bird?'

Thomas shook his head, and walked off towards the kitchen door. But at once his way was blocked by the portly frame of Nicholas Capper, who was coming out. Thomas stood aside to let the man pass – but the other addressed him, and in a politer tone than he expected.

'Falconer – master Giles wishes to speak with you. He asks you to wait for him by the falcons' mews.'

Thomas looked up, but saw no hostility in the man's gaze. 'He will likely change his request when he hears what my master has done,' he replied. 'I'm ordered to leave at once . . .'

But Capper merely shook his head impatiently. 'He knows of that already, yet still wishes you to attend him. May I tell him you will wait?'

Thomas showed his surprise, then nodded. As Capper went away, he turned about once again and walked to the stable.

He waited a half-hour beside the mews, and was on the point of wondering whether some mistake had been made when he heard footsteps. The unmistakeable figure of Giles Baldwin rounded the stable wall – and to Thomas's surprise, he was displaying the same smile he had worn the night before.

'Falconer . . .' The man's manner was brisk. 'I'm glad you have waited. I would have some private speech with you.'

Thomas inclined his head. The other hesitated, glancing about as if to make certain they were alone. Then when he did speak, Thomas received a jolt.

'You should not go home,' Baldwin told him. 'For your master needs you more than he realizes. He may even be in danger.'

Thomas opened his mouth, but the man stayed him. 'Ask me not for details – I will not give them. Though it seems best you leave my house for the present, yet we must find a means for you to remain close by. I have given the matter some thought in the last few minutes, and this is my proposition: that I take you into my own service, as a temporary falconer. You can make a start by doctoring the haggard. Will that serve?'

His keen eyes gazed into Thomas's. And now Thomas grew aware of the sharp intellect behind the man's stare – and sensed something more: that this court official carried the heavy weight of responsibilities which he could not share. Once again, Thomas wondered why Giles Baldwin had invited Sir Robert here as his guest. He tried to order his thoughts.

'It will serve well, sir,' he answered after a pause. 'And it may be that I can find lodgings in the village . . .'

Baldwin nodded quickly. 'That's wise. As soon as you have a place, send word to me.' He fumbled in his gown and drew out a small purse. 'There's enough here for your immediate needs.'

Thomas took the purse. Though he had many questions,

he saw they would not be welcome. Yet he decided to risk one. 'Forgive me, but this danger to Sir Robert that you speak of,' he began, 'does it have any connection to a Lady Imogen Semple?'

Baldwin blinked. 'The best advice I can give you, falconer, is not to think on that lady,' he said dryly. 'Even though she will be my guest at Sayes Court from tomorrow.'

Then as Thomas started, he added: 'I say this, because I believe you're a man I can trust to keep his mouth closed when need arises. Even if you are called upon to serve the lady at hawking – for now I think on it, that may be likely . . .' He frowned suddenly, as if the matter irritated him. Reasoning as he spoke, he went on: 'Perhaps it's best this way . . . and it's a good reason for hiring you. I will take her out to Shooter's Hill. Do you know it?'

Thomas shook his head.

'No matter. It's a few miles to the south-east, beyond the royal hunting ground. One wild spot is much the same as another to a falconer who knows his craft, is it not?'

Thomas frowned. 'Indeed sir – yet will not Sir Robert wish to ride out, as one of the party?'

Baldwin nodded. 'No doubt he will, but what objection can he make to your presence? You work for me now. And remember, we are within the Verge – that is, within twelve miles of the Sovereign's seat. Here every man, no matter what his station, must mind his behaviour and govern himself accordingly.'

Growing brisk again, the Clerk of the Green Cloth – which innocent title seemed, to Thomas's mind, to hide more duties than it described – glanced at his falcons on their perches.

'Now – I will leave you to your work.'

But as Baldwin was about to take his leave, the events of last night rose suddenly in Thomas's mind. Seizing the chance, he voiced his thoughts.

'Sir – are you aware of the body that was washed ashore in Deptford, but a week ago?' Noting Baldwin's startled expression he added: 'They're saying murder was done—'

'Enough!' The man half-raised his hand, bidding Thomas be silent. 'What do you know of this?' he asked sharply.

Thomas drew breath and told him what he had learned the previous night. By the time he had finished, the other's brow was creased in a deep frown.

'I have said I will trust you,' Baldwin murmured, 'so listen well. The constable of Deptford made me a report of the death you speak of, on the day the body was found. To my knowledge, he has done nothing further . . .' He hesitated. 'Though the gossips may say murder was done,' he went on, 'there is no proof – and I hope there will not be! Because if a capital offence were committed here, within the Verge, it would be a matter for the Crown, not the magistrates. And those of us who serve the Queen at Greenwich will not have her troubled with such matters – especially at this time. She has more than enough to contend with – do I make myself plain?'

After a moment, Thomas nodded. In his mind several things began to fall into place, but he kept silent. Baldwin looked away briefly – then turned as a thought struck him.

'Unless . . .' He hesitated. 'It would be most helpful if someone of discretion were to find out who the unfortunate victim is, so that we may report the death as an accident.'

Now, Thomas saw it, and at once, he began to revise his opinion of master Giles Baldwin. For expediency's sake the young woman would be buried, her family paid off, and an end put to the business without the Queen even having to hear of it. That was how the Court operated: nothing must trouble Elizabeth's temper during the time of festivities.

He met Baldwin's eye. 'Someone of discretion?' he repeated.

The other gave a wan smile. 'Your reputation precedes you, falconer,' he said. 'Sir Robert has sung your praises at supper-time on more than one occasion. As old soldiers will spin tales of their victories, so hawking men will boast of their catches, and the prowess of their falconers.'

Thomas said nothing.

'You would do good service,' Baldwin said quietly. 'If not for the State, for me personally. And I feel sure we could find a way to reconcile you to your master, and see you restored to his service.'

Again Thomas said nothing, prompting a look of impatience on the other man's face. 'If you prefer not to involve yourself,' he began, 'then—'

'Do you give me leave to poke about where I will,' Thomas asked bluntly, 'and uncover what there is to be uncovered?'

Baldwin frowned. 'I suppose so . . . and should you—'

But again Thomas presumed to interrupt him. 'And suppose I uncover a murderer?'

There was a silence. 'Unlikely, isn't it?' Baldwin countered. 'If the woman was indeed murdered – which as I've said, is not proven – then surely the culprit will be long gone?'

'Yet, if I did uncover such?' Thomas persisted. 'And if he made confession of his crime, then might the matter still not be despatched without troubling the Queen?'

Baldwin blinked. 'You reason well, falconer,' he allowed at last. 'So be it.' And with that he walked away, hunching his black gown about his shoulders. Thomas watched until he had disappeared, then turned to see the big female falcon looking straight at him.

'Aye – glare away, mistress,' he said softly. 'I will heal your sore . . . yet how I might carry out the other task, is a puzzle only a conjuror would attempt – and a mad one at that!'

Thomas treated the haggard's eye to the best of his skills, then having fed and watered both birds left them alone. After a bite of dinner, he walked into Deptford. So deep in thought was he after his conversation with Baldwin that he did not even look at the garden of Sir Ralph the ark-builder as he trudged past, nor in the grimy windows of the Sea-Hog. But a moment later the door opened, and a shout drew him from his reverie. He looked round to see Lorel Cox in the doorway.

'Thomas – come and warm yourself!' the player called. 'I've not thanked you for aiding me last night.'

Thomas shook his head. 'I've business to see to . . .' he began, then stopped. 'Do you know where I can find the constable?'

Cox pointed, away from the waterfront. 'He lives behind the strand row, on Deptford Green . . .' He turned to go inside. 'Come back when you're ready, and I'll treat you.'

Thomas half-raised a hand, and looked around for a path away from the riverside. Passing between two houses he found himself on the wide green, still hard with frost. The church stood at one corner, and another line of cottages straggled westwards, towards the royal shipyard. Seeing an old man dragging a bundle of firewood he asked for the house of William Rycroft, and was directed to the cottage at the end of the row. He was about to knock at the door when he heard a sound from the rear. Moving round the side of the house he found a garden cluttered with baskets, fishing tackle and an upturned rowboat. There stood Rycroft, in workaday clothes, moving things about in a disconsolate fashion. When Thomas hailed him he looked round in some surprise, before recognition dawned.

'You again,' he muttered. 'Not more trouble, is there?'

Thomas shook his head. 'Not of the kind you mean, master Constable. May I speak with you? I'm come from Giles Baldwin, at Sayes Court.'

Rycroft looked surprised. Wordlessly he pointed to a gate built of driftwood. As Thomas stepped through, he noticed a small hut at the end of the garden, and guessed that that was where the body lay; the young woman with neither name nor face, whom he must try to identify. More, if she had indeed been murdered, he was to seek out the killer . . . Only now, he realized, was the enormity of the task sinking in. Why he had been so quick to volunteer for it, he barely knew.

Rycroft was watching him suspiciously. As briefly as he could, Thomas explained his business. And to his relief, having frowned at him since his arrival, the constable seemed to relax. 'If you're offering your help, then it may be you're an answer to a prayer, master,' he said, and turned towards the little hut. 'Are you sure you're ready for this sight?'

Thomas nodded. Without further word, the other led the way.

*　　*　　*

She was like a statue. That was the first thought that came to Thomas, standing beside the rough wooden box as Rycroft lifted the lid off. He gazed down upon the slim body that lay within, still fully dressed and packed tightly about with ice from the frozen river. It was the first time he had ever seen a corpse more than a week old that was so well preserved. The young woman might merely have slept.

'I've an ice-pit by the house,' Rycroft told him. 'Good for keeping fish. They've been known since ancient times – beats me why more folk don't build one.'

Thomas nodded absently, gazing upon the terrible, disfigured face. But one conclusion he had already drawn. Turning to the constable, he said: 'Whoever she was, she wasn't burned – at least, not by fire. This scarring was caused by some caustic substance . . . a liquid, I would guess.'

The other stared. 'Like what?'

Thomas shrugged. '*Aqua Fortis*, perhaps, such as goldsmiths use. It's a mighty dangerous brew.'

Rycroft looked puzzled. 'Do only goldsmiths use it?'

Thomas raised his brows. 'Nay – many folk do. Falconers use it at times to burn out a frounce. That's a hawk's ailment – an ulcer in the mouth.'

The other man looked helpless. 'This don't help us much, though, does it?'

But Thomas was peering closely now, taking in details of the woman's dress: the good quality and cut of the cloth, the richness of the embroidery. He noted the delicate hands, unsullied by household drudgery. And as for the rings . . . he turned to Rycroft again.

'Have you thought much upon how the poor girl ended up here, master Constable?' he asked.

The other gave a shrug. 'Washed downriver on the tide,' he replied. ''Twas my son and his friend who found her – old Lowdy pulled the body from the water, reckoned she'd been there all night . . .'

Thomas was nodding. 'But look at these silver rings – it was no robbery, was it?'

Rycroft hesitated. 'If you ask me, master Finbow, 'twas likely a suicide. The most heinous of crimes, to my mind.'

Thomas met his gaze. 'To *my* mind, when a man – or woman – is driven to such despair as to lose their wits, we should not judge them too harshly,' he said.

But the other was wearing a stern look. 'The sin of despair,' he muttered. 'Even this poor, ruined wretch had no cause to take her own life. It's for a higher power to choose when we must leave this earth!'

Thomas sighed and resumed his examination. After a moment he stiffened, and pointed to the young woman's neck.

'These bruises,' he began, but Rycroft nodded impatiently.

''Tis Lowdy's belief she was strangled. Her neck was already broke when he fished her out . . .' He frowned. 'That's how the rumours started – well, I say there's no proof, and no reason to go off hunting for a murderer!'

Thomas stood up and faced him. 'And yet, you will not object if I make some investigations?'

The man shook his head. 'Nay – if you've the time. If you can discover who she was, that I may restore her to her kin, you'd earn my gratitude. Let them bury her – meanwhile . . .' He grunted. 'She can stay here a while, though the sooner she's gone the sooner my wife will give me peace. She don't take kindly to what I do here. Even though it was at Baldwin's bidding!'

Thomas decided not to speak of master Baldwin. He followed Rycroft out, squeezing himself through the door of the tiny hut. As he went, he threw a last look at the body. Seldom had he come upon anyone who had been so cruelly used as had this young woman. A proper burial, he thought, was not the only thing she deserved: the other was justice.

The sky was overcast, and spoke of a snowstorm. Thomas walked back to the strand and turned eastwards towards the mouth of the little river Ravensbourne, known hereabouts as Deptford Creek. The cottages petered out, giving way to rough ground that would have been marshy in warmer weather. There were osier beds about the river's mouth – and across it, between there and the Queen's huge palace, a great ship lying at an alarming angle, its timbers weathered and streaked with mould. Thomas stopped abruptly, realizing what it was: the *Golden Hind*, that had circled the world . . . For some minutes he stood gazing at it, before his sixth sense told him he was being watched. He looked round and saw a little, roughly-thatched house some yards along the Creek. Outside its door, an old man in a rough cap and woollen jerkin stood motionless, staring at him. At least Lowdy Garth was easy to find, he reflected, as he raised a hand and started towards the cottage; he could only hope he was as easy to talk to.

To his relief, formalities were not important to the old man. Intentions were important – those, and the prospect of someone who could be bothered to listen to him. And once he had learned Thomas's purpose, Lowdy wasted no time in conducting him to the place where he had first come upon the body of the unknown woman. As they stood gazing at the frozen river, Thomas glanced behind him, and saw that Sir Ralph Monkaster had spoken the truth: the spot was indeed only yards from his garden with its famous ark. In fact, it was almost directly opposite.

He listened in silence while Lowdy recounted the events of that gloomy morning, a week ago. And he showed no disappointment when he realized that the old man could tell him little he had not already learned. Finally, when they reached the point where William Rycroft had come down to the strand to take away the body, Lowdy fell silent for a while.

'Poor maid,' the old seaman muttered at last, and gave a cough. 'I've seen folk washed up before, but none that looked as she did . . . 'twas like some savage beast had mauled her face.'

Thomas nodded. Then taking his time, he began to voice his questions. 'You say you've seen bodies washed down-river before, all the way from London?' he asked. When Lowdy gave a brief nod, he went on: 'How long does it take, would you say, for one to reach Deptford?'

Lowdy shrugged. 'Depends on the tide,' he answered. 'A few days, sometimes a week or more . . .' He swung his body round to face Thomas. 'I see which way your mind moves, master. And before you ask it – I don't believe she could have floated all the way down. Even with the water close to freezing, she'd have been in a worse state than she was . . . you want to know what I *do* think?'

Thomas eyed him. 'I do indeed.'

'What I think,' Lowdy told him, 'is that someone wanted it to look like she drowned, only she was already dead before she went in. And that same someone wanted it to look like the tide carried her down from London – when more likely, it carried her no further than from over there!'

He raised his arm and pointed, across the water to what looked like a desolate, uninhabited waste. But as everyone knew, the Isle of Dogs was far from uninhabited. Though a man would have to be in desperate straits indeed to wish to go there.

Thomas nodded, and turned back to Lowdy. 'If I heard aright, you also think whatever happened to the woman's face was done so that she could not be recognized. Only when I viewed the body, they looked like old scars to me.'

Lowdy met his eye. 'Even so, master,' he answered. 'Yet still I know in my heart that the poor maid was murdered.'

Thomas nodded again. 'I think so too,' he said quietly, and glanced up at the sky as the first flurry of snowflakes came down. Then he clapped the old man on the shoulder, and walked with him towards the Sea-Hog.

Six

Thomas did not stay long at the inn. Having bought Lowdy a mug and seen him settle down by the fire, he drew Lorel Cox aside and asked him if he knew of somewhere he could find lodgings. But the player had been drinking for hours, and his wits were not at their sharpest. After frowning at the floor for some moments, he shook his head. 'There's no room where I stay, nor any other house I can think of. Deptford is bedded in tight for the winter . . .' He brightened. 'What of Simon Lovett's?'

Now Thomas frowned. 'Where Mallam lodges? I think not . . .'

Cox shrugged. 'Then you'd best ask about you . . .' He waved a hand to indicate the Sea-Hog's customers. Though on past experience, Thomas held out little hope of a welcome from any of them. He was about to take his leave, when the player seized his arm clumsily.

'I was going to treat you to a mug, for aiding me,' he said.

'Another time, my friend,' Thomas said; then an idea struck him. It seemed a rather wild notion, but the task that lay before him was such, he was in no position to be particular. To Cox's surprise he withdrew his arm, placed it about the other's shoulder and drew him closer.

'How would you like to do some real work as an intelligencer?' he asked.

The player blinked. 'What d'you mean?'

'I mean, help me hunt for a murderer.'

Cox jerked his head up, peering at Thomas through narrowed eyes. 'You jest with me,' he mumbled. 'Ever since I came upon you by the shipyards, you've mocked me . . .' But he broke off as Thomas shook his head.

'I do not mock you. And what I tell you is true, as it is secret. Will you hear me, or not?' When after a moment Cox nodded, he went on: 'I'm charged by Baldwin with finding out who the girl was – she whose body was found on the shore. I need someone who can play a part, move about unnoticed, ask questions—'

'Someone to be your angler?' Cox put in, starting to get excited.

'If you will,' Thomas nodded. 'I'll pay you what I can . . .'

'Ask no further!' The player's eyes were wide with delight. 'For the experience alone, I would do it!' He put out his hand and Thomas took it, wondering now whether he had been somewhat hasty.

'Remember, this is between ourselves,' he said, but Cox was nodding vigorously. Adopting the exaggerated dignity of a man who tries to look sober, Cox said: 'You may count on me to the death – my sworn friend!'

'Then . . . I'll speak with you later,' Thomas said, with a dampening of spirits. 'When I've found somewhere to lodge.'

At the door he looked back to see Cox gazing after him with a broad smile. With a sigh, he stepped out into the falling snow.

A matter of minutes later, having no better plan, he entered Simon Lovett's shop a short distance along the waterfront. The interior was gloomy and he could see little, since the place was stacked untidily from floor to ceiling. Making his way between boxes and bundles, he found two men standing by a table in low conversation. One was the chandler himself. As Thomas approached the man peered with his one eye, not recognizing him. But when Thomas gave him greeting, he knew the voice at once. 'Falconer – if you seek your friend Mallam, he's within.' He pointed to the rear door, which led to the Lovetts' own rooms.

'It's you I would speak with, master Simon,' Thomas replied. 'You and your wife, that is . . .'

The other nodded. 'She's also within – go through, pray. I'll attend you after I've done business here.' Briefly he indicated the other man, who now turned to look at Thomas.

Thomas looked at him in turn . . . and felt the hairs on the nape of his neck spring up.

Peering at him with sharp little eyes over a face covered in a black, wiry beard, was a man he would not have trusted under any circumstances. For a few seconds they exchanged stares. Nothing was said, though Thomas felt himself being speedily assessed as to his status and character. Then with a quick, mocking smile the fellow dropped his gaze and turned back towards Lovett. Thomas had only the fleeting impression of galley-slop breeches and a pair of scuffed boots, before he made his way out to the back.

But there was no one in the kitchen. Thomas walked past the table where he had sat the night before, and through another doorway. There was a small parlour opening off it, but that too was empty. To his right were the stairs, and it was there that he stopped dead, berating himself for not guessing what was afoot. From somewhere overhead came muffled voices, followed by sounds which, though indistinct, were easy enough to interpret. Cursing Ben Mallam silently, he retraced his steps softly, back to the kitchen. Then he began clumping about, knocking a stool over and calling for mistress Lovett.

From upstairs there was a sudden silence, then the thud of feet on bare boards. A few moments later came footfalls on the stairs, and Alice appeared in the doorway, flushed in the face, with wisps of hair poking out from under her linen cap. 'Master Thomas . . .' She was trying to get her breath without appearing to do so. 'What do you here?' Then seeing the look on Thomas's face, her gaze dropped.

'Forgive me,' Thomas said. 'I see my choice of time to come a-calling was a poor one.'

'Nay – you're right welcome . . .' Alice pushed past him and began busying herself, finding a jug of beer and mugs. 'Master Ben's unwell – I was taking a posset up to his chamber.'

Thomas nodded gravely. 'It was you and your husband I came to speak with,' he said. 'I saw him in the shop—'

'Indeed?' The chandler's wife looked even more flustered. 'No matter – whatever you lack, Simon will have it. If not

64

he will point you to it.' She put the mugs on the table, looking round uneasily. With a wry smile, Thomas picked up the stool he had knocked over.

'Clumsy of me,' he said apologetically, and sat down.

Alice poured out the beer, and already her customary smile was beginning to appear. 'We're all given to clumsiness at times – what is it you seek?'

Thomas accepted the cup. 'A roof, mistress,' he replied. 'I need lodgings, for which I'm prepared to pay a fair price – and I hear your attic chamber is big enough for two.'

Mistress Alice was taken aback. 'I thought you served a wealthy master, who stays at Sayes Court . . .' she began.

'No longer,' Thomas said curtly. 'I serve master Baldwin as falconer now – yet he has no bed-space for another servant.'

Alice sat down while she digested the information. Her initial anxiety at being caught in embarrassing circumstances seemed to be evaporating. After a moment she glanced towards the door to the shop. 'I'll confess we could do with the money,' she murmured, and her face clouded. 'Simon's a poor head for business. Some men take advantage – like they do of his eyesight.'

Thomas frowned slightly, and ventured an observation. 'There's a fellow there now,' he said. 'Wide breeches, and a black beard almost to his eyes . . .' He stopped, for Alice Lovett's smile had vanished.

'Daniel Skeeres,' she said. 'The times I've told Simon to have naught to do with that man, I couldn't count.' She met Thomas's eye. 'He's a *knight of the post* – know what that is?'

Thomas nodded slowly. 'A false perjurer – one who'll swear anything you like, for a price.'

Alice sighed, then looked away. 'I'll speak with Simon,' she said. 'You'll likely be at your work in the day, won't you?'

Thomas nodded. 'A place to sleep is all I want.'

'Well then . . .' Alice picked up a mug, and Thomas raised his. As they clinked cannikins, she said: 'I believe we can do business, master. Only what Ben Mallam will make of the arrangement, I know not.'

65

At that moment footsteps sounded from behind, and Thomas turned to see the jingler himself in the doorway in his shirt and hose, his hair awry. There was a brief silence, before Thomas decided to break it.

'That posset of yours must have done wonders,' he said to Alice. 'Looks like he's made a full recovery.'

In fact, Ben Mallam accepted the arrival of his new chamber-fellow without comment. The reason for his apparent good humour Thomas discovered that night, after he had collected his belongings from Sayes Court and moved them to the Lovetts' attic. The two of them talked briefly, lying on their pallets on either side of the brick chimney-breast, which afforded some welcome warmth. And it was then that master Mallam broke the news which, he insisted, heralded a change in his luck.

'There's a Galloway nag upriver, at Redriff,' he said. 'Worth six or seven nobles at the least – only, after I looked it over for the old maid who's selling, she thinks it's on its last legs. I promised to take it off her hands, save her the bother of feeding it through the winter.'

'That's mighty generous of you,' Thomas said, fancying he could see Ben's broad grin even in the pitch dark.

'Now master Thomas,' he said. 'If we're to room together, I can do without your passing judgment on me and my trade.'

Thomas yawned, determined to put aside his cares and get a night's rest. For some reason, he thought of his encounter with the black-bearded Daniel Skeeres that afternoon in the shop. In passing, he mentioned the fellow to Mallam – whose reply was scathing.

'That whoreson rogue . . . he's lucky to be alive. There are men in prison on his testimony alone – innocent men, who'd tear his heart out if they could get at him!'

'Then you know what he does,' Thomas muttered sleepily.

'I do, for it's a poorly-kept secret,' Ben answered. 'He's laying low here for the winter . . .' He snorted. 'Someone ought to pay him in kind, and swear a warrant out on him! He wouldn't last a half-hour in Newgate . . .'

The jingler turned to Thomas in the dark, eager to return to the subject of his Galloway nag. But all he heard was a gentle snoring.

The next day the folk of Deptford woke to clear, sunny skies and a carpet of glistening snow.

It lay thickest on the frozen river, a deceptively tranquil stretch of pure white that hid the danger beneath: that of thinning ice. For the temperature had risen, bringing the likelihood of a thaw, and the breaking up of the ice-sheet. Thomas stood on the strand in the early morning, sniffing the clear air, and once again found himself gazing across to the Isle of Dogs. Lowdy's testimony of yesterday, about the likely direction from which the nameless woman's body had drifted, was uppermost in his thoughts. And his expression was grim as he realized that soon he would have to cross over and take a look for himself. But for now, he had more immediate tasks. Turning from the waterfront he began the short walk to Sayes Court, and his duties as temporary falconer to master Giles Baldwin.

To his relief he saw no sign of Sir Robert that morning, nor of Capper the steward. The grooms, gardeners and house servants were his occasional companions, and they treated him no differently to the way they had before. Master Giles, he learned, was at the palace, but would return by the afternoon, for important guests were expected.

Throughout the day as Thomas tended the falcons, his thoughts turned continually to the arrival of the one important guest whose name he knew: Lady Imogen Semple. From casual enquiries he learned that she would bring her own steward, a man by the name of Malvyn Wyckes who had some knowledge of falconry. There was also a waiting-woman, who was something of a riddle: younger than her mistress, and as beautiful, the grooms told Thomas. Not only that, but she was foreign too . . . in fact she was from the far side of the world, with huge dark eyes and a skin the colour of walnuts.

At midday he took dinner with the kitchen folk, and learned the name of the other distinguished guest: Sir John Amyot, a wealthy Kentish landowner and frequent attendant at the Court. He too was a hawking man, who would be one of the party that would ride out to Shooter's Hill. Thomas, it seemed, would be kept busy. But when he rose to go out, Bridget, the youngest kitchen wench, stayed him and spoke low in his ear.

'You should mind yourself, falconer,' she murmured. 'For Lady Semple's a dreadful scold, and hard to please. She's of a cruel heart; even master Giles cannot abide her. Why he invites her I cannot guess – lest it be to please Sir Robert . . .'

Then abruptly the girl reddened, but Thomas favoured her with a kindly look. 'Don't fret yourself, mistress,' he said. 'I well know my master, and what he does.'

Bridget nodded and went about her work, but as Thomas turned to go outside, his face clouded. How he was to fulfil the task that had first brought him here, and make his master see this lady for what she truly was, still appeared a mountainous undertaking.

Not to mention the small matter of finding the murderer of the faceless woman.

In the afternoon, he finished his tasks and was walking across the kitchen yard when he grew aware of a commotion from the front of the house. At that moment one of the grooms appeared.

'Thomas – stir yourself. We're ordered to attend the arrival of Lady Imogen!'

The man vanished round the corner of the courtyard wall. Thomas followed, quickening his pace, and arrived to see the entire household gathering near the main entrance. As they formed up in silence, Nicholas Capper appeared at the doors, followed by Giles Baldwin dressed in a smart midnight-blue gown. And at his heels, hurrying down the steps with a broad smile, came Sir Robert. But as Thomas took his place, he had no time to stare at his master's garish suit of flame-coloured satin – nor the hat with the gold plume, nor the cloak of yellow velvet: for hooves sounded, and all eyes turned as a coach drawn by steel-grey horses swung out of the lane, churning up the snow, and slowed to a halt before them. A servant darted forward to open the door – and Thomas could barely suppress his surprise: for the woman who stepped out was so small, she barely reached to the man's shoulder. And that was his only glimpse of the Lady Imogen Semple: a tiny figure in a fur-trimmed cloak, before Sir Robert came to make his bow and masked her from sight. Instead, Thomas's attention was caught by a horseman who rode in behind the coach. This man drew rein and dismounted in relaxed fashion, staring about until one of the grooms came to take his horse. He guessed that this was Wyckes the steward, which was soon confirmed when Capper, at his most pompous, strode up to greet the man. Together the two mounted the steps to the house where Lady Semple, Sir Robert and Baldwin were already disappearing. Only now, as the Sayes Court servants began to disperse, did Thomas see the last member of the party: the slim waiting-woman, muffled in a cloak and hood, who followed behind her mistress with short, rapid steps. Then they were inside, and the doors closed.

But if his curiosity about the new arrivals was aroused, it was soon to be satisfied. For within the hour he was ordered to prepare master Baldwin's falcons, and get himself horsed: Sir Robert and the Lady Imogen wished to go hawking.

He waited by the falcons' mews, while in the stable yard the grooms scurried about readying mounts. Soon a murmur of voices rose, and a jingling of harness told that the party were ready. When they appeared, he was surprised to see three people: Sir Robert, who had changed into more sober hunting attire; the Lady Imogen in smart riding clothes, mounted on a small grey pony; and her steward.

As they drew rein Thomas made his bow, trying not to let his spirits falter, for his master seemed bent on ignoring him. And now Thomas noticed he was riding the fine new Neapolitan horse that Martin had told him of – an animal whose worth he could only guess at. But he kept silent, as Sir Robert merely leaned down and allowed Thomas to place the hooded haggard on his gauntlet, before moving off. Thomas sighed, then turned as the steward rode up to him.

'Falconer – I'm Malvyn Wyckes, steward to Lady Imogen. With your leave, I'll take the tercel.'

Thomas found himself looking into a broad, handsome face framed by blonde curls and a well-trimmed beard. The man was younger than he expected, with smiling eyes and an easy manner. Quickly Thomas made his bow.

'As you please, master,' he said, and taking the male falcon from its perch, lifted it on to the man's outstretched arm. Wyckes took the bird upon his wrist in a confident manner, then turned to indicate Lady Imogen, who was sitting some distance away.

'My Lady has her merlin,' he said. 'It travelled in the coach. I would ask that you care for it well during our stay.'

Thomas tensed. Thus far he had avoided looking at the diminutive Lady Imogen. Now he saw that she indeed carried her own falcon: a sleek little merlin in a beautifully embroidered hood topped with a tuft of feathers. He bowed stiffly and walked forward, realizing too late that behind him Wyckes was quickly clearing his throat, as if to stay him.

'A fine bird, my Lady . . .' Thomas began, then broke off abruptly, wondering whether he had misheard. For it seemed to him that the Lady Imogen had uttered an oath under her breath that would not have been out of place in the Sea-Hog. Finally he looked up, and froze. For staring at him was a terrible little woman; beautiful indeed, as he had expected – but with a pinched mouth and furious green eyes, which bored into his.

'Did I give you leave to address me?' she snapped.

Thomas blinked. 'No, my Lady . . .'

'Then learn, and learn quickly, that you do not speak to me unless called upon!'

Thomas stared, then glanced to where Wyckes sat some yards away, shifting in his saddle. But when he looked to the lady again, she had already turned away.

'Sir Robert!'

It was almost a shriek. At once Sir Robert touched spurs to his horse and urged it towards her. 'Madam . . .' He wore a glassy smile. 'Has aught distressed you? Pray tell me . . .'

70

'This fellow,' Lady Imogen cried, 'has shown a marked lack of respect! Since I understand him to be one of your servants, I naturally thought—'

'You are mistaken, my Lady, for I serve master Baldwin.'

The words were out before Thomas could check them. And it was then that he realized how little he cared if he were dismissed from Baldwin's service too, and sent packing. To see his master apparently in thrall to this woman was more than he could bear. And in the tense silence that now fell, he remained calm, which only enraged her further.

'You hear that!?' Lady Imogen was almost quivering with rage. 'Such insolence – I will not bear it!'

Sir Robert's eyes were blazing, but he would not meet Thomas's gaze. 'Your pardon,' he said thickly. 'I will deal with the man later, I swear . . . now I beg you, let us ride. There are but a few hours' daylight left . . .'

But Lady Imogen sat her trim little pony, still glaring at Thomas. And since his height was such that, even on foot, his face was level with hers, this only enraged her further.

'You'll pay, fellow!' she shouted. 'With a word I could have you jailed and flogged – do you doubt that?'

'Do I have leave to answer, my Lady?' Thomas asked gently, prompting a muffled curse from Sir Robert. But then, as matters seemed to be getting out of hand, there came a respectful little cough, and Malvyn Wyckes eased his horse forward.

'My Lady, please . . . the matter is scarcely worth your attention. Do us the honour of riding forth, so that the folk hereabouts may see you, and admire your skill at hawking.'

Lady Imogen bristled, then half-turned towards her steward. 'I wish only for rightful obedience,' she said. 'You know that!'

'And you shall have it,' Wyckes replied with a smile. 'Let Sir Robert deal with the fellow – we must work up an appetite for supper. Our host has taken such pains with tonight's table. He promises all your favourite dishes!'

There was a moment, before the lady finally relented. And Thomas was almost astonished at the change in her manner.

'Sweet Malvyn . . .' she sighed, breaking into an

71

affectionate smile. 'Your counsel prevails as always, for I know you love me.'

She turned absently to Sir Robert, who had sat in silence during the exchange, looking quite miserable.

'As do you, sir, of course . . . come, ride alongside me, and soothe my unquiet spirit.'

And despite himself, Thomas's heart sank at sight of the foolish grin that spread over Sir Robert's face. His only shred of relief was that he himself was now ignored, as all three of them – the lady, her attentive steward and her hapless lover – rode away across the fields, bearing their hooded falcons. Thomas, it seemed, was not needed upon Shooter's Hill after all; in fact, it seemed as if he had been entirely forgotten.

Seven

It was Saturday night, and as soon as he had settled the falcons, including the Lady Imogen's treasured merlin, Thomas went down to Deptford. So preoccupied had he been throughout the evening with Sir Robert and Lady Imogen that he had forgotten the other important guest who was expected at Sayes Court, Sir John Amyot. That worthy had apparently been delayed on the Queen's business, and did not arrive until the others were at supper. Hence Thomas saw nothing of him, but was told to expect another hawking party on the morrow. Feeling low in spirits he walked to the Sea-Hog, thinking to speak with Lorel Cox. Already he was regretting his rashness of the day before, in recruiting the man to help him with his investigations. So it was with no little embarrassment that he found the player waiting eagerly for him. Barely had he entered the door than Cox came up and gripped his arm.

'Thomas – I've been at the palace, putting my ear to the ground. And there are matters you—'

'You've what?' Thomas looked aghast, but the other stayed him with a quick shake of his head.

'Hear me out, will you? This touches not on the . . .' He lowered his voice. 'The other business. Rather it touches on your master, Sir Robert Vicary.' When Thomas hesitated, he went on: 'I fear he is sailing into very dangerous waters.'

But to Cox's disappointment, Thomas merely shrugged. 'I know it, as it seems does everyone else. My master is bewitched.'

Cox frowned. 'You mean his infatuation with Lady Semple.' When Thomas made no response, he said: 'That is not the whole of it, my friend.'

Thomas frowned in turn. 'What do you mean?'

'I mean,' Cox told him, 'that Sir Robert's not the only one to whom that lady gives her favours. And if rumours are true, the other is a man he would be well advised not to tangle with!' Glancing round the crowded taproom, Cox put his face close to Thomas's and whispered: 'He is Lord Beauchamp, son of the Earl of Hertford. And in the eyes of some people, he's the rightful heir to the throne!'

Thomas stared at him, then shook his head. 'Nay . . . surely it cannot be so . . .'

But Cox was nodding vigorously. 'It is so! His mother was Lady Seymour, sister to Lady Jane Grey, and through the Order of Succession declared by King Edward her male heirs—'

'Stop!' Thomas said aloud, prompting curious looks from the nearest drinkers. Taking a breath, he bent his head close to Cox's. 'I don't mean the business of heirs to the throne – what's that to me? I mean it cannot be that my master . . .' He checked himself. 'That Sir Robert would fall so hopelessly for someone who . . .' But he was faltering. In his mind's eye he saw again the foolish look on Sir Robert's face, and the enraged features of Lady Imogen, as he had seen them that very afternoon, and his heart seemed to sink.

Cox was nodding, and his eyes gleamed. 'You have made her acquaintance, I see. Can you now doubt what that woman is capable of?'

Thomas had no answer. His thoughts whirling, he allowed Cox to lead the way to one of the tavern's darker corners, which seemed fitting enough. They sat down, and the player called for a mug. The swelling on his jaw seemed to have lessened since the fight two days ago, and despite the occasional looks of hostility he received, he was in good spirits.

'If it were naught but idle Court gossip,' he said, 'I would treat it with the same caution that you do, my friend. But it seems clear that Lady Imogen is the bedfellow of His Lordship, and frequents his town house – as he does hers. Of course, Beauchamp's married with a son, so she can hold out no hope of snaring him in that way . . . yet, doubtless she has her reasons.'

Thomas was staring at the floor. Now the words of Giles Baldwin came back to him with some force: that his master could be in danger. Telling himself that Sir Robert was no longer his master was futile. He thought of Lady Margaret and faithful old Martin, back at Petbury: their anxiety, and the trust they had placed in him. Like it or not he must do his utmost to help – but where was he to begin?

'What more do you know of Lady Semple?' he asked finally.

Cox shrugged. 'She's the widow of Sir William Semple. He was not of a grand family; rather a merchant, who never had much luck. Nor was he a wealthy man – left her little but a coach, and a house in Hart Street, by the Tower . . .'

'Yet clearly,' Thomas put in, 'she has connections well above her rank.'

Cox nodded. 'And for someone who's barely taller than Queen Mary's famous dwarf, she casts a mighty shadow.'

At that moment the drawer appeared with two mugs, and as he held them out he looked hard at both men. 'That tussle the other night caused a good deal of damage,' he said. 'And I'm looking at the ones who started it all!'

Thomas came out of his reverie, and with a sigh fumbled for his purse. 'Will an angel help pay for it?' he asked.

The drawer stared at him, then his face cleared. 'By the Christ,' he muttered. 'You're a rare one . . .'

Thomas handed him the coin. 'Just give me warning next time that burly fellow's in, will you?'

The drawer grinned. 'I will, master,' he replied. Then shaking his head, he moved off. But when Thomas turned to Cox, he saw the player was looking decidedly nervous.

'Now every cutpurse in Deptford will have his eye on you,' he muttered.

Thomas tilted his mug and took a long, welcome draught. By the time he had lowered it again, he had begun to order his thoughts a little better. And the primal urge that rose in him was one of anger. It took him aback.

'So – Lady Imogen has a thirst for power,' he said.

Cox took a pull from his own mug. 'And is aiming at the very seat of it,' he said quietly. 'Everyone knows King James of Scotland is the likely successor to our Queen – shrewd men have been backing him all along. But still there remain other claimants: Lord Strange was one, who died this year. And some favour Beauchamp; his difficulty is, he's illegitimate. His parents' marriage was declared invalid years ago.'

'Then what hope has he?' Thomas asked.

'He and his friends have tried hard to establish his legitimacy. If they succeeded he'd have a true claim to the throne . . .'

'Whereupon those friends would no doubt be well rewarded,' Thomas finished. He frowned. 'Surely the Queen's loyal servants are aware of the matter . . .?'

'I would guess so,' Cox answered. 'If I know Bossive Robin.'

'Bossive Robin?' Thomas repeated, then remembered. 'Master Secretary . . .'

'Sir Robert Cecil,' Cox nodded. 'Another one it's wise not to meddle with.'

Thomas turned to him. 'Are you still willing to help me?' he asked abruptly.

Cox was looking uncomfortable. 'I am. Yet you have seen I'd not be much use if . . . if I got into danger . . .'

Thomas nodded. 'I ask no man to take risks on my behalf,' he said. 'Information is what I need – and you have entry to places I cannot go.'

'You mean the palace . . .' Cox was looking uneasy. But Thomas shook his head.

'I have in mind the city, which you know better than I. The taverns and ordinaries . . . say, those about Hart Street by the Tower?'

Cox met his eye, then sighed and looked away. 'Ben Mallam was right,' he murmured at last. 'All men have appetites, yet yours seems to be for hidden knowledge. Or perhaps it's merely for following a scent.'

Thomas raised his brows. 'Provided it leads to justice.'

The following morning, the Sabbath, Thomas rose early from his bed at the Lovetts'. Having come late to his lodgings the previous night, he had seen nothing of his hosts. Nor had he set eyes on Mallam, who had not been there at all. Dismissing that matter he walked the path up to Sayes Court, thinking instead of the Lady Imogen, who it now appeared, took to her bed a Lord who claimed succession to the English throne. What, he asked himself as he had done a dozen times already, could she truly want with a man like Sir Robert?

Having taken breakfast, he went to tend the falcons and found a new bird – a magnificent passage hawk with a great hooked beak – staring at him from its perch alongside the others. Then he guessed that this belonged to Sir John Amyot. The notion was confirmed when one of the grooms arrived an hour later and told him to make ready: a hawking party would ride out as soon as the company came from their prayers. And their host, master Baldwin, would be among them.

While he busied himself readying the falcons, Thomas found his thoughts drifting. In the cold light of day, he wondered whether he had been wise in asking Lorel Cox to go enquiring into the Lady Imogen's affairs. Had he not made a promise to the constable, and to Baldwin too, to look into the death of the young woman washed up on the strand? That task sat uneasily beside his personal desire: to find some way to make his master see what kind of woman he was entangled with. And as the morning wore on, he began to wonder if his reasoning were at fault. Surely he was letting his heart rule his head? Hence it was almost a relief when the hawking party appeared with a jangling of harness, and rode up to the mews talking quietly among themselves.

First to draw rein was Giles Baldwin. As they exchanged greetings, Thomas sensed that their earlier conversation was all but forgotten. Today the man was playing host, and must attend to his guests. As Thomas was placing the big haggard, now recovered from the soreness in her eye, upon his outstretched gauntlet, Baldwin turned to the nearest of them.

'Sir John – pray come forward and let the falconer serve you!'

Now Thomas got his first sight of Sir John Amyot, who was reining in his fine hunting horse. The tall, well-dressed man looked down at him with a sardonic smile, then addressed his host. 'So this is the fellow you've taken on, master Controller,' he said in a slow, nasal drawl. 'From what I hear, you'd best keep a close watch on him.' He turned again to Thomas. 'I trust you've looked after my Hermia, falconer. She's worth more than your year's wages.'

Thomas met his eye. 'She's a fine bird, sir,' he answered. 'Though she seems a little edgy . . . perhaps it's the chill.'

He took the passage hawk from its perch and handed it to Amyot – and was at once on his guard as he read the warning in the other's eye: here was a hard man, and one to be wary of.

But there was no time to dwell on it, for now he had to take the tercel over to Sir Robert, and the merlin to Lady Imogen. The two sat together some yards away, smiling and talking low. Both ignored Thomas pointedly as they took their falcons, and quickly rode off on the heels of Baldwin and Amyot. That left only the Lady Imogen's servants, who would follow behind without birds: Malvyn Wyckes, who gave Thomas a brief but courteous greeting, and the waiting-woman. She was the last to draw near; a slim, dignified figure on a borrowed chestnut mare from the Sayes Court stable. As she reined in, she threw back her hood and looked at Thomas, who met her eye – and froze. Seldom had he seen a face of such beauty . . . and rarely one of such deep sadness.

She was not the first African he had encountered; slaves brought from the Indies and sold as house servants were not unknown in London. But this young woman, who could have been barely above twenty years, was special. Her clothes may have been plain – a worsted cloak, and hand-me-down shoes – but her bearing was that of a princess. She did not speak, merely gazed at Thomas with large, cherry-stone eyes, then looked down at the mudded ground.

Remembering that he must get himself horsed, for he was to accompany the party, Thomas was about to go when Wyckes addressed him. 'You must not mind Mouka, falconer . . . she is somewhat nervous on horseback.' He turned to the young woman. 'Master Finbow will follow us – you may trust him to see you safe.'

Since yesterday's encounter, Thomas had found himself developing a grudging respect for Lady Imogen's steward, whose patience, he imagined, must be almost infinite to deal with such a mistress. The way the man had soothed her spoke of his shrewdness as well as his tact. Thomas nodded, and met the man's eye. 'I will mount up and ride along with you, master Wyckes.' To the silent Mouka, he said: 'You need not fear, mistress; the mare is docile, and will not bolt.'

But the young woman merely looked away.

It was a long morning; and for Thomas, a tense one.

The party left the fields beyond Deptford, crossed the Kent Highway and climbed steadily through wooded ground up to Shooter's Hill. The day was fair and the terrain good, and though Thomas expected poor hunting at this time of year, a few pheasants and partridges came in sight. Baldwin and Amyot, he noticed, stayed together, seemingly at ease in each other's company, letting their birds soar and swoop. They paid little heed to Sir Robert and Lady Imogen, who despite the difference in their ages might have been taken for newly-weds, so wrapped up in each other were they. It was all Thomas could do, when he saw the simpering face of the man he still thought of as his master, not to turn and ride off in disgust. Instead he kept himself busy, dismounting to bag up the meagre catch, while keeping one eye on the figure of Mouka, in the rear.

Towards midday, when the party would return to Sayes Court, Thomas's attention was drawn to the waiting-woman. Unaccustomed to riding, she had dismounted and was leading the mare by its rein. When Thomas rode by she stopped, then caught him off guard by looking up and addressing him.

'I am told you used to serve Sir Robert.'

The voice was soft, with an unusual lilt that Thomas found appealing. He smiled at Mouka. 'I did, mistress,' he admitted, and dismounted to stand beside her. Only then did he see the warning look in her eyes; at first he misinterpreted it, thinking she meant him to keep his distance. But then she confounded him by saying: 'If you care for him still, you must get him away from her.'

For a moment, he wondered if he had misheard. Glancing round, he saw Baldwin and Amyot sitting their horses some distance away, deep in conversation. Of Sir Robert and Lady Imogen, as well as Malvyn Wyckes, there was no sign. He faced Mouka again.

'You're not the first to warn me . . .' he began, but she gave a little shake of her head.

'The longer you delay,' she said, 'the harder it will be.'

He stepped closer, half-expecting her to flinch away, but she stood her ground. 'What is it you're afraid to tell me?' he asked. 'I swear that none shall know from whom I heard it—'

'I will not say more,' she said. 'For my courage has run into the ground like water.'

There came hoof-beats. Half-turning, Thomas saw Sir Robert and Lady Imogen emerging from a grove of trees. Further off, Malvyn Wyckes was spurring his own mount to join them.

'Then, tell me one thing,' Thomas persisted. 'What does your mistress want from Sir Robert? Surely it's not merely that he pays court to her, and spends lavishly upon her . . .?'

Mouka hesitated. 'She means to get a husband – one who'll give her everything she wants.'

'But he is a married man,' Thomas countered. 'With children – even a grandchild . . .' He stopped. A thought had occurred to him, that seemed at first ridiculous. But fragments of his conversation with Lorel Cox came to mind: *Can you now doubt what that woman is capable of . . .* He bent his face low, towards Mouka's. And now, she did flinch.

'If he were to become a widower,' she said, 'there would be no barrier – would there?'

Then she turned away, tugging at the mare's rein, and prepared to greet her mistress. And Thomas could only wait as Lady Imogen rode up, and watch as Mouka made her curtsey. Behind, still wearing a foolish grin, came Sir Robert. And Thomas's heart sank to its lowest since he had left Petbury.

* * *

That afternoon, having no further duties, Thomas left Sayes Court and hurried into Deptford. But as he was striding along the strand towards the Sea-Hog, a reedy voice hailed him. Absently he looked round to see Sir Ralph Monkaster standing by his gate with arm raised. 'Hawksman!' he cried. 'Have you pondered further upon my words?'

Thomas was about to make an excuse and walk on, when another figure appeared behind Sir Ralph. It was Lowdy Garth, who peered at Thomas for a few moments before recognizing him. On an impulse Thomas checked his stride, turned and stepped to the gate.

'The air grows warmer, sir,' he said. 'Better for your work, perhaps . . .?'

But Sir Ralph snorted. 'Sun or snow, rain or hail – nothing the Almighty sends shall impede my task,' he said sternly. 'Remember, you have little time to prepare. Make not the mistake of scoffing like these village clods – order your affairs against the storm!'

Thomas made no reply, but cast his eye over the untidy bulk of the ark. In daylight, he saw only too well how crudely built the vessel was. Simon Lovett was right: it was unlikely to sail anywhere. He sighed, as Lowdy came shuffling up.

'Your friend the jingler's bought a nag,' he said. 'It's here, in Sir Ralph's outhouse.'

Thomas blinked, then saw Sir Ralph was nodding. 'He's promised me another,' he said. 'To start my menagerie . . .'

'And Will Rycroft was looking for ye,' Lowdy added helpfully, as if Sir Ralph had not spoken. He was looking hard at Thomas. 'Could it be I know what that's about?'

Thomas did not reply. Instead he glanced at the frozen river, noting that its covering of snow was already thinning. He turned to take his leave, and saw that Sir Ralph had wandered off to select a length of planking from a pile. To Lowdy, he said: 'I'll speak with Rycroft – you haven't set eyes on the player, have you? Master Cox?'

But before Lowdy could reply Sir Ralph spun round, raising his fist in the air. 'That scoffing popinjay!' he shouted. 'All those who strut upon the stage for the amusement of fools deserve the wrath of Heaven! And he will get his deserts, make no mistake!'

The outburst was sudden, and it was over as quickly. Lowdy Garth shook his head and moved off, while the ark-builder, after glaring at Thomas, turned back to his ark. Overhead, gulls wheeled and shrieked.

The man's mad, Thomas thought, and walked off towards the Sea-Hog. But before he reached the door he halted, staring ahead. Some distance along the strand Alice Lovett, in outdoor clothes, was waving to him. Quickening his pace he passed the inn and strode to the chandler's shop. Alice walked forward to meet him.

'Someone's been looking for you, Thomas. He said 'twas important, so I told him he could wait in the kitchen.'

'Mallam?' Thomas enquired, but the woman shook her head.

'Nay – Lorel Cox.'

Thomas hurried past her, into the shop.

Cox was nervous. He sat at Alice's kitchen table opposite Thomas, sipping a mug of ale. And only when Alice had left the two of them and gone out again, would he speak.

'I went to London early,' he said. 'I thought the Sabbath morn was a good time to poke about, talk to people as they came from church . . . I played an innocent, up in town for the Christmas Revels. Played him rather well, I thought . . .'

'You went to Hart Street?' Thomas broke in. 'To the Lady Imogen's . . .?'

Cox nodded. 'Only it's not Hart Street proper where her house lies – rather the poorer end, by Crutched Friars. The rich don't live where you can hear the din from the artillery yard, over the walls. Not that her house is small; it's big – an old, rambling place, in poor repair . . .'

He broke off, and Thomas watched him. 'You've learned something,' he said, but the other would not meet his eye.

'Your pardon, Thomas,' he muttered. 'But I . . . I don't believe I can help you further in your investigations.'

Thomas said nothing.

'It's not that I'm afraid,' Cox went on hurriedly. 'It's more

82

– well, I am afraid, I freely confess it. I'm a player, and not really suited for . . . well, it wasn't what I expected, is what I mean . . .' He was almost stammering now, and finally he fell silent.

Thomas leaned forward. 'I'm in your debt already,' he said quietly. 'And despite what you think of yourself, you're no coward. You tamp your fear down, and go where you must – I'll not ask more of you. Tell me what you've learned, that I may decide what to do.'

Cox met his eye, and took a pull from his mug. 'There's evil in that house,' he said.

Seeing Thomas's brow furrow, he went on: 'Or there was . . . and people still shun the place. Took me a while to get any sense out of those who live nearby – in the end I had to use all my guile on a little kitchen-maid next door. She it was, who told me about the demon that lived on the top floor, under the roof.'

Thomas sat back. 'A demon?'

Cox looked uncomfortable. 'She wasn't the only one who saw it. Others told of it . . . mostly at night, they'd see this fearful creature at the window, clawing at the panes. The maid said it screamed sometimes . . . once the glass broke, and after, it had bars over it.' He shuddered.

Thomas stared at him. 'How long did this go on?'

'A year or more . . . but now, they say it's gone. No more faces at the window.'

'Did you learn anything else?' Thomas asked after a moment.

'Little I didn't know already,' the player told him. 'Lady Imogen's private rages, and the way she torments her poor servants – everyone must fawn upon her and swear their love and devotion, if they know what's good for them. Though they say that new steward of hers has done a lot to keep her in check.' He sniffed. 'Mayhap he's more than a steward – for a small woman, she's one of fierce appetite!'

'New steward?' Thomas asked. 'You mean Wyckes?'

'I know not the name,' Cox answered. 'He came into her service a few months back. A good-looking fellow, by all accounts – curly hair, an easy manner . . .'

'We've met.' Thomas was frowning again. 'This . . . the figure on the upper floor . . .'

'The demon,' Cox nodded. 'Did I say it was kept under lock and key, and fed through a hatch in the door?'

Thomas sighed. 'No, it must have slipped your memory.'

Cox stiffened suddenly. 'You don't believe me!'

Thomas shrugged. 'I know not what to think, where the Lady Imogen's concerned . . .'

'That's no answer!' the player countered. Picking up his mug, he drained it, then set it down with a thud.

'I went to the city to help you – to be your intelligencer!' he said hotly. 'Then when I bring intelligence, you refuse to hear it!'

'Nay, wait . . .' Thomas raised a hand, but Cox was already on his feet.

'The devil with you!' the player said. 'I've a perform-ance to give before the Queen this night – I'm for the palace, where my talents are better appreciated. So, master Sceptic, I give you good-bye!' And before Thomas could say another word the man had flung his tattered cloak grandly about him and walked out, banging the door behind him.

Only one of the theatre folk, Thomas thought ruefully, would know how to make such an exit.

Eight

By evening Thomas was back at Sayes Court, seeking an urgent audience with Sir Robert. He stood in Nicholas Capper's chamber, cap in hand and his pride firmly under control, while the portly steward frowned at him. 'I understood you and your former master were . . .' The man fumbled for the words. 'At some pains to avoid one another . . .'

'Yet my concern for him is undiminished,' Thomas said. 'And I have news he must hear.'

, Capper shrugged. 'Well, it must wait. Sir Robert, Sir John and my master are gone to Greenwich Palace to see the play, like everyone else. The Lord Chamberlain's company are most highly regarded in Court circles.'

Thomas sighed. 'No doubt Lady Semple is gone too,' he muttered. But Capper gave a shake of his head.

'The Lady Imogen is unwell, and has retired to her chamber. Her woman attends her.'

Thomas showed no surprise. Seeing there was nothing to be done here, he was about to take his leave when a thought struck him. 'Is there any means by which I can get a message to my mistress – I should say, to Lady Vicary?' he asked.

Capper gave him a blank look. 'All the way to Petbury, in mid-winter?'

'Never mind.' Thomas started for the door. 'I merely ask that as soon as you may, you tell Sir Robert I have a matter of importance to put before him.'

Capper bristled as if forming some sharp riposte, but he was too slow. All he heard was Thomas's boots echoing on the flagged passage outside.

* * *

Needing to collect his thoughts, Thomas went to the falcons' mews and stood in the chill night air, gazing at his charges. All the birds seemed docile after their day's exertions, and merely stirred before accepting his presence. His troubles were not their concern; after a while they forgot about him altogether, and dozed on their perches.

The words of Mouka rang in his head; in fact they had been in his thoughts since the morning. Was it truly possible that Lady Imogen looked forward to Lady Margaret's death, in order to marry Sir Robert? She could hardly be expected to wait for Lady Margaret – twelve years younger than her husband, and as fit and healthy as anyone at Petbury – to die of natural causes. In which case, was the woman capable of arranging her murder? It seemed absurd; yet he believed he knew enough of Lady Imogen now not to discount it. The notion chilled him to the bone.

Barely knowing what he did, he found himself walking away from Sayes Court, across the fields into open country. Soon the lights of Deptford were only a faint glow in the distance, while beyond, the great frozen mass of the Thames gleamed faintly. Finally he stopped beside a fallen elm-tree and sat down upon it. Seldom, he realized, had he felt so alone; what now could he do?

After a while he looked up and saw the towers of Placentia to the east, stark against the night sky. Lights showed at many windows. He could almost fancy he heard the sound of distant revels, but knew it was only the breeze. He imagined Lorel Cox on stage in a great hall, taking his bow before a delighted audience, including Sir Robert. And slowly, to his relief, a resolution began to form.

He would go back and wait for Sir Robert, if he had to wait all night; no one would stop him conveying what he knew – as well as what he suspected. Then at least his obligations would be fulfilled, and Sir Robert could rant all he liked; let him take what steps he wished. Thomas would then focus his efforts on finding out who had murdered the poor woman whose body lay in Will Rycroft's hut. Whether he succeeded or failed, he would have discharged that obligation too – and would owe Giles Baldwin nothing. Hence he would pack his belongings and leave for Berkshire, on foot if necessary. Nell at least would be glad to see him, as would Eleanor. Then the Finbows could decide together what to do.

The thought cheered him, and in a moment he had risen and was retracing his steps. A half hour later he was on Deptford Strand again, walking to the door of the Sea-Hog . . . and an old saw came unbidden to him, that almost made him smile. *Men make their own luck*, his father used to say. For on entering the inn, the first person he set eyes upon was Ben Mallam; and he knew now what he would do.

'Thomas – welcome!' the jingler cried. 'You're in time to toast my good fortune!' He was standing among a group of unsavoury-looking fellows, most of them the worse for drink. Catching the drawer's eye, Thomas called for a mug, then eased himself through the throng until he was close to Mallam.

'Could we have a private word?' he murmured.

'Anything for you, my friend . . .' Mallam turned to the others. 'Standing before you, is the best falconer in all England, even if he's a mite too serious for his own good!' He clapped Thomas on the shoulder. 'You see me at the turning of the tide,' he grinned. 'I'm now the lucky owner of a neat little Galloway, that will sell for ten nobles at the least, and put me back in business!'

'I heard,' Thomas replied. 'I also hear you've talked Sir Ralph into giving you free stabling.'

Ben's grin widened. 'Where's the harm in that? I'll be moving the jade in a day or two, and the old fool will forget all about it.' He tilted his mug and took a pull, as Thomas's own drink arrived. Taking it from the drawer, he bent close to Ben's ear.

'I'm going on a little trip across the river,' he said. 'And I want you to accompany me.'

Ben started, and turned to face him. 'Across the river . . . you mean to the Isle of Dogs? You're as cracked as Monkaster . . .' Then he flinched as Thomas gripped his shoulder.

'I need your help.'

Mallam shook his head. 'I'm not going there!'

87

'I need your eyes and ears, as well as your knowledge,' Thomas persisted. And before Ben could protest further, he added: 'Else in my ignorance, I might just let slip to master Lovett what you and Alice do behind his back.'

Mallam froze. The other drinkers, seeing he was now engaged in what looked like business, were turning away from him. Frowning, the jingler met Thomas's eye.

'You wouldn't . . .'

'Believe it, I'm desperate enough,' Thomas told him. 'Do you truly want to try me?'

The two stared at each other, until at last Mallam lowered his gaze. 'I won't forget this, you whoreson hawk-prigger,' he muttered.

Thomas merely drained his mug, and led the way outside.

They had no lantern; only the light of the waxing moon, and its eerie reflection from the frozen river. Soon they had ventured upon its surface, and the lights of Deptford were receding at their rear. Though the ice seemed solid enough, there was an alarming creak from it at intervals. Not for the first time, Mallam cursed roundly.

'You cross-biting cove,' he said. 'If I don't fall through to my death, I could get my throat cut on the other side, just for the clothes on my back. My only consolation would be, you'd likely get yours cut too!'

Thomas ignored him. They were almost at the other side now. Peering ahead into the darkness, he made out two or three faint points of light. 'So long as we stick to our tale,' he said, 'we'll pass for a couple of knaves fleeing the law . . .'

'And then what?' Mallam demanded. 'You think anyone there's going to give us a bed for the night—'

'I told you,' Thomas said tersely. 'I want to know about the dumping of a body in the river, around a week back.'

'You're mad.' Mallam was tapping his forehead. 'The Isle isn't the kind of place you go asking questions—'

'Well, we're about to find out.' Thomas pointed and at once Ben stiffened, peering towards the lights. Ahead of them the riverbank rose in the gloom, and standing upon it, staring down at them, were two figures in ragged clothes.

Mallam gulped, but Thomas stopped and raised a hand. 'We're seeking refuge, masters,' he called softly. 'Can we come ashore?'

After a moment one of the fellows gestured to them to walk forward and climb the bank. As they did so with some difficulty, the man grew less threatening. He was lame, and leaned on a forked stick for a crutch. His companion was a shivering, skinny little runt who looked as if he would keel over at any time.

The lame one peered at them. 'Where've you come from?' he grunted. Thomas was about to reply, but Mallam cut in quickly.

'There's a *stalling ken* above Billingsgate, run by one Malter,' he said. 'You know it?' When neither man spoke, he went on: 'I had a bit of plate – worth two angels or more . . . I was taking it to him, when the cove I found it from shows up with a constable at his back . . . that's my luck for ye. I can but thank Christ for the dark, and for the ice!'

He gave a chuckle, then fell silent. The lame man did not react, but the skinny one was peering at Thomas.

'What of your friend?' he whined.

Thomas snorted. 'He's no friend of mine,' he said. 'He owes me – and I'm not letting him out of my sight until he sells that plate and pays up in full.'

The other two looked at each other, and finally the little man nodded. Only then did Thomas notice the poniard in the lame one's hand; it glinted as he stowed it away.

'You'd best come in and make yourselves known,' he said. Turning to Mallam he added: 'There's a stalling ken here, of a kind . . . only I doubt you'll get two angels for your trouble.' He frowned. 'Where's the stuff?'

Mallam drew a breath. 'It's safe,' he replied. 'You don't think we'd carry a sack of plate over here, do you? The place is full of thieves.'

He laughed again, and after a moment the two men relaxed. Turning awkwardly, the lame one hobbled away towards the lights, and the others followed.

* * *

The lights, it turned out, were cooking-fires. A short time later, having thrown two half-pennies into a cracked jar as contribution, Thomas and Ben were sitting huddled beside one such blaze, sharing a platter of meat and onions in a thin sauce. Though what particular animal had furnished the meat, neither of them dared to ask.

It was not the only encampment on the Isle. There were others further inland, among the marshes, which Thomas was not inclined to enquire about. This sorry collection of tents and makeshift shelters was nearest to the riverside, and the only one opposite Deptford. And it was nearby, he felt sure, that someone had thrown the body of the faceless woman into the water. Though now that he was here, making enquiries about such an event seemed somewhat rash. For though Thomas had spent as much time in bad company as he cared to recall, never in his life had he found himself in such a nest of thieves and rogues.

Some sat by the fire, eating or drinking from cannikins. Others wandered restlessly to and fro, or disappeared into the shelters as the night wore on. Without seeming to, Thomas took the measure of them: discharged soldiers, deserters, beggars and fugitives of every sort. Some were clearly sick, and would not last the winter. Others were angry-looking, desperate men whom it would be wise to avoid. One or two were better dressed than their fellows: ruined clerks or scriveners, even parsons whose crimes had put them outside the bounds of civilized society, and which it were best not to dwell upon too much.

No one addressed them, and after they had supped and shared a cup of poor watered sack, Mallam spoke low to Thomas. 'What did I tell you?' he muttered. 'You'll get no information here that's worth a bent farthing. Let's cut our losses and get out.'

But Thomas remained seated. 'The stalling ken,' he said. 'That might be worth a visit . . .'

Mallam hesitated. 'I'll find out where it is – but once we're there, you're on your own. This place makes me jumpy as a hare.'

With an exaggerated movement he stood up, stretched,

and walked off, fumbling with his breeches as if about to make water. Thomas waited. He waited several minutes, until Ben startled him by appearing out of the dark, from another direction. But at his brief nod, Thomas too stood up and walked away from the firelight. Nobody paid him any attention.

The 'stalling ken' – the receiving house for stolen property – turned out to be nothing but a sheet of patched sailcloth stretched over a low framework of poles. Inside it was stuffy and dim, lit by a single lantern. But there was no mistaking the tent's purpose, for almost filling it were two heavy, iron-bound chests, securely locked. And sitting upon one of them was the proprietor: a weasel-eyed old man with long grey hair and an untrimmed beard. As Thomas and Ben lifted the door-flap and entered, he raised a hand swathed in a tattered woollen mitten and called out: 'Stop, and state your business!'

Mallam halted, spreading his hands to show he was unarmed and said: 'We've a bit of plate for sale, master. Good silver . . . heard you might know of someone who'd buy such.'

The old man peered at them. 'So where is it?' he grunted.

'Safe, upriver,' Ben said, and knowing how lame his answer sounded, turned to glare at Thomas. 'My friend here's the one to do business with. I'm but his bawker.'

The man's gaze shifted to Thomas, who took a step forward. 'The plate can wait,' he said. 'It's information I'm after, and I can pay for it.'

Ben's mouth fell open. But before he could curse Thomas's apparent foolhardiness, Thomas had pushed his way past him to stand over the old man. The next moment, however, he was staring down at the point of a dagger, which had appeared in an instant.

'Peace, master,' he said. 'I mean you no harm, and here's the proof.' Meeting the old man's eye, he put his hand slowly into his jerkin and drew forth a silver coin.

But the other did not move, only stared hard at Thomas. 'I need only whistle,' he growled, 'and you'll be taken and bound. And I wager you wouldn't care to think what some of those back there in the marshes would do to ye . . .'

'I know it,' Thomas said. 'Yet I'm a man seeking vengeance for a young girl murdered. I deem her worth any risk.'

He held out the coin, and after what seemed an eternity the old man's eyes shifted towards it. Then suddenly, he took it.

'Another sixpence when I find out who dumped a body in the river here, a week or so back,' Thomas said.

The old man was frowning, but slowly he lowered the poniard. 'I know naught of it,' he said. 'You've wasted your money.'

'Another tester,' Thomas repeated.

There was another wait. Thomas heard Ben Mallam shifting on his feet, but kept his eyes on the old man. Finally the fellow sniffed, turned his head and called out.

'Matty!'

There was a sound from outside. Thomas and Ben both started as the door-flap lifted, and a young boy in his teens stepped inside.

'Take these two to the jetty, tell the apple-squire I said to aid them.'

The boy nodded. And without further hesitation, Ben Mallam went out. The old man meanwhile, held out his hand until Thomas had produced another coin and given it to him. And there was a glint in his eye as he said: 'There was no silver plate, was there?'

Thomas merely turned from him and went out.

They followed the young boy back to the cooking-fire, then away from it, to Ben Mallam's relief, along the path that led towards the river. Nobody followed them. But when they reached the bank, the boy turned briskly to his right and led the way along it, past clumps of dead, frozen bushes, until there was no light except that of the moon reflected off the ice. After some minutes, by which time both had grown very uneasy, they emerged above a gravel slope. Below them a crude jetty was thrust out into the Thames, and beside it lay a small boat, stuck fast in the ice. But the boy walked on, around a stand of broken rushes, gesturing them to follow. To their surprise a light appeared – and there was a house, of sorts, set back from the river, with a sagging roof and a stack of firewood by the door. The boy signalled to them to wait while he walked forward and knocked hard upon the door. Immediately there came an answering call from within, followed by voices . . . most of which were unmistakeably female. And swiftly Thomas and Ben turned to each other; for only now, had they understood.

'A trugging-house,' Ben snorted. 'Which men can reach from the city by boat . . . cosy, eh?' He rounded upon Thomas, unleashing his fear and frustration. 'I should've known – and I should've left you at the riverside and gone straight back to Deptford!' he cried. 'Now we've been led on a wild goose chase! My only consolation is, it's cost you a shilling!'

Thomas ignored him. He was watching the door, which had opened, allowing a dim light to spill out. The boy was speaking low to someone within; finally a figure appeared, wrapped in a heavy cloak, peering up the slope towards him.

'To hell with you, Thomas . . .' Ben was turning away. 'You can make your own way back!'

Then he stopped in his tracks; and Thomas looked round, for he too had heard voices – not from the house, but from upriver, in the direction of London. The next moment three men appeared out of the gloom, and Mallam gave a loud groan. For their leader was a very short, thickset fellow in a broad-brimmed hat. And as he drew near, he too let out a cry of recognition.

'Mallam, you dunghill knave – you owe me, still!'

'Tom-tit!' Ben backed away, gripping his left arm as if the very memory of who had broken it made it hurt afresh. He threw Thomas a look of desperation. 'It's Peter Sly – leg it!'

'Wait.' Thomas's voice brooked no argument. 'He wouldn't start anything here . . .' He looked towards the house, and saw now that the boy was gesturing to them. 'Come on, let's get inside. It's your best hope.'

Without waiting he strode to the doorway, and with a gulp, Mallam followed. His long sigh of relief as the door closed behind them was audible enough for the personage in the cloak to step back in alarm. But quickly, Thomas took charge.

'There are a couple of coves out there we'd rather not

see, master,' he explained. 'Though I doubt they'll trouble you . . .'

But as the cloak was thrown back, he had to revise his use of the word 'master'. He was looking at a hard-faced woman of middle years, her cheeks heavily painted with ceruse. Grey hair showed under the edge of the red periwig atop her head.

'Any scores here, are settled outside,' the woman snapped. 'All who use my house know the rules!'

Thomas nodded. They stood in a little outer room, with a door from beyond which came women's voices and a shout of male laughter. Only now did he realize the boy Matty had vanished.

'State your business,' the woman said.

Thomas's eye moved downward, to the stout knobbed stick she carried. Aware of Mallam breathing hard at his back, he began to explain his purpose once again, but found it difficult to keep frustration from his voice. The task was indeed looking hopeless. After a moment, however, the woman stayed him. 'This the boy has told already,' she said. 'I say to you what I said to him: there's one within who may help, if you'll await him. There's little goes on he don't know about.'

But Ben Mallam had other ideas. As Thomas hesitated, the jingler stepped forward, putting on the easy smile he always employed when dealing with the opposite sex.

'My friend will wait if it pleases him, my duck,' he smiled. 'All I ask is the use of a back door or window, so I can get myself out and across the river in one piece.' He slapped his pocket. 'I'll pay the rate for your ugliest callett, and not even tumble her – now, is that a bargain?'

The woman frowned. 'You must be hard pressed indeed,' she muttered, then held out her hand. 'Threepence will cover it . . .'

The coin was out in an instant. Taking it, the bawd turned and rapped on the door with her stick. The moment it was opened a mere crack, Ben pushed his way inside. As he went he called over his shoulder to Thomas: 'I told you, you're on your own. And it's the last time I aid you!'

The door slammed shut. But before either Thomas or the woman could speak there came a banging on the outer door: Peter Sly and his fellows, Thomas guessed. At least Mallam would give them the slip if he got out the back . . .

The woman gestured to him to move aside, so she could answer the door. Having resolved to take his leave in any case, he did so. But at that moment the inner door opened again and a man came out – to stop dead as he and Thomas came face to face. Thomas blinked, at once recognizing the heavy beard almost to the eyes: Daniel Skeeres.

'He's the one I meant,' the bawd said to Thomas in a matter-of-fact tone, and jerked her thumb towards Skeeres. ''Twas him brought the boat, and got it stuck in the ice . . .' She threw Skeeres a leering smile. 'Overstayed your welcome, didn't you, master Butter-Mouth? Only 'twas one situation you couldn't talk your way out of!'

She turned to open the door, and the cold night air flooded in. On the threshold, the diminutive figure of Peter Sly was poised to enter, with his two companions close behind. But seeing Thomas's tall frame looming above the bawd's head, he fell back – and that brief moment was all Daniel Skeeres needed. For whatever was about to be asked of him, it seemed he was not keen to hear it. Twisting past Thomas like an eel, he thrust the bawd aside and stepped quickly out of the door. In the process he also shoved the Tom-tit and his fellows, who reacted angrily. But already Skeeres had ducked his head and was running towards the river. And in a moment, for no other reason than his instinct, Thomas had leaped through the door and was running after him.

Behind him came shouts: the old bawd's cry of indignation, and the Tom-tit's bellow. But Thomas did not look round until another voice, one he recognized, called to him from ahead and to his left, beside the jetty: it was Mallam, also bolting for the ice, cursing loudly as he realized his escape had been short-lived. For his enemy Peter Sly, with his two fellows close behind, had started in pursuit.

But Thomas kept his eyes on the retreating back of Skeeres, who had scurried off to the right, in the direction of London. And whatever happened, he did not intend to let him go.

Nine

Confusion reigned on the frozen, moonlit Thames, for there were two separate pursuits. Skeeres, skidding on the ice, falling and scrambling up again, showed increasing desperation as he realized Thomas was the surer of foot, and was gaining on him. Meanwhile Ben Mallam, in the rear, showed similar desperation as his own pursuers came doggedly on. Finally he drew near enough to Thomas to shout between breaths. 'This is your doing, you . . .'

Then he yelped in alarm. For there was a loud crack, like a cannon-shot: except that it came from somewhere close to their feet. 'The ice!' Ben gasped. 'It's breaking up!'

Thomas checked his stride, glancing swiftly about. Ahead of him Skeeres had slipped again and was struggling to his feet, his panting audible from twenty yards away. On either side, the riverbanks showed ghostly in the dark. Only a distant, twinkling light spoke of any nearby habitation.

'Where are we?' Thomas shouted.

'Redriff's up ahead . . .' Ben nodded to their left, then risked a look behind. 'By the Christ, they're gaining!'

He began to move nervously forward, but Thomas pointed. 'Run beside me, but keep a few feet apart. Take long strides . . .'

And to Ben's horror he stepped out into the centre of the river, to its deepest part, then veered towards the south bank and began trotting forward.

'Have you lost your senses?' Ben yelled. 'We'll fall through!'

But already Thomas was disappearing into the gloom. Cursing again, the jingler followed. With each step, he now expected to hear a cracking that heralded an icy death.

Looking round he saw his three pursuers, in a tight body, coming on fast. And even as the notion struck him, he heard another great crack – which was followed by another . . . then Ben Mallam halted, hearing screams, and turned about in time to witness the terrible sight: two men falling through a patch of thin ice.

There was a flurry of spray, and what sounded like the breaking of shards of glass as the two bigger men thrashed about, up to their necks in the icy river. Even as Mallam gazed in horror, one of them disappeared. The other man was clawing feebly at the edge of the great hole that had formed. Only Peter Sly the Tom-tit was still safe, hopping about from one place to another, as if performing some sort of dance. Finally, whimpering, the little man turned from his lost fellows and ran for his life towards the north bank. In a moment he had disappeared into the dark.

With a sick feeling in his vitals, Ben Mallam looked down at his feet, fancying he heard another crack. Then at last, his powerful instinct for self-preservation made him look up, and he began to make straight for the south bank. He took long, loping strides, half-expecting each to be his last. Only when he had fallen over a rotting log did he realize that he had reached the river's edge. With a cry he flung himself forward on to soggy, slush-covered ground, almost weeping as he felt the hardness beneath. Then he turned and sat down heavily in melted snow, his legs shaking, staring out at the treacherous expanse of ice which had almost become his grave. And only after that, did he begin to think about his companion.

'Thomas . . .?' Ben got slowly to his feet, glad even to feel the icy wetness of his breeches. He had faced danger more times than he could have remembered; but only now did he know what it truly meant to have come close to death, and lived. Never again, he vowed, would he walk out upon the frozen Thames, not even to a fair. He peered into the darkness. Across the river, a few faint lights showed, but there was no answer.

'Thomas!' he shouted, more urgently. An unpleasant thought was forming: not only that Thomas too was lost under the ice – but that it was somehow Ben's fault. After all, he had survived, while . . .

'*Thomas!*' he yelled, looking wildly from left to right; but still no answer came. Ben swallowed, and took a few unsteady steps along the riverside. Then he was walking faster, stumbling over stones and tussocks, squinting upriver into the gloom. He opened his mouth to shout again – then at last, to his huge relief, there came an answering cry from barely a dozen yards away.

'Here!'

Heart in mouth, the jingler hurried forward, to see Thomas standing over a slumped figure sitting head in hands on the shore, gasping for breath.

'By the Christ . . .' Ben put a hand out, as if to assure himself that Thomas was alive. 'I thought . . .' He broke off, shaking his head, and looked down at the seated figure. As he watched, the man lowered his hands and turned a haggard, heavily-bearded face towards him. Ben blinked.

'Dan Skeeres?' he stared at Thomas. 'This was who you were chasing?'

Thomas, who was recovering his own breath, nodded briefly.

'But why?' Ben wore a blank look. 'He'd swear anything you like for—'

'So I've heard.' Breathing deeply, Thomas straightened up and faced him. 'What happened to your friends?'

Ben shuddered, and told him. Then he sat down on the gravelly shore. After a moment Thomas turned back to Skeeres, whose eyes were busily assessing his chances of escape.

'Why did you run off?' he asked. 'I only wanted to ask you a few questions.'

Skeeres said nothing, and finally Ben Mallam gave a snort.

'You'll get naught out of him unless you pay dear for it,' he said. 'And even then it's likely a pack of lies!'

'Says who?' Skeeres muttered, with a glare at Ben. 'And since when have jinglers been famous for their honesty?'

But Thomas was not about to listen to these two trade insults. He was tired, he had wasted hours on a fruitless errand, and this man represented his last shred of hope. With a sudden movement, he leaned down and grabbed the startled Skeeres by the collar.

'A body was dumped in the water, from the Isle, just before the river froze over,' he said. 'Could be it was close to that jetty where your boat's stuck. What do you know of it?'

Skeeres gulped, feeling the strength of Thomas's grip. Thomas knew that the perjurer had almost fallen through the ice himself, and hence was likely feeling very shaky. The fellow moistened his lips and looked up. 'There's no need for this,' he muttered. 'You want answers, friend – you can have them.'

Ignoring Ben Mallam's grunt of derision, Thomas bent his face closer. 'What do you know of it?' he repeated.

Skeeres hesitated. 'Would it be the body of a man or woman?' he enquired innocently.

Thomas watched him closely. It may have been the poor light, but he believed he saw a look in Skeeres's eye that told him the man knew something after all. He turned abruptly to Ben.

'What say I shove this cove out upon the ice while you crack it with a rock, and we watch him drown?' he asked. 'We'd be doing all London a favour, would we not?'

Mallam eyed Thomas, and stiffened. 'That we would,' he agreed. 'And there are no witnesses!'

Skeeres put out his hands to grab Thomas's wrist. 'Don't try and cog me,' he sneered. 'You're not the kind—'

'What kind am I, then?' Thomas asked, tightening his grip. 'The kind who'd break a poor maid's neck and cast her into the water – or the kind who'd ruin her face first, so she couldn't be recognized?'

Skeeres frowned. 'I don't know what you're—'

But at that moment Ben Mallam got to his feet. Skeeres's eyes darted towards him as he stooped to pick up a large stone, then stood hefting it in his hand.

Skeeres turned to gaze at Thomas again. 'If you already know so much, why ask me?' he demanded. 'I've killed no one!'

Mallam sniffed. 'That much at least, is likely the truth,' he observed. 'He hasn't the spine for murder.'

'You've a plain choice,' Thomas told Skeeres. 'Tell me what you know, and you walk away; waste any more of my time, and I'll shove you through the ice myself.'

There was a moment. The word *murder* seemed to have alarmed Skeeres. And, it being the habit of practised liars to tell as much of the truth as they can afford to, he seemed to relent.

'I put her in the water,' he said.

Thomas drew a breath. 'You!'

'Yes, me!' Skeeres looked angry now, which somehow gave his testimony the stamp of truth. 'Only I know not who she was. I was paid to do it, and I didn't ask questions. She was already dead, and her face was like that before I set eyes on her – *finis*!'

The other two stared. Thomas let go the man's collar, and straightened up. 'Who paid you . . .?' he began, but with a muttered curse, Mallam stepped closer to him.

'More lies,' he said harshly. 'The only way he'll talk is if we crack a hole in the ice and dangle him over it—'

'It's truth!' Skeeres spat, with a malevolent look at the jingler. 'And ask not who paid me, for I'm carrion if I tell that!'

Mallam glared at him. 'You're frozen carrion if you don't!'

Skeeres was rubbing his neck, his eyes darting everywhere. But he saw that the moment he tried to scramble to his feet, Thomas would seize him. He hesitated, then:

'I'll tell what I can. I was paid a sovereign to bring a boat after dark to Petty Wales, by the Tower – just above the water-gate. Two were waiting, with the . . . with a bundle, tied up in buckram. My part was but to ferry it downriver to Woolwich, untie it and heave it over the side—'

'Woolwich?' Thomas leaned forward, startling the man. 'Then why did it wash up at—' He stopped, and turned towards Mallam, who was wearing a wry look.

'If you knew our friend a little better,' Ben said, 'you'd not trouble to ask. Once he's got paid and rowed out of sight, he dumps his cargo overboard at the first opportunity – by the trugging-house jetty!' He turned to Skeeres. 'Couldn't wait to spend your sovereign, could you, Dan?'

Skeeres made no reply, but Thomas saw it clearly now. Of course the poor woman was not supposed to wash up at Deptford, close to a royal palace, but further downriver, where the tide would carry her out to sea . . . then a notion struck him.

'There was a deal of silver about her fingers when she was found,' he said quietly. 'I'm surprised you let that go into the water.' And now, Skeeres's startled reaction was all he needed.

'Was that what you were doing at Lovett's?' Thomas went on. 'Trying to sell him something you took off the corpse?'

Skeeres looked away, until Ben Mallam's snort of contempt made him turn in alarm. The jingler dropped his stone and took a step forward, but Thomas shook his head. Instead he leaned down and spoke to Skeeres in a hard voice.

'Give me a name,' he said. 'None will know it came from you.'

But Skeeres shook his head. 'I swear I know not who she was, nor do I wish to—'

'The one who paid you,' Thomas cut in harshly.

Again the man shook his head. 'I don't know his name!'

'You're lying,' Thomas snapped. 'You said you were carrion if you told . . .'

But there was a wild look about Skeeres now, which put Thomas and Ben on their guard. 'I cannot name him!' he cried. 'Now in God's name, let me go!'

'Why can't you?' Thomas countered. 'You're no stranger to risk – who is it you fear so much?'

Skeeres cursed under his breath. 'Who do I fear?' he threw back. 'The Queen's Privy Council, that's who! And rackmaster Topcliffe, who'd pull me to pieces and smile while he did it, to think I'd named one of their best projectors—'

Then he smacked his fist on the ground, furious at having said more than he wished. And throwing caution aside now, he did scramble up. At once Ben Mallam darted forward, but Thomas put out a hand to stay him. Unfortunately it was the jingler's left arm he caught . . . and too late he remembered, as Ben yelped with pain. And it was Thomas's turn to mutter an oath as Ben sank to his knees, clutching his arm. Then he whirled round in time to see Daniel Skeeres running away along the riverbank, stumbling and cursing, until the night swallowed him up.

But there was no point in giving chase, for Thomas knew in his bones that he had learned all he could from the knight of the post. With a sigh, he turned to help the groaning Ben Mallam.

In the morning Thomas was up before dawn, having snatched a few hours' rest in the Lovetts' attic. Ben was exhausted, and he left him sleeping. Neither Simon or Alice were yet awake, which suited Thomas well enough. Any enquiries he might need to make about the chandler's dealings with Daniel Skeeres would have to wait. Grimly he set himself to his task of confronting Sir Robert.

He was at the mews as the Sayes Court household began to stir, to tend the falcons. Seeing all was well he walked to the kitchen yard, just as young Bridget emerged from the back door with a slop-pail. 'Falconer!' she looked startled. 'You're an early one!'

He gave her good-day, then asked for tidings of her master and his guests.

'Master Giles and Sir Robert came in only an hour or two since,' the girl answered. 'Seems the Queen kept everyone up all night, dancing and such! Do you mark it, at her age?'

Thomas hid his disappointment. 'Then, they'll be abed all morning . . .'

Bridget shrugged. 'Not Lady Imogen,' she muttered. 'She was up early, calling for her woman.' She shook her head. 'How that one stands it, I don't know . . . they say she beats her almost every day, whether she done wrong or no.'

Thomas winced. He was trying to decide whether to wait for Sir Robert to rise, or find something more useful to occupy him. He was on the point of deciding to return later, when a thought struck him.

'Tell me,' he asked in a casual tone. 'Have you heard the tales about Lady Imogen's house in London?'

'You mean, that it's haunted? Everyone knows that – only you'd best keep it to yourself. Master Giles don't like gossip.'

Thomas nodded, and decided not to ask further. 'I've business in Deptford,' he said. 'I'll come back when Sir Robert's awake.'

Bridget grinned. 'That'd be business at mistress Lovett's, would it?' She gave Thomas a sly look, and before he could reply, walked off towards the pig-pen.

Simon Lovett had opened up his shop, though there were no customers yet. When Thomas walked in he was lighting a lantern against the gloom of a cloudy morning. Having hung it on its hook, he turned to peer at the incomer before nodding a greeting. 'Alice said you were out early,' he said. 'Mallam's still snoring like a bullock.'

Thomas came closer, until Lovett made out his expression and frowned slightly. 'You look like a man wanting to do business,' he observed.

Thomas nodded, unsure as yet how to broach the matter. Finally he said: 'I had a long talk last night with a fellow *you* were doing business with – on Friday, was it not? Name of Skeeres.' He paused. 'Tried to sell you something, didn't he?'

The other's frown deepened. 'What if he did?'

'Supposing it was stolen?' Thomas suggested.

Simon said nothing. And without taking his eyes off him, Thomas pointed over his shoulder. 'Supposing it was stolen from the one who was found washed up on the shore, not fifty yards from here?'

Lovett drew a sharp breath. 'If you're trying to accuse me of something, master Thomas,' he said quietly, 'you'd best come out and say so.'

'I don't accuse you,' Thomas replied. 'Unless it be of carelessness.' When the other bridled, he went on: 'From what I've heard, you're not born to a life of business. You take too much on trust, ask too few questions. A man like Skeeres . . .' He broke off, for Simon Lovett had taken a step forwards. And his one good eye blazed like a coal.

'What else have you heard?' he said in a harsh voice. 'That

I'm short of money? Who in Deptford isn't? That don't make me a brogger – nor any other kind of cozener!'

Thomas met his eye. 'Agreed,' he said. 'Nor do I think you knew where it came from . . .' He hesitated, then: 'All I ask, is you let me look at it.'

'I haven't said there's anything to look at,' Lovett retorted. 'How do you know I didn't tell Skeeres to take his goods elsewhere?'

'I don't,' Thomas admitted. 'I suppose I'm asking you to take me on trust, too.'

There followed a long moment; then to Thomas's surprise, Lovett gave a sigh and dropped his gaze. 'I bought it for Alice,' he said.

Thomas stared. 'Bought what?'

The chandler did not look up. 'You think like everyone else,' he muttered. 'Because I've only one eye that works, I don't see what goes on under my own roof . . .'

A look of understanding crossed Thomas's face. 'I ask your pardon,' he began, but the other raised his head.

'Save your pity! I'm a fool to myself, looking away, making out I don't hear things . . .' He sighed. 'Mallam's not the first,' he said.

'I still ask your pardon,' Thomas said after a moment. 'If only for keeping my own mouth shut—'

Lovett shook his head. 'The jingler's your friend, and any man can see what a wandering eye Alice has,' he said in a tired voice. 'If I'd been more of a husband . . . seems I can never give her the things she wants. And you're right – I'm the worst ships' chandler on the river!'

Thomas gave a wry smile. 'Where's the shame in that?' he asked. 'A man who hides his troubles and puts on a good face, gets through each day as you do, has my respect.'

Lovett said nothing. After a moment he moved to a chest that stood against the wall, opened it and began lifting out pieces of old clothing: salt-stained sailors' jackets and breeches, tarred jerkins and hats . . . finally from the bottom, he drew out a little canvas bag. Then gesturing Thomas to draw near, he went to a small table under the lantern, where the light was good.

'You were on the scent,' he said. 'I knew 'twas likely stolen, but I never guessed it came from the dead maid – I swear that to you.'

'I believe you,' Thomas said. 'I've only just learned of it myself . . .' He broke off, bending closer as Simon opened the bag and laid out its contents, then drew breath. He was staring at a finely worked gold necklace of tiny, filigree bows interlinked with red enamelled hearts. In the centre, where it would lie on the wearer's chest, was a larger heart, bearing two gold letters: *J.D.*

Neither man spoke. Finally after a glance at Lovett, Thomas took up the piece and examined it.

'Is it not the most wondrous thing?' Simon murmured. 'To think it was about the neck of one so hideous . . .' He shook his head. ''Tis hard to fathom.'

Thomas's mind was busy. His first thought was that the killer of the young girl was careless to let something that might identify her remain upon her body. Unless the grisly business had been despatched quickly, in poor light, perhaps . . . small wonder, he reflected, that Dan Skeeres could not resist taking it. The rings on the girl's fingers would have seemed but trifles next to this . . . He looked up. 'Could you guess at its value?' he asked.

Lovett shrugged. 'More than you and I earn in a year, put together,' he said. 'I gave Skeeres two angels on account, said there might be more later. I'd a mind to get it valued.'

'Well, I doubt he'll be back for further payment, now I've uncovered his little secret,' Thomas told him. ''Twas he threw the poor maid in the river, though she was already dead.'

Lovett gasped. 'Nay . . . you're mistook! He's a rogue, right enough – but mixed up in murder?' He shook his head.

'Mixed up with murderers, though likely not one himself,' Thomas replied. 'But now . . .' Gently he laid the precious necklace down. 'If I haven't a name, then at least I have some initials: *J.D.* It's a beginning.'

'What will you do?' the other asked.

Thomas considered. 'Could I borrow it for a while? I'll bring it back – you've my word on it.'

Simon hesitated. 'You won't say where you got it?'

'You have my word,' Thomas repeated. And after a moment, the other nodded.

But no sooner had Thomas stowed the necklace inside his jerkin, than the door flew open. Both men looked round, as the unmistakeable figure of William Rycroft filled the entrance.

'Master Constable,' Thomas murmured. 'That's odd, for I would have come looking for you . . .' Then he stopped, seeing the man's agitated manner.

'Will?' Lovett was peering at him through his one eye. 'What's the matter?'

Rycroft took a breath, looking from one man to another. 'Someone got in my hut last night,' he said to Thomas, 'and broke open the casket. All that's left is melted ice.'

When neither man made a response, he raised his voice. 'I mean the poor maid's body – it's gone!'

Ten

Thomas stood beside the constable again in his little hut, staring down at the wooden box. But now, as Rycroft had said, there was nothing but a pool of water to show where the young woman had lain. After a cursory glance about, Thomas faced the other man. 'And you and your family heard nothing?' he asked.

Rycroft shook his head. 'Whoever did it, must have been in and out quick – and mighty quiet. Then, there was no lock on the door – why would there be?' He wore a baffled look. 'Who'd wish to steal a corpse?'

The two of them walked outside. Rycroft closed the door of the hut and led the way through his cluttered garden. At the gate he hesitated. 'I'll poke about the village, find out what I can,' he said.

'And I'll tell Baldwin,' Thomas said. 'I've other business there, anyway.' Grim-faced, he set out for Sayes Court.

Having expected a long wait, Thomas was surprised to learn that Giles Baldwin had risen already. It seemed the demands of the Christmas Revels at Placentia allowed him little time for sleep. So a short while later, Thomas was conducted to the main hall, where the Clerk of the Green Cloth was taking a hasty breakfast alone.

'Falconer?' Baldwin looked up in surprise. 'If it's not an urgent matter, then it must wait. I'm for the palace within the hour.'

Thomas made his bow, and told him of the disappearance of the body. But when he came to the end of his tale, the man's reaction was not what he expected. If anything, he looked unconcerned.

'Extraordinary,' he mused. 'Why would anyone do that, do you think?'

Thomas shook his head. 'I know not, sir. Unless it be to conceal some evidence – something I've missed . . .'

Baldwin nodded, wiping his mouth with a napkin. 'Well, let Rycroft make his enquiries. At least it relieves you of a tiresome task, does it not?'

Thomas frowned. He had been about to tell more: of Dan Skeeres, and all the discoveries of the previous night; but for some reason he held back. 'You mean, you no longer wish me to look into the girl's death?' he asked finally.

'I did not say so,' Baldwin replied quickly. 'But without a corpse there can be no burial, can there? Which relieves some of us of a nuisance, including the poor rector of St Nicholas . . .' He took a drink from a silver mug, and set it down carefully. 'In any case, you have enough to occupy you for the present – especially if my guests wish to go hawking again.'

Thomas's spirits sank. 'Do they wish to ride out today?' he asked, but Baldwin shook his head.

'They have other plans, I believe,' he said vaguely. 'Now, if there's nothing further . . .?'

Seeing he was about to be dismissed, Thomas spoke quickly. 'Master Giles,' he began, 'I recall our conversation when you said Sir Robert may be in danger. Since then I have learned more . . .' He trailed off, then: 'I've thought much upon it, and it's most urgent that I speak with him – whether he wishes to see me or no.'

But at that, Baldwin looked uncomfortable. 'Sir Robert will be in my company day and night, at the palace,' he said. 'Have you forgotten it's the eve of Christmas?'

Thomas blinked. 'I believe I had, sir,' he answered.

'Then pray – allow yourself a little relaxation, with my blessing!' Baldwin put on a smile, but to Thomas it appeared somewhat forced. 'So long as you keep an eye on the birds, your time is your own.'

Thomas stared, but could read nothing behind the steady gaze. The change in Baldwin's attitude, he could not fathom.

Finally he said, 'Then with your leave, sir, I will ride into London . . . to the markets, perhaps . . .'

'Of course,' Baldwin nodded. And without further word, Thomas made his bow and went out of the hall.

As he passed the foot of the main staircase, he had a mind to cast caution aside and march straight upstairs to Sir Robert's chamber. But at that moment a door opened above – and then came a shriek, which stopped him in his tracks.

'You worm! You ignorant savage!'

Thomas froze, for there was no mistaking the voice. And even as he looked up, there followed the sound of a hard slap. He blinked.

Two figures had appeared on the landing. One was Lady Imogen, in an elaborate morning gown. The other was Mouka.

'Is there no end to your clumsiness?' Lady Imogen screamed. 'Take it away, and wash it anew!'

And Thomas could only watch in dismay as Lady Imogen's hand shot out to strike her servant again, a sharp blow across the face. Mouka flinched, but made no sound. She merely took the white linen shift which Lady Imogen thrust at her. And then, Lady Imogen glanced down and saw Thomas. For a second their eyes met, before she turned swiftly and vanished. Almost at once, a door slammed.

With small steps, Mouka descended the stairs towards him, head down.

'Mistress?' Thomas stepped forward, whereupon the girl started in alarm. Then recognizing him, she lowered her eyes.

'Will you let me pass?' she asked.

He stood aside, seeing the red mark upon her smooth cheek, and drew a breath, controlling his anger.

'Are you hurt, mistress?' he asked, but Mouka did not seem to hear. In a moment she had rounded a corner, heading for the kitchens.

Thomas stood alone in the passage for a long moment. Then with a sigh he turned away, realizing that he no longer had any stomach for an audience with Sir Robert. Despite his resolve of the previous night, he decided that it could wait a few more hours.

*   *   *

109

The ice was breaking up. Had Thomas not already had first-hand knowledge of it, he would have learned of it the moment he rode the gelding through Bankside, and halted at the approach to London Bridge.

The river was transformed. The booths and tents of the Frost Fair were gone, as were the skating children, the riders and folk on foot. Instead figures could be seen in boats, hacking at the thinning ice with poles. The thuds and cracks were audible from a mile away, as by slow degrees the jubilant watermen broke up the great ice sheet that had almost ruined their livelihoods. Even now the first boats were forcing a channel across, toward the Southwark shore. Their shouts and laughter could clearly be heard.

Thomas watched them for a moment, then shook the reins and eased the horse forward, to mingle with the great throng crossing the Bridge. Soon he was riding through the busy thoroughfares: Fish Street, Gracechurch Street, then a left turn into Lombard Street, where he had to force his way through the crowds in the Stocks Market. Ten minutes later he had reached his destination: Goldsmiths' Row on West Cheap, between Bread Street and Friday Street. Then, having given a penny to a boy to hold the horse, he began his search – which proved more difficult than he had imagined.

The goldsmiths were busy men, bent on serving their wealthier customers. They looked askance at the tall man in humble garb as he entered their shops, and quickly despatched servants to attend him. At first, when he drew out the gold necklace they thought he was trying to sell it, and quickly assumed that it was stolen. Then, when he managed to convince them otherwise, they grew impatient. Did he not know what the season was? A time for gifts and giving, and here he was seeking information. And in any case, those that bothered to look at the object told him, the workmanship was indifferent, and could have been by any of half a dozen hands. But that narrowed it down somewhat, and he began to proceed with renewed hope – only to find that none of those he visited would own to the piece being theirs. By the time he had worked his way almost to the end of Goldsmiths' Row, by the Saddlers' Hall, he had only two names left on his mental list. Feeling dispirited, he entered the second-to-last shop.

The goldsmith was an elderly man, in a dark gown and skull cap, with more than a look of the alchemist about him. At the least, when Thomas stated his business, the man listened attentively. Finally he gestured him to a little table by the window, and when Thomas drew forth the necklace, to his relief the other nodded at once.

'Derrick,' he said. 'He was a friend . . . I remember him making this very piece, for his own daughter.'

Thomas stiffened, but kept expression from his face. 'You said he *was* a friend . . .?'

'He died, almost two years ago. The daughter was broken by his death, for she was his only child . . .' The goldsmith gazed absently through the window. 'They were the most loving father and daughter I ever knew.'

'And her name was . . .?' Thomas waited for the old man to look his way again.

'Jane,' he replied. 'Jane Derrick, daughter of William.'

Thomas's heart was racing. At last he had put a name to the dead girl: *Jane Derrick.*

Suddenly the goldsmith frowned. 'What are you doing with her necklace?'

Thomas drew a breath. 'I'm sorry to tell you that, like her father, the poor girl is dead.'

The other looked shocked. 'Dead? No! So young, and so pretty – how did she die?'

Thomas hesitated. 'I know not . . . I've merely been trying to establish her identity—'

But the man broke in sharply. 'Her identity? How can that be? After her father died the girl went as waiting-woman to a lady of means. She is – she was – easily recognized . . .'

Thomas blinked. 'Do you know the name of this lady of means?'

Just then the shop door opened, and the goldsmith's attention was diverted. But before moving away, he answered Thomas quickly.

'Lady Semple. Beyond that, I can tell you little. She dwells near the Tower . . . you should seek further information there.' He shook his head. 'Poor Jane . . . a most clever girl, and of a kindly disposition. Perhaps you would return at a quieter hour, and tell me more of what befell her?'

Thomas managed a nod. Then stowing the necklace away, he quickly thanked the man and got himself outside.

He retrieved the horse and led it through the teeming streets, scarcely noticing where he walked. His mind was in turmoil; for now, the two matters that had pressed upon him for the past few days were suddenly joined. How this could be, he had no idea. And the more he dwelt on the matter, like earth that is turned over too often, the less it yielded.

He retraced his steps, until he was in Lombard Street again with the great bulk of the Tower visible above the rooftops. Finally he stopped, bought a pie from a stall and ate it standing up. Then he bought a bag of grain for the horse, and while he waited for it to eat its fill, formed a resolve: he would go to the Lady Imogen's house, as Cox had done, and take a look for himself. Now he thought upon it, he realized it would have been better if he had gone there at the outset.

The house was easy to find, from what Cox had told him. It stood near the East Wall, where Crutched Friars narrowed to become the street known as Poor Jewry. It was larger than he expected, with a walled garden about it overhung by old yew trees. Having tethered the horse to a post, he found that the iron gate was not locked, so he walked boldly to the front door and knocked. After a moment it was opened by a middle-aged serving-woman in a grimy apron, who started at the sight of Thomas towering over her.

'My Lady isn't here,' the woman began, but he shook his head.

'I'm seeking mistress Derrick,' he said. 'Jane Derrick.'

He had expected a reaction of some kind – but nothing like what followed. For the poor creature almost leaped back from the doorway. And she would have shut the door at once, if Thomas had not put out a hand to stop it.

'I mean you no harm,' he said in a gentler tone. 'I merely want to know what happened to mistress Jane—'

But the woman looked terrified. She backed away into the

hallway, shaking her head. 'There's none of that name here, fellow! Be gone!' And with that she heaved the door shut, slamming it in Thomas's face.

He stood on the step, debating with himself whether to knock again. He even considered walking around the house and peering through windows, then rejected the notion as a probable waste of time. But the house-keeper's reaction was all he needed to know that he was on the brink of some discovery. There were answers in Lady Imogen's house – and sooner or later he would have to return and seek them.

He walked back to the street, untied the gelding and climbed into the saddle. Deep in thought as he rode away, he barely noticed when the horse decided of its own volition to turn left into Woodruff Lane, which led south to Tower Hill. When he realized what had happened he halted, and chiding the animal softly he turned it round, preparing to retrace his way towards Crutched Friars. But as he reached the corner, three riders on good horses clattered past him in the direction of Poor Jewry – and at once he drew rein, turning his head to avoid being recognized. But the riders were bent on quiet conversation among themselves and paid him no heed – which was fortunate, for he had recognized two of them: Sir John Amyot and Malvyn Wyckes. The third was a squat, dark-bearded man in black riding clothes, whom he did not know.

Tense with anticipation, Thomas let them ride on a few yards, then eased the horse forward out of the turning and halted it. As he watched, the three men stopped outside Lady Imogen's house, dismounted and led their horses through the gateway.

Thomas too dismounted, tethered the gelding again, then walked cautiously back to the house. There was no one in the garden, but from the rear he could hear the sound of hooves, followed by the banging of a door.

For several minutes he stood in the street, pondering the matter. Perhaps it was all quite innocent, Wyckes returning to the house on some business of Lady Imogen's, but his instinct told him otherwise. And besides, why would Amyot accompany him? And who was the other man?

But the day was drawing on, and he had yet to speak to Sir Robert. Tamping down his natural curiosity, he remounted and rode away towards the Bridge.

Within the hour he was back at Sayes Court, where more frustration awaited him. It seemed Sir Robert and Lady Imogen had gone out riding, and no one knew where. So Thomas went to the mews and fed the falcons, then walked down the path into Deptford. He had a mind to find Cox, and question him further about Lady Imogen's house. Perhaps there was some detail he had missed? But on looking in at the Sea-Hog, he learned that no one had seen the player since the day before. So needing somewhere to sit and think, he walked along the strand to the Lovetts'. The moment he entered the shop, Simon Lovett stopped what he was doing and came forward. Thomas drew out the necklace.

'Thanks to this, I've put a name to the dead girl,' he began, and handed it to Simon. But as he took it, the chandler fixed him with his good eye and spoke urgently.

'Rycroft's been looking for you . . . you'd best go to him now. You'll find him at Monkaster's.'

Thomas raised his brows. 'I just passed there, and saw no one about . . .' he said, then noticed the other's agitation.

'Simon – is something amiss?'

Lovett hesitated. 'Your friend Cox, the player . . . he's dead.'

He found Will Rycroft at the back of Sir Ralph Monkaster's cluttered yard, by the stern of the ark. There were three men standing beside the dilapidated outhouse that served as a stable: Rycroft, Sir Ralph himself – and for some reason Ben Mallam, all of them looking shaken. As Thomas arrived the constable turned towards him.

'You've heard, then.'

Thomas came forward – and saw the congealed blood; in fact, it would have been difficult to miss, for the ground was almost awash with it. Heart in mouth he followed it with his eye, towards the prone figure of Lorel Cox, lying against the stable wall on his back. His eyes were open, the face pale as marble.

Thomas was numb. A dozen notions flew to his mind – but the picture that quickly gained mastery over the rest was of the excited player agreeing to help him in his investigations: *count on me to the death, my sworn friend . . .*

'He was stabbed,' Rycroft was saying. 'A poniard in the back, so it's my guess he saw not his assailant. Looks like he fell, then he was turned over and finished off with a couple of stabs to the heart. Whoever did it was taking pains to despatch the matter.'

Thomas barely heard him. He looked now at Sir Ralph, who looked pale. 'Such evil, on my land . . . it cannot be borne!' The old man shuddered. 'The Lord knows I disliked the player, but . . .' He broke off and turned away, then began whistling to himself. 'I . . . I must work on my ark,' he said. 'This may be an omen of some kind, bidding me make haste—'

'Nay – hold fast, sir!' Though shaken himself, Rycroft's expression was severe. 'I've questions to ask . . .'

Sir Ralph faced him. 'I've told you all I know! He is as I found him – I heard nothing, and I know not how he came to be here! How many times must I say such?'

Rycroft drew a breath, but did not reply. Thomas glanced at Ben Mallam, who was looking stunned. But when Ben spoke, Thomas learned that the cause of it was not merely Cox's death.

'My Galloway nag . . .' Ben gestured helplessly towards the stable. 'They've killed that too!'

Thomas stared, then felt his anger rise, and had a mind to shout: *Is that all you can think of – your wretched horse?* But he bit the words back as Rycroft addressed him.

'You were one of the last to speak with Cox,' the constable said, 'were you not?' When Thomas nodded, he went on: 'Did he say aught? I mean, did he have any enemies . . .?'

He trailed off, seemingly finding his own words foolish, and Thomas felt sympathy for the man. A simple village constable, he was unused to dealing with such matters. His eyes strayed again to the blood-soaked body.

'None that I know of,' Thomas replied. 'We talked over a mug, and he went off to the palace . . .' He frowned. 'He gave a performance last night with the Lord Chamberlain's Men. They must be told . . .'

'I've sent word,' Rycroft put in. 'Someone will be here soon . . .' He sighed, and looked again at Sir Ralph. 'You're certain you can tell me nothing?' he asked, which prompted another expostulation from the ark-builder.

'Nothing!' he cried. 'What would you have me say?' He looked down suddenly. 'This blood . . . I must wash it away! My land has been defiled . . .'

'When did you find him, Sir Ralph?' Thomas asked abruptly.

'This morning,' the old man answered. 'As soon as I came from the house . . . and Mallam is right!' He nodded towards the jingler. 'Whoever did it stabbed the poor horse as well – a most brutal deed!'

He turned away, shaking his head, and walked off towards the ark. Thomas turned to Ben Mallam. 'Mayhap it was to keep the jade from making a noise,' he said.

There was a bleak expression on Ben's face. Finally he looked at Rycroft and said: 'I'll get some fellows to help me take it away, bury it by the Creek . . .'

But the constable shook his head. 'No need for that,' he said. 'The slaughterhouse, just beyond the shipyard – they'll take it off you. My brother-in-law Jukes is slaughterman there.'

But instead of showing gratitude Ben merely let out an oath. He looked grimly at Thomas. 'Don't it sound a mite familiar to you?'

Thomas said nothing. When Rycroft asked him if he would break the news to Baldwin, he nodded absently. A terrible guilt was threatening to overwhelm him. And after a moment the other two men sensed his unease.

'Come – let's first to the Sea-Hog and get something strong down our gullets,' Mallam said.

Rycroft looked as if he was of similar mind, but before he could speak, Thomas glanced from one to the other, and drew a long breath.

'Nay,' he said. 'I'm going to search the yard, see what I can find.' He clenched his fists, and forced himself to look down again at the body.

'This man tried to help me,' he added, allowing his anger to show. 'Even though he was afraid, he helped. He told me things I found hard to believe, and we parted on bad terms. Now . . .'

He looked up. 'I owe it to him to pursue this matter to the end,' he said. 'To unravel every thread of it – and I will not rest until I find where it leads!'

And watched by the other two, he dropped to one knee beside the remains of Cox, still clad in his moth-eaten cloak, and bowed his head. He had wanted to play a spy, Thomas recalled – and for a while he had been one, of sorts.

Unfortunately, this was the way spies sometimes ended up.

Eleven

After the others had gone off, Thomas began to examine Sir Ralph's yard. He had already looked over the body, and agreed with the constable's deductions. Cox had been stabbed in the back with a poniard, but that alone might not have brought about instantaneous death. The wounds in his chest, directly into the heart, would have put an end to him, and also caused the huge loss of blood. And it was the pattern of the blood which gave him a start. For on walking backwards from the place where Cox lay, he found a sporadic trail of droplets leading along the ground beside the ark, towards the gate. Ignoring Sir Ralph, who was seated inside the vessel hammering feverishly, he followed the trail outside to the strand, then stopped and bent low. It seemed to him there were marks in the gravel, of a scuffle of some kind – and here, the blood trail petered out. After a while Thomas stood up, feeling the breeze on his face, and nodded to himself.

It seemed clear enough. Cox had been walking homeward to his lodgings, the previous night. Perhaps he was slightly drunk, or at least tired and elated from giving his performance at the palace. He would not have been alert to the figure – assuming there was only one – who came up behind him. Then when the blow was delivered he fell, and had been dragged or forced off the strand into the nearest gateway – Sir Ralph's. There the killer had shoved him to the end of the yard and finished him off, out of sight behind the ark. For some reason he had also chosen to stab Ben Mallam's poor nag. That part Thomas found hard to fathom, unless the animal threatened to draw attention to the deed, as he had first surmised . . .

He walked a few paces, towards the river. The ice was broken now, and beginning to move on the tide, a sluggish, untidy flow downriver. For a while he listened to the harsh cries of the sea-birds, wheeling overhead. Then he turned and began to walk back to Sayes Court.

He had intended to seek an audience with Giles Baldwin, but was not surprised to learn that the Clerk of the Green Cloth had been called to his duties in the palace. Nor was Nicholas Capper to be found; so having nowhere else to go, Thomas strode restlessly to the falcons' mews. The birds roused at once, thinking he was about to take them out for exercise. But when he merely sat on a stump and stared at them, they settled back into sullen silence.

The afternoon was wearing on, and he had no clear plan other than to tell Baldwin everything: he had resolved to do that much, then let the man take what action he would. But now, he knew he could not leave for Berkshire. He was caught up in some turn of events, the causes of which he could not begin to guess. But somehow he must see them to a conclusion – even if only for the sake of his friend of but a few days, Lorel Cox.

He sighed, looking up at the cloudy sky, thinking of their last words together. Crows flew overhead, towards the tall oak trees that bordered Deptford Green. Closer to, Baldwin's dogs barked in their kennels. He glanced idly about – to see a slim figure in a brown worsted cloak rounding the stable wall, walking with small steps.

He stood up quickly, whereupon the woman saw him and stopped. In fact, she turned about at once and would have walked away, had not Thomas hurried to overtake her.

'Mistress Mouka,' he said, and planted himself firmly in her path. 'I must speak with you – and I will not bear a refusal.'

Mouka blinked. 'I was taking a walk,' she began, then seeing the look on his face, she faltered. 'What do you want of me?'

'All you can tell,' he replied. 'About your mistress, and her house in London – and about Jane Derrick.'

With a sharp movement, she drew her cloak about her throat. 'Ask me not of her,' she muttered, then flinched as Thomas leaned forward.

'She is dead,' he said. But when Mouka gasped, he went on: 'I know who she was. I know she was Lady Imogen's waiting-woman, that she was clever, and pretty – yet she was not pretty when her body was found, washed up here on the strand. I also know how it got there, after she was cast into the river—'

'Stop!' The young woman fell back with a little shake of her head. And now, Thomas saw the anguish in her large eyes.

'Stop,' she repeated. 'For you torment me . . . you know not what you speak of!'

'There's no one else I can ask!' Thomas almost shouted. Then seeing her flinch, he drew a deep breath. 'A man is dead too – one who was my friend. It could be he was killed because he went to Lady Imogen's house, seeking clues . . . and it was to help me that he went there. Now – I beg you: I need to know whatever you know!'

Mouka gazed at him. Then her expression changed, and he knew that this was the person who could give him what he needed, to begin making sense of the clutter of events. After a moment, to her surprise he offered her his arm.

'You wished to walk,' he said gently. 'And I am but master Baldwin's servant. So let me be your guide and protector, for the night will draw in soon. Let's walk together across the fields, so that you can tell me what you will. And none shall hear it but me.'

There was a silence, broken only by the crows calling as they settled to roost. After what seemed an eternity, Mouka looked up and met Thomas's eye. Then quickly, she seemed to come to a decision. She nodded and took his arm, and together they walked across the lane and into the open fields, until the manor was out of sight.

It was a tale the like of which he had never heard. It chilled him as it revolted him, and finally it alarmed him, for its implications were worse than he could have imagined. Yet as they walked, and dusk fell, he could only listen to the lilting voice of Mouka, who, though but a child when she was snatched from her homeland, had nevertheless not lost the power of her people to tell stories.

'I was sold to Lady Imogen,' she began, 'as a maid of all work, to do humble tasks, after her husband died. I asked for nothing more, since I had a place to live, and food and clothes; and even though I was at times cold, and sore from the beatings she gave me, yet it was better than what I had known . . .' She shook her head. 'But that was in a far country . . . let us speak then, of the house by the City Wall, from where you can hear cannon-fire. It frightened me, until I knew what it was.' She threw Thomas a sidelong glance, which was the closest he had seen to Mouka smiling.

'The artillery yard,' he nodded.

'There I dwelt,' Mouka said, falling into a rhythm of speech which Thomas would not interrupt again. 'Until one day, more than a year ago, I was told my Lady had engaged a waiting-woman, who would rule over me and order my tasks. And I was frightened at first, fearing more beatings and more harsh words . . . until Jane came. For she was like a warm breeze, in the chill of that house. And she was my one true friend.

'Now the days went quickly – for though my Lady was as heartless as ever, Jane bore it with a good grace, and we would even laugh together, at night in our chamber in the rooftop. And so we might have stayed, keeping to our duties, had the changes not come.'

Thomas walked slowly, keeping pace with her small, delicate steps. But he showed no reaction, for if anything Mouka seemed glad to speak now.

'The changes,' she continued, 'began but a few weeks after Jane came. And they had to do with a handsome Lord, who started to frequent the house with his followers . . . and at times he came alone, to spend the nights with my Lady in her chamber. His name I will not tell.'

Though he kept silent, Thomas guessed it: Lord Beauchamp.

'In those days,' Mouka said, 'my Lady changed too. She

was still vain and cruel, yet she was now shrill, and taut like twine that is pulled too tight, that it might snap . . .' She glanced up at Thomas. 'You, too, have seen how she is.'

He nodded, and let her continue.

'In those days, other men began to come to her house. One that came, was master Wyckes, to be her steward. Though why she needed such, none of us servants knew, for she had no steward before. And also came the tall man with the hard face, that stays here – you know him. Amyot.'

Thomas caught his breath, biting back questions. But in the next moment, she answered one of them.

'Another was a little heavy man like a toad, always in black. He was strange, with an accent I could not always understand. Then I learned he was from Portingale. His name is d'Avila.'

Mouka hesitated, and Thomas sensed her discomfort now, as she seemed to come to the nub of her tale. He waited.

'So there was a coming and going in my Lady's house, and these men would often be in quiet talk with her, at supper and late into the night. And sometimes we waited upon them . . . and this is how it happened.' She took a sharp breath, struggling with the memory, then:

'Jane was pretty, as you know . . . and my Lord is a handsome man, with an eye for well-bred ladies even though he is married. And so one night they smiled at one another, for perhaps a little too long – only smiled. Yet for my Lady, it was enough.' She had stopped now; but meeting Thomas's eye, she forced herself to go on.

'It was my Lady who took her beauty away. For after her Lord was gone the next morning, she came to Jane screaming, and called her harlot and callett and words I did not know, and she said she would spoil her for ever! And she seized her by the hair, and dragged her to the still-room, and . . .'

She choked on the words. But Thomas too had stopped, and took her shaking hand in his.

'You need not say it,' he murmured. 'For I can guess. She took a certain liquid, and threw it over her . . .'

Mouka said nothing; but large tears welled from her eyes. And Thomas felt his stomach tighten; for now, in Lady

Imogen, he knew the kind of woman he was dealing with. Then suddenly he started, for something else sprang into focus.

'The demon . . . the face at the attic window,' he said. 'It was Jane! She was locked away, kept out of sight like a prisoner—'

'Nay – like a beast!' Mouka finished, nodding at him. 'My Lady tried to conceal what she had done, for Jane was from a good family, and known to some. A physician came in secret, and he could do naught for her terrible burns. Then master Wyckes took charge . . . he it was put out the tale that Jane had gone away. And all the while she was locked up – fed through a hatch like a dog! I was made to sleep in the kitchens after, and told never to speak of it, or I would be sent back to whence I came . . .' She lowered her eyes. 'They knew I could not bear that.'

Thomas nodded, gazing at the dark bulk of Shooter's Hill ahead of them, without seeing it.

'I should have guessed as much,' he muttered. 'As I should have gone into that house – forced myself in if necessary, and gone to that room and searched it.'

But Mouka shook her head. 'There's naught to see,' she said sadly. 'Save the marks she made on the walls, in her growing madness . . .' She let out a sob. 'They caged her like a beast, and she became little more than one . . . I am glad she is dead. For her spirit is free!'

Though Thomas was chastened by the tale, there was a growing anger inside him now, against the Lady Imogen. He would fight her, and free Sir Robert from her, no matter how difficult it was. He turned again to Mouka.

'Did you ever get the chance to speak with Jane again?' he asked.

She nodded. 'Once only . . . I crept out of the kitchen at night, and stole up to the attic. We talked through the hatch in the door . . . whispers only . . .' She cried softly. 'She was near madness by then, for she talked only of one thing: that there was a plot to kill the Queen.'

Thomas froze.

'I bade her forget such foolish notions, and talk of how

123

we had been happy, when she first came,' Mouka went on. 'Yet she could only talk of plotting and murder, and such dark matters – her mind was filled with darkness, like the room. She had begun to bang on the windows, and folk nearby talked of foul spirits in the house . . . so in the end, my Lady had to get her away. I believe it was master Wyckes who arranged it. And one morning – not so long since – Jane was gone.'

She turned to face Thomas. 'I say again, that she is better dead.' She frowned, as if she had only now wondered at Thomas's knowledge of it.

'But how do you know she is?' she asked.

He told her quickly: of the body on the strand, and the necklace, and his enquiries at the goldsmith's which had led him to discover the identity of Jane Derrick.

Mouka was silent. Finally she said: 'I would like to go back now.'

Thomas nodded, and they turned to begin retracing their steps. It was almost dark, and already the lights of Deptford twinkled in the distance.

Suddenly Mouka stopped. 'What will you do, falconer?'

For a while, Thomas made no reply. Then he said: 'I will find out who killed Jane, as I will find out who killed my friend – that they may both have justice.'

Then he started, for Mouka gripped his hand suddenly.

'If you do, you will heal my heart,' she said.

Then the two of them walked in silence, back to the manor.

But he could not tell Mouka now of his feelings; for her words rang in his head, and he knew instinctively that there was more to them than the ravings of a poor girl driven to madness:

A plot to kill the Queen . . .

It was true; he knew it in his heart, even though his head tried to dismiss it. He remembered his conversation with Cox in the Sea-Hog, about Lord Beauchamp's claim to the throne, and how some still worked to prove his right of succession. And so, he reasoned, Lady Imogen, as Beauchamp's lover, was a part of the scheme – as was their friend Sir John

Amyot. As for the man Mouka had described dressed in black, the Portuguese . . . was it not a fair description of the other man he had seen riding to the house, along with Amyot and Wyckes? Hence it seemed likely that Wyckes was part of it, too. As for Sir Robert – did they intend to draw him into the business? The notion filled him with despair.

Darkness had fallen, and the windows of Sayes Court glowed. Mouka went quickly into the house. After looking in on the falcons, Thomas followed, and learned that Giles Baldwin had come home to take a brief supper before returning to the palace. So at once he seized his chance, and without asking anyone's leave, strode to the main hall.

Baldwin and Nicholas Capper were seated together at the table. Both looked up in surprise when Thomas walked in, and the steward frowned. But Baldwin read Thomas's expression, and after a moment, gestured him forward. Thomas made a brief bow, then asked for an audience on a matter of grave importance.

'Speak then, falconer,' Baldwin replied. 'For I must return to the Queen's service soon.'

'Sir . . .' Thomas hesitated. 'It's on the Queen's business that I make bold to come here.'

Baldwin and Capper exchanged glances, but before either could speak Thomas added deliberately: 'And it must be for your ears alone. I can but ask that you trust me in this.'

Capper glared and would have made some retort, but he looked round in some surprise as his master touched his arm.

'I will hear the falconer,' Baldwin said.

There was a moment, before Capper rose abruptly, pushing his chair back from the table. Then signalling to the two serving-men that stood by to follow him, he swept out of the room without looking at Thomas.

Now they were alone. Stepping forward, Thomas met the other man's eye and said, 'Sir – I believe I may have uncovered something . . .' he hesitated, aware of how it would sound. 'Something terrible,' he added lamely.

Baldwin frowned. 'What is it?' he demanded. 'Speak up now!'

Thomas drew breath, then: 'It's a plot to kill the Queen.'

But whatever reaction he had expected, it was not the one that followed; for Baldwin did not flinch. He merely put down his napkin slowly, leaned back in his chair and gazed squarely at Thomas. 'Indeed,' he said quietly. 'Then perhaps you had better tell me of it.'

So Thomas told him.

He told of his discovery on the Isle of Dogs; of Daniel Skeeres, and the necklace he had taken off the body washed up on the strand, which had now disappeared. He told of his investigations in London, of his identification of Jane Derrick, and his visit to the Lady Imogen's house. Then – though he was careful to omit Mouka's name – he told what he had learned of Jane, and of her terrible fate. And finally he told of the death of Lorel Cox, and how he believed it was bound up in his investigations. He also spoke, albeit reluctantly, of what Cox had told him concerning Lady Imogen and Lord Beauchamp. Then, feeling a good deal of relief at having shared his burden, he fell silent and waited.

The silence was long, and now Baldwin was not looking at Thomas. In fact, he realized, the man had ceased to look at him halfway through his tale. Instead he had fixed his gaze on a half-empty platter before him, and seemed intent upon keeping it there.

Finally Thomas could bear it no longer. But as he was about to speak, the other man looked up suddenly. 'I should have known better than to ask someone like you to poke around,' he said in a dry tone. 'Yet I never expected you to dredge up such nonsense as this.'

Thomas froze. 'Sir – the matter appears as fantastical to me as it must to you! Yet the more I turn it about, the more I've come to believe that the Lady Imogen, Sir John and others are at the nub of the scheme – and hence Sir Robert—'

'Enough!' Baldwin snapped; and the change in the man's demeanour was so abrupt, Thomas blinked.

'Do you not realize,' the other said coldly, 'that I could have you arraigned for what you have just said? Impugning the honour of men such as Sir John Amyot, a friend to our Queen – let alone my Lord Beauchamp – amounts to treason!

And such would mean not merely imprisonment, but your death!'

Thomas drew breath. 'I see that, sir,' he replied. 'Yet might I remind you that it was you who warned me that my master – for such he was then – might be in danger. And now I believe Lady Margaret too could be at risk, if what I have learned of the Lady Imogen proves true—'

'No more!' Baldwin had risen now, and raising his hand, he pointed a finger directly at Thomas.

'No more, falconer, for you will incur my wrath, and that would be very unwise indeed!' After a moment he sat down again. 'I was told of your reputation,' he said. 'Of your skill at uncovering what others miss. Yet never did I imagine that you would make whole cloth out of such scraps: rumour and gossip, and the testimony of rogues and thieves, compounded with your frantic imaginings! And I find truth in Sir Robert's accusations, of your pride and presumption. You're but a servant here, have you forgotten?'

Though he was in turmoil now, Thomas remained outwardly calm. For he began to believe that he had misjudged the Clerk of the Green Cloth – and badly.

'Nay, sir,' he replied. 'I have forgotten nothing.'

'Then listen to me, and listen well.' Baldwin's voice was low, but he was smouldering. And the warning Thomas read in his eyes, reminded him suddenly of the one he had read in Sir John Amyot's gaze, only the day before.

'Sir Robert is a guest under my roof,' Baldwin continued. 'As are Sir John and the Lady Imogen. You insult me as their host and protector, as you do them. As for the implication that the Lady Imogen means harm to Lady Vicary, in order to somehow entrap Sir Robert—' He broke off with a look of contempt. And at that Thomas made to speak, but immediately the man raised his voice, cutting him short.

'It is preposterous, falconer! Preposterous and foolish, and I will not have such matters aired! Do you mark that?'

Thomas said nothing.

'Now you will listen, as I have listened,' Baldwin continued. 'I am known here as a generous man, who puts up with more impudence than would most in my position.

Hence I do not cast you out. Instead I will give you a choice: you may keep your place here as falconer, and serve my guests at hawking for the period of the Revels – until Twelfth Night. After that you must leave, and go where you will.'

Thomas stood very still. Finally, seeing the other man appeared to be waiting for him to speak, he said: 'You mentioned choice, sir – what other course have I?'

'The other course, falconer,' Baldwin answered, 'is to leave now, and get yourself from the Verge – I care not where. But understand this: if you keep on worrying at this bone you have turned up, piling rumour upon rumour and prating of it, then I will have you arrested and gaoled, your fate to be decided at Her Majesty's pleasure.'

And with that he sat back again, deliberately picked up a cup and drank from it.

But for Thomas, there was no choice. Despite all that had happened, he could not leave Sir Robert to whatever danger might befall him. Nor would he forsake the memory of poor Jane Derrick, and of Lorel Cox. Though how he could help any of them, he was now at a loss to discern.

Do nothing, he said to himself. *That is what I am ordered to do, and that is what I must appear to do.*

With an effort he faced Baldwin, and bowed. 'Your pardon, sir,' he murmured. 'I meant not to offend. I have allowed my distress at losing my master's favour to muddy my thoughts.'

But Baldwin, he saw, was not convinced by his sudden contriteness.

'Indeed, falconer,' he said. 'So you have. And hence, you may mark this: that so long as you remain here I will have an eye upon you, wherever you be. Now go to your duties.'

And with that, the man picked up his cup again and called for his servants. The door was opened at once; and Thomas could only make his bow, and get himself outside.

Twelve

Thomas walked down the dark pathway into the village, and made straight for the Sea-Hog. There, as he had expected, he found Ben Mallam drowning his sorrows by the fireside. Calling for a mug of strong ale, he sat himself down beside the jingler, who barely looked up.

'If you're in search of conversation you'd best go elsewhere,' Ben muttered. 'I'm fit for naught but drinking my last penny. Then I'll sleep it off, and tomorrow I'm moving on. Looks as if Deptford's been unlucky for me after all.'

The drawer arrived with a mug, and handed it to Thomas. When he had taken a long, welcome draught, Thomas wiped his mouth and said: 'That'd be a pity, for I need your services still. And I'll pay you – say, half as much as the nag was worth.'

There was a moment, before Ben turned to him with a look of suspicion. 'Why would you want to do that?'

'Because there's no one else to aid me,' Thomas told him. 'And I've business to finish, before I move on too.'

The jingler emptied his mug and sat staring into it for a moment. 'I don't understand why the whoreson had to kill my little Galloway too,' he said quietly. 'What's a dumb beast got to do with Cox?' He paused. 'There's one thing, mind: he knew Dan Skeeres. Liked to mix with all sorts – for his work, he said.'

Thomas stared. 'Why didn't you mention that sooner?'

Ben shrugged. 'I didn't know you had business with Skeeres, until I found you chasing him up the river . . .' He shuddered.

But Thomas's mind was busy. He thought over Skeeres's testimony the previous night, by the frozen Thames. That rogue, he now believed, would be a party to murder if the fee was high enough. Then he thought again, of Skeeres's blurted statement, about his fear of the Queen's Privy Council, and one of their 'best projectors' . . . but that made no sense to him at all.

'Have you any idea where Skeeres might be now?' he asked.

The jingler thought for a moment. 'Keeping well out of sight,' he muttered. 'Which means, at none of his usual haunts. So . . . yes, I've a notion where he'd be.'

He met Thomas's eye. 'You want me to take you there?'

Thomas said nothing, which prompted a snort from Ben Mallam.

'Jesu, master hawksman . . .' He shook his head. 'I don't know who's the madder: you or Monkaster – or me!'

An hour later, they had walked three miles upriver, along its south bank to the little hamlet of Redriff.

There were few lights, and only the barking of dogs to challenge them as they made their way through muddy, narrow streets to a very poor neighbourhood. Thomas was wary: these were the sort of alleyways where a man was easily taken, for his purse or merely for his dagger and belt. But there was not a soul in sight as the two men stopped outside a little, dilapidated dwelling, whose jetty leaned over their heads at a crazy angle.

'Another trugging-house?' Thomas looked sceptical, but Mallam was shaking his head as he knocked upon the door.

'Old Sarah's a drab right enough,' he said, and gave his lopsided grin. 'But she's also Skeeres's mother.'

Thomas had barely time to register the information, when the door was opened a few inches, and a sour-looking old woman in a ragged cap stuck her face into the gap. And even Mallam almost recoiled at the stench of poor sack on her breath.

'No one here,' she said in a slurred voice, then frowned as she recognized Ben. 'What d'you want, horse-prigger?'

'I'm looking for Dan, Sarah,' Mallam answered in a casual tone. But the woman scowled.

'Not here . . .'

Ben pulled his mouth down. 'That's a pity, my duck. For I've a bit of business he might be interested in.'

The woman peered at him with rheumy eyes. Then noticing Thomas for the first time, she drew back. 'Who's this?'

'I'm a friend of master Skeeres too, mistress,' Thomas said, fumbling for his purse. 'And I'd be sorry to miss him. I've brought something on account, for his trouble.'

He drew out a coin, and held it up. There was a pause before the old woman snatched at it, but Thomas was quicker. Closing his hand upon it, he managed a smile, and said: 'Can we talk with him first? It's a matter of import . . .'

The woman scowled again, then seemed to relent. In fact to both men's surprise she sagged suddenly, as if all the fight had gone from her. After a moment she pulled back the door, and said in a hoarse voice: 'You'd best see for yourselves.'

Thomas and Ben exchanged glances as they stepped into the house. They were in a dark, foul-smelling passageway with a narrow stair. Sarah closed the door behind them, and pointed towards the back.

'In there,' she said. But she did not move.

With growing unease they walked past her and through a doorway into a small room lit by a rush-light. At first, Thomas could see little except a low truckle-bed against the wall . . . then he drew breath sharply, and stepped forward. Behind him, he heard Mallam utter an oath.

Daniel Skeeres was stretched out on the bed with his eyes open, and he was dead.

'One I didn't know brought him,' Sarah told them. 'Said he fell through the ice, below the Bridge. I told him it's not like Dan . . . he may be clumsy, but he's nobody's fool.'

They stood in the hallway, watching her drink from an old leather horseman's flask, standing up. Then she lowered it and added: 'Or he wasn't, I ought to say . . .' She frowned. 'Least he won't be coming here troubling me when I've a customer. He only used this place to hide stuff, anyway.'

But Thomas had questions; and despite Ben Mallam's look,

which spoke clearly of his wish to get out as quickly as possible, he bent and addressed the woman.

'What kind of fellow was it who brought him, mistress?' he asked.

Sarah peered dully at him. 'What's it matter?' She looked away. 'Dead now, and there's an end to it.' She coughed. 'Have to do summat about that . . .'

Thomas reached for his purse. 'I'll give you something towards the burial,' he said. 'But will you tell me first, how he looked when he was brought in? I'd like to know.'

Sarah stared at him. 'Why so?'

'Because like you, I doubt he fell through the ice,' Thomas told her. 'More likely—'

'More likely some whoreson rogue he'd crossed caught up with him, you mean!' Sarah nodded sagely, and took another pull from her flask. 'That don't be a surprise – do it, horse-prigger?'

She leered at Ben Mallam, who threw Thomas a helpless look. But this time, Thomas would not be deflected.

'Why don't you go and wait for me?' he said. 'Back to the Sea-Hog, if you like.'

Ben showed his relief. Clearly the surroundings, as well as the discovery of another body, had unnerved him. Pushing past Sarah, he headed for the door. But as he pulled it open, the old woman had a parting shot for him.

'Can't get out quick enough, can you?' she cried. 'Yet there was a time you'd have used Dan readily enough to cog some mark out of a nag, wouldn't ye? And you know that's gospel truth!'

But Ben was gone in an instant, closing the door behind him and leaving Thomas and the old woman alone. After a moment she turned to face him. And despite the amount of drink she had taken, he sensed that her reason was not dulled.

'You're no friend of Dan's,' she muttered. 'So what's your interest? And why so ready to part with your money?'

Thomas drew a breath, then: 'A friend of mine was murdered, last night. And it could be by the same hand as your son.'

Sarah met his eye, then suddenly she sagged again. In fact

this time she swayed, and Thomas caught her. And she offered no resistance as he steered her awkwardly through the doorway into another dingy room, facing the street. Since there was naught here but a fireplace and a couple of stools, he laid the wretched creature down on the carpet of stale rushes, and knelt beside her.

'Is there anyone I can fetch, Sarah?' he asked.

Sarah had closed her eyes, but now she opened them again.

'Leave me be,' she mumbled. ''Tis the eve of Christmas, and I wish for no one.'

He sighed, and was about to rise, then suddenly she lifted a hand, and took hold of his collar. And although she was near to falling into a stupor, she spoke to him in a low voice, so that he had to bend close to hear her.

'You showed kindness,' she said, 'which I've not known in a long while . . . so listen.' She drew a long breath, then:

'Dan was caught up in summat . . . a blind bit of cozenage, I thought. But he said 'twould make him enough to clear all he owed . . .' She coughed. ''Twas no plain figging law, nor curbing, he said – this time he'd be paid in gold!'

She closed her eyes again, and let go of his collar. And as her hand sank on to her breast, it was all Thomas could do not to try and shake her awake. But then she half-opened her eyes, for the last time. And to his surprise, she smiled.

'Said he was working for someone important,' she whispered. 'And come Accession Day he'd get his reward . . .' She gave a slow shake of her head. 'Then, I never could believe a word he said . . .'

Then she gave a sigh, and slipped into unconsciousness.

Thomas watched as her features relaxed into an expression of peace. And through the creases seamed with grime, the pretty woman who had once inhabited this sorry, raddled body was revealed to him briefly; and he understood why men had sought Sarah Skeeres out and used her, until by degrees she had become the creature she now was.

He took the coins from his purse, and laid them beside her. Then he stood up and went once more to the back room, to take a proper look at the body of Daniel Skeeres.

First he felt the man's clothes, which were indeed wet.

Yet the corpse, if it had been submerged, was not cold enough
. . . he began to examine it, but saw no trace of blood or
even of bruising, unless . . . he frowned, stood up and brought
the tiny rush-light. Then holding it close to the man's neck,
he bent down, and found the marks. Reaching out, he touched
Skeeres's cheek, feeling the thick beard like rough wool. At
once the head rolled to one side, and now he saw it: the
man's neck had been broken, and the life choked from him.
Moreover, the clothes stank – but not of the river; rather, it
was a stale smell, like that of water that has stood in a tub
for too long.

He rose, snuffed out the light and set it down. Then he
left the room, walked down the passage and out of Sarah
Skeeres's house.

He did not go back to the Sea-Hog. He had formed a resolve,
and would see it through: to seek out Sir Robert at last, and
refuse to leave until he had told him everything. But it was
past midnight by the time he returned to Deptford, and he
knew he needed to rest. So he went to his lodgings at the
Lovetts', and finding Alice and Simon already abed, climbed
up to the attic and fell into an exhausted sleep. Only when
he awoke at dawn, did he remember that today was Christmas
Day.

Ben Mallam was spread-eagled on his pallet, snoring.
Without waking him Thomas dressed quickly and got himself
downstairs, then stepped out on to Deptford Strand. The day
was fair, and within minutes he was striding up the path to
Sayes Court.

Uncertain yet of how he might gain access to Sir Robert,
he went first to the falcons' mews to feed and water the
birds. Then he walked to the stable yard and found the grooms
already at their work. Upon enquiry he was told that master
Giles and his guests had been at the Queen's Christmas Revels
all night. But to his satisfaction, he learned that while Baldwin
and the Lady Imogen had returned before dawn and retired
to their chambers, Sir Robert and Sir John Amyot had yet
to appear. So Thomas stationed himself outside the stables,
and set himself doggedly to waiting.

Mercifully, he did not have to wait long. Barely a half hour later, as smoke began rising from the chimneys of Deptford, the two knights rode slowly into the yard together and dismounted. Whereupon to Sir Robert's surprise and irritation, Thomas presented himself.

'Sir – I must speak urgently with you.'

Sir Robert was wearing a new burgundy cloak over his red and gold clothes. Deliberately he handed his reins to a groom, then stifling a yawn, faced Thomas. 'But I've naught to say to you – now let me go to my bed, before I sleep where I stand.'

Sir John Amyot had handed his horse over to the other groom. Now he looked round, took in the situation and addressed Sir Robert. 'Servant troubles again, sir?'

His tone was sardonic, and Sir Robert bristled. 'No servant of mine, Sir John,' he muttered, and began to move away. But to his amazement Thomas blocked his path.

'Sir Robert – you trusted me once,' he said in a low voice. 'And despite what has passed, you may still. I pray you let me speak, for it concerns your own safety and that of others – perhaps even the Queen's.'

Sir Robert's jaw dropped. 'What in the devil's name do you mean?' he began. Then seeing Thomas's expression he frowned. There was a moment before he glanced at Amyot, who was moving away towards the house. But as the man looked back with eyebrows raised, Sir Robert said: 'I'll to my bed soon, sir – we'll continue our discourse at dinner.'

The other merely yawned, and walked off.

Sir Robert turned to Thomas. 'It had better be urgent,' he said curtly. 'For I'm in no humour for time-wasting.'

Taking a breath Thomas followed him, away from the yard until they stood by the mews. Sir Robert stopped, gazing for a moment at the falcons. But when he turned to face Thomas, his expression was cold.

'Speak, then. And make it short.'

Leaving out certain matters, and certain names, Thomas started to tell him what he had told Giles Baldwin the day before. But the moment he mentioned the Lady Imogen, he knew he had made a mistake. For Sir Robert stepped back as if he had been struck, and his eyes blazed.

'You . . . how dare you harp on that! I should have you arrested for what you suggest—'

'What do I suggest, sir?' Thomas countered, managing to keep desperation out of his voice. 'There's naught that I've learned, that you cannot verify for yourself. I'm convinced these people – Sir John and Lady Imogen, a Portuguese named d'Avila and perhaps others – are in consort with Lord Beauchamp to bring about his accession—'

'Enough!' Sir Robert's mouth was twitching. 'You know nothing of my friends,' he cried, 'nothing! And if you persist in spreading such slander, you'll end up under lock and key . . .' Suddenly, he drew breath. 'Who else have you told?'

Thomas hesitated, then without knowing why answered: 'No one, sir. For my loyalty is to you, not master Baldwin, even though I serve him as falconer. And I beg you for the last time – for Lady Margaret's sake, to think upon what I say—'

But he had gone too far. Furiously Sir Robert raised his gloved hand and pointed at him.

'You dare to suggest . . .' He broke off, almost speechless with rage. Then to Thomas's dismay, he turned to walk off. But a second later, he swung round again.

'Who told you of Beauchamp's claim?' he demanded.

Thomas eyed him. 'A man who has since been murdered, sir,' he answered. Then for good measure he added: 'And there's another who may have blundered, or found out more than was good for him – he too is dead. I saw his body for myself last night, in a poor house in Redriff – his neck was broken. You may verify that too, if you wish.'

Sir Robert stared at him. And suddenly, Thomas felt a stirring of hope in his vitals. For something he had said, had unnerved the man; he saw fear in his eyes – and emboldened, he went on.

'Sir Robert – you must know in your heart, that you and Lady Imogen are the subject of malicious gossip, at Court if not across all of London. The moment your back is turned men scorn you for what you have become – a plaything for a woman who aspires to greater riches than you can ever give her! And if you would have me arrested for my impertinence, then let me make it easier – for I will tell you what kind of woman she is!'

He stopped, half-expecting the knight to strike him, for there was a wild look in the other man's eye now. But after a moment, it was Sir Robert who spoke.

'Tell me, then,' he said softly.

Thomas drew breath, and told him everything he had learned of poor Jane Derrick. And all the while Sir Robert listened, without meeting his eye. When Thomas had finished, there was a silence. Thomas found himself looking at the falcons on their perches, all of which were staring at him as if they too had heard his tale. On Deptford Green, rooks were calling from the tree-tops.

Finally, when he could bear the silence no longer he faced Sir Robert. But the knight seemed to have forgotten he was there, and was staring vacantly at the ground. At last he raised his head – and now Thomas saw in him a great tiredness; of the kind that could not be relieved by mere sleep. But the next moment, the man's question surprised him.

'Who told you of the Portuguese?' he asked in a voice so low, Thomas could barely hear him.

He hesitated; whatever happened to him, he would not mention Mouka's name. Finally he said: 'The same who told me of Beauchamp's attempts to prove his right to the throne.'

After a moment, Sir Robert nodded slowly. But Thomas was alarmed now, for the change in the other's manner was striking. His anger seemed to have evaporated, leaving only a bleakness, the like of which Thomas had not seen before in the man he knew – or thought he knew . . . He opened his mouth, but Sir Robert shook his head. And now, he did walk away.

Thomas waited a while, then followed him to the stables. But even as he rounded the yard wall and heard the sound of hooves on cobbles, he knew that his former master had got himself mounted. And the next moment he had to step aside quickly, as Sir Robert appeared on his new Neapolitan horse, urging it to a canter, away from Sayes Court.

Then he could only watch as the horse broke into a gallop, bearing its rider away across the fields.

And Sir Robert did not look back.

Thirteen

The bells of St Nicholas were ringing lustily in celebration of Christmas, but Thomas barely heard them. He walked down to the strand, head bowed, making for the Lovetts'. But as he passed Sir Ralph Monkaster's yard, someone hailed him. He turned to see William Rycroft standing by the gate.

He paused, intending to make some excuse and walk on, for his mind was in turmoil and he had no wish to speak with the man. But something in the constable's demeanour stayed him. He waited as the other approached.

'It's turned up,' Rycroft said in his phlegmatic voice. Then when Thomas appeared not to understand, he added: 'The body.'

Thomas was nonplussed. 'Cox's body . . .?'

'Nay! The players came already and took him away – I mean the young maid's, that was taken from my hut.'

Thomas stared. With all that had happened, he realized, he had almost forgotten Rycroft's promise to 'poke about'. Though he had already judged the constable as being a man of his word. But he frowned when the other went on: 'There's devilry in this business, master Finbow. And I'd be obliged to you, if you could shed some light upon it.'

After a moment, Thomas nodded. 'I will. But first, will you tell me where you found the woman?'

'The woman . . .?' Rycroft shook his head. 'From what I've been told there isn't much to tell whether she was male or female, or even human.' With an expression of distaste he pointed upriver. 'In the shambles, there beyond the ship-yard. Where they slaughter livestock for the Queen's table.'

Then, with a look which Thomas interpreted as an invitation to follow, the constable walked off along the strand.

The slaughterhouse was a noisome place, and Thomas was thankful that it was closed up for the holiday of Christmas. From somewhere behind the open-fronted building where the slaughtermen worked, came the bellowing of cattle in their holding-pens. But the gate was unlocked, and in the yard which faced the river, a stout man in an apron was waiting for Rycroft. On seeing the two men arrive he came forward, but his face clouded as he recognized Thomas. Then Thomas stiffened as he recognized him, too: one of those whom he and Cox had done battle with in the Sea-Hog.

'What's he doing here?' the fellow demanded, jerking his thumb in Thomas's direction.

'Who I bring with me is my business,' Rycroft retorted. 'Now, show me where you found it.'

After a moment the man shrugged and gestured to the constable to follow. So the three of them walked across the yard, to where stood a cart covered with an old ox-hide. Here they stopped.

'Best look for yourself, Will,' the slaughterman said. 'I haven't touched it since I saw it, at first light . . .' He shook his head. 'I only came in to take the cart over to the pit.'

'The pit?' Thomas asked, prompting a contemptuous look from the other.

'It's where we take the foul meat, to burn it,' he answered shortly. 'The best meat goes straight to the palace, to the Queen's kitchens. After Deptford folk have taken all they want, this is what's left.'

There was a moment, before Rycroft gestured to the fellow to remove the cover. But even before he did so, Thomas had grown aware of the stench of putrid flesh. And both he and the constable gagged as the man threw the hide back, to reveal a rotting pile of assorted animal parts.

Seeing their reaction, the slaughterman laughed. 'Need a good strong stomach to work here,' he said, grinning. 'Want me to save you the bother of poking about?'

Reaching out, he lifted a sheep's leg aside, and pointed to what lay beneath. After a moment, Rycroft turned and walked a few paces away. But Thomas stared, and saw what he had seen: a human arm and hand, discoloured but still delicate. A woman's hand, right enough, and very likely, Jane Derrick's.

Now he too turned away, and walked over to join Rycroft. The slaughterman watched them both, then tugged the cover back in place and joined them.

'It's an odd business, right enough,' he allowed. 'I wouldn't have looked twice as a rule, save that the hide wasn't tied on right. So I pulled it off to re-tie it – and saw what you did.' He brightened suddenly, facing the constable. 'I told 'ee there was a leg, too, did I not? Likely the rest of it's in there, if you want to look . . .'

'I do not!' Rycroft was glaring at him. 'Now tell me who loaded up the cart.'

The man shrugged. 'That's Dick Jukes's job. Looks like he was in a hurry, tying it off crooked like that.'

Thomas stiffened, recognizing the name of the bullying fellow he had tangled with at the Sea-Hog, and whom he had first mistaken for a shipwright. Then he remembered: Rycroft's brother-in-law. He turned to the constable, who seemed to have paled suddenly.

'Dick?' Rycroft muttered. 'It can't be . . .'

The slaughterman's eyes narrowed. 'You saying I'm a liar, Will?'

Thomas faced him. 'No one's saying that,' he replied, then voiced the question on his lips. 'Who usually takes the foul meat to the pit – you?'

The man shook his head. 'Nay – 'tis Jukes's task. He should be here – only the amount of sack he took last night, I didn't see him getting in before noon, so I thought I'd best move it.' He snorted. 'That'll cost him a supper – or a mug, at least.'

Thomas turned to Rycroft, who was gazing unhappily towards the river. Finally he looked round, drawing a long breath.

'Will you walk over to my house, master Finbow?' he

141

asked. 'I believe I'm in need of something to settle my stomach.'

To the slaughterman he said: 'I'd be obliged if you would retrieve all that's human, and place the poor soul's remains in a box. I'll have someone bring one to you anon.'

The man nodded his agreement, then frowned and said: 'There won't be no trouble for the rest of us, will there? 'Tis only an old corpse – been dead for a long time, by the looks of 'n . . .' Then seeing the look on the constable's face, he fell silent. Wordlessly, Rycroft turned and walked to the gate. Thomas followed.

A short while later the two men were sat in Rycroft's tiny kitchen, taking breakfast. Only now did Thomas realize how hungry he was, and gratefully accepted mistress Rycroft's offer of bread and hot porridge. When they had finished, the constable gestured Thomas outside to the cluttered garden. The man had said barely a word since they left the shambles. Now he turned to face Thomas.

'I've been going over it in my mind,' he said. 'About whoever took the body from my hut . . .' He gestured briefly towards it. 'How they'd have to know the ground, so to speak, to get it out through this yard without making a racket. And if it were just one man, he'd have to be mighty strong . . .'

'Not only that, master Constable,' Thomas replied. 'He'd have to have good reason too, would he not?'

Rycroft eyed him. 'You promised to shed some light on the business,' he said finally. 'Isn't it time you did so?'

Thomas nodded, and suggested they take a walk.

And as they walked along the strand, and he told the stolid constable the grisly tale, he found that he was relieved at last to have a listener who neither interrupted him, nor berated him. So he ended up saying more than he had at first intended, and laid bare almost all of what had befallen him since he first rode into Sayes Court, five days earlier. Only when he had finished did he realize what a curious turn of events it amounted to. Having told it, he found he was barely able to believe the whole of it himself.

They stood looking across the river at the Isle of Dogs, which appeared in daytime as lifeless as ever. Finally the constable turned to gaze at Thomas.

'It seems to me you have carried quite a burden on your shoulders, master Finbow,' he said finally. 'Could you not have come to me sooner, and asked for my help?'

Thomas met his gaze. 'Mayhap I should have done,' he admitted. 'And I ask your pardon for it.'

The other turned towards the cottages behind them. 'Well now,' he murmured. 'I've a mind to go and see master Jukes, and ask him for his version of events. Would you like to assist me?'

With a nod, Thomas followed the man away from the riverside, towards Deptford Green. From a distance he heard a familiar hammering; it seemed that on Christmas Day as on every other day, Sir Ralph Monkaster still laboured at the building of his ark.

Dick Jukes lived in one of the older, poorer cottages on the green, near the church. At Rycroft's knock the door was opened by a shrivelled rake of a woman in a gown too large for her, who started at sight of Thomas and the constable. And as she admitted both men, she was already making excuses.

'I pray you, Will, be not too hard on him,' she gabbled. 'For whatever happened last night, 'twas the drink that's to blame – he's a devil when it's took hold of him, you know he is . . .'

But Rycroft's expression was stern. 'I must speak with him, Katherine,' he said, and nodded towards the staircase. 'Is he above?'

Katherine bobbed in a bird-like fashion. 'I daren't wake him when he's like that.' She glanced at Thomas, but did not address him. And now he saw the dark rings beneath her eyes, and the old, yellowed bruise on her cheek. Her nervousness, he guessed, was borne as much out of concern for what her husband might do to her, as for what he might have done already.

Grimly he followed Rycroft up the stairway, which gave

on to a single room taking up the whole floor. And there was Jukes lying sprawled on a pallet, fully clothed. The room stank of drink and stale sweat. Without hesitating, the constable walked over and shook the man awake, and to Thomas's surprise he was conscious almost at once. In fact he awoke as if surfacing from a near drowning, flailing his arms and shouting.

'Get off me, you whoreson . . .' He blinked, then stared wide-eyed at the intruders.

'Sit yourself up, Dick,' the constable ordered. 'I've questions for ye – and I'll have the truth.'

Jukes sat up, his brow creasing. He glanced at Thomas, but if he recognized him, he gave no sign. 'What's the coil, Will?' he muttered, then coughed. 'By the Christ, my mouth's full dry . . .'

But Rycroft was in no mood for delay. 'The body of that poor maid that was washed up on the tide,' he snapped. 'Why did you take it?'

Jukes swallowed. 'What . . .?'

'Why did you take it from my hut, Dick?' Rycroft repeated. 'Who told you to get rid of it?'

The other glanced from his relative to Thomas, and now he did recognize him. And at once his mouth twisted in a snarl.

'Who accuses me?' he demanded. 'This cove?'

'Answer me!' the constable cried. 'For in God's name you've shamed your sister and me – as you shame the whole village!'

Jukes's face fell. 'Listen,' he began, wetting his dry lips. 'Let's you and I speak . . . send this one out, for 'tis naught of his affair—'

But Rycroft had stepped forward rapidly, and Thomas blinked as he leaned down and seized Jukes by the collar of his dirty, sodden shirt.

'You're for a gaol this time,' he breathed. 'And none will miss you – not even Katherine, for she'll not have to lie any more to save your miserable skin!' The constable was beside himself. 'Now I ask you for the last time – why did you take the body?!'

'Let me go!' Jukes spat. With a sudden movement he grabbed hold of Rycroft's wrist with one hand and raised the other in a fist – but he was too late; for Thomas had darted forward to seize him. Together the two men yanked the wretched fellow to his feet and drove him backwards against the wall, making him cry out. The whole cottage shook alarmingly.

'Enough!' Jukes was panting like a wrestler. ''Twas not my plan – I swear to ye, Will! I wanted no part of it, save that he forced me; he could have me clapped up for nothing, he said, and I believed him . . . he's not a man to take refusal!'

'Who isn't?' It was Thomas who spoke, tense with excitement – and not merely from his exertions. For he sensed at last, that here was the information he had wanted . . . controlling his eagerness, he pressed his face closer to Jukes, who was sweating now. The fellow looked from one man to the other, then gave his answer.

'The steward.'

Thomas drew breath. 'Baldwin's steward – Capper?'

'No!' Jukes shouted, shaking his head. 'The fellow that serves her Ladyship – the little shrew that stays at Baldwin's, and rides to hawking—'

Abruptly, Rycroft let go of the man and stood back in surprise. After a moment Thomas did the same, but as he did so he let out a sigh, and lowered his gaze to stare at the pitted floorboards.

Wyckes . . . Wyckes, who served her Ladyship so faithfully; who smoothed all her affairs so cleverly, even to arranging for the disposal of poor Jane Derrick, whose corpse was not supposed to be found on the shore . . . and who must now disappear again, this time for ever.

With a glance at Rycroft, Thomas faced the culprit again. 'I'll not ask if you were paid for your trouble,' he said wryly. 'Whatever the sum was, I'd guess you drank it all last night – which was your own undoing. If you'd driven that cart away as you were supposed to, no one would have known of it.'

Jukes's jaw dropped.

'Was it Wyckes's instruction that you burn the body?'

Thomas persisted. 'Or was that your idea, since it was your job to get rid of the foul meat?'

But Jukes lowered his eyes, lapsing into a sullen silence. And having mastered himself, it was Rycroft who spoke up.

'Does it matter?' he asked Thomas. 'For me, it's enough that he was ready to do such . . .' He threw Jukes a scathing look. 'Let the Queen's guards take him . . . I want him not in my sight!' He grimaced. 'I'll set matters in motion – but how I'm going to break the news to my wife, as to what depths her brother has sunk to, I know not.'

'Do you wish for my help, to bring him out?' Thomas asked. But the other shook his head.

'It's my duty, master Finbow. I can but thank you for what you've done.' He hesitated. 'We'll speak further, of what you told me . . .' He signalled with his eyes. And with a nod, Thomas turned and made his way down the rickety stairs.

As he left the cottage, he caught a glimpse of Jukes's wife, sitting alone in the downstairs room, staring at the floor. She did not look up.

By mid-morning Thomas was back at Sayes Court. His intention was to avoid the house, and to find out Wyckes's whereabouts. So he went first to the stables, and learned that the Lady Imogen had gone riding. But as he was about to walk off to the mews, one of the grooms stayed him. 'Master Baldwin sent word, Thomas,' he said in a low voice. 'That the moment you returned, you should go straight to him. And I'd do his bidding, if I were you.'

Thomas nodded, but went to look in on the falcons anyway. Needing to think, he busied himself with simple tasks: sweeping the mews, putting fresh water out. The birds needed exercise – but how long would he be here, to tend them? He was still turning matters over when he heard hooves, and glancing round, saw two riders approaching across the fields: the Lady Imogen and her steward, Malvyn Wyckes.

He stiffened, unsure of how to proceed. But having half-expected some sharp words from the lady, he was surprised when she reined in her pony and sat calmly, looking him over.

'Falconer . . .' Her tone was languid. 'You have been remiss once again.' When Thomas said nothing, she added: 'We thought you would serve us, but it seemed you had business elsewhere . . . perhaps I will take my merlin out later. I trust you have fed her correctly?'

'Any bird in my care will be well looked after, my Lady,' Thomas answered stiffly.

His gaze wandered towards Wyckes, who had pulled up some yards away. Struggling to master his feelings, he turned back to Lady Imogen, who wore a sad little smile.

'Now – what have you done with Sir Robert?' she asked.

Keeping expression from his face, Thomas replied: 'I have not seen him, my Lady.'

'Nor I,' Lady Imogen said. 'It's most remiss of him . . . the moment you see him, you will tell him I am distraught that he neglects me so, on Christmas Day.'

Thomas gave no answer, but to his relief she shook the pony's reins and let it carry her towards the stable. As she went, she called over her shoulder to Wyckes.

'Sweet Malvyn – have them make me a posset, and send Mouka up with it. I must rest now.'

Then without looking back she disappeared round the wall of the stable yard. Wyckes was about to follow – but now Thomas seized his chance. Stepping forward, he took hold of the horse's bridle.

'I would speak with you, master steward.'

If Wyckes was alarmed he mastered it well, and merely looked down at Thomas with a slightly puzzled expression.

'Yes . . .?'

'I was with the Deptford constable this morning,' Thomas said flatly. 'I helped him arrest the man who stole Jane Derrick's corpse and butchered it.'

There was a silence. The puzzled look left Wyckes's face, to be replaced by a thin smile.

'I'm afraid I don't understand . . .'

'I think you do,' Thomas told him. 'For it was you arranged for her to disappear in the first place, was it not? Unluckily for you, the men you picked to do your handiwork were not up to their tasks. Skeeres a rogue, and Jukes a sot – how

147

long did you think it would be, before the truth leaked out?'

Wyckes said nothing, but there was a look in his eye that made Thomas's hackles rise. Then without warning, the man sprang agilely from the saddle and landed on his feet in front of him. Thomas let go of the bridle, and took a step back.

'Falconer . . .' Wyckes's voice was low, but there was steel in his tone. 'I'm about to give you a warning, and I strongly advise you to heed it.'

Thomas faced him, feeling every muscle in his body tense. And now realization dawned – for he had faced killers before, and knew in his vitals that this man was one. Instinctively he went into a crouch, whereupon Wyckes gave a short laugh.

'What in God's name did you think I was about to do?' he asked. When Thomas made no reply, he gave a shake of his head. 'Falconer – whatever you have turned up in your burrowings, it's but half a tale. You may take my word on that.'

But Thomas's thoughts were leaping like crickets now – and even as he reasoned, he began to give them voice.

'You killed Skeeres,' he said. 'I saw his body . . .'

But Wyckes's expression merely hardened. 'I've no intention of repeating myself,' he said. 'So listen well: you know not what you meddle with.'

But to the man's surprise, Thomas ignored him. 'You killed Skeeres,' he went on, 'because he was a risk – and because he'd betrayed you by not taking the body downriver as you paid him to.' Then he drew breath sharply. 'Was it you killed Lorel Cox, too?'

Wyckes took a step closer, and began to speak rapidly. 'That's quite enough, falconer. Now listen to me, and listen well, or you'll find yourself in more trouble than you could ever imagine. These foolish investigations of course will stop, at once. For I say for the last time, you know not what you deal with. And you are nothing—' The man emphasized the word with a crack of his fingers. 'Nothing, falconer, in the scheme of things . . .'

'What scheme is that?' Thomas asked. 'The one to kill our Queen, and place Lord Beauchamp on the throne?'

148

Wyckes froze, and a pained look came over his face.

'You killed Cox because he poked his nose in,' Thomas cried. 'And he did so because I asked him to—'

'Ah . . .' Wyckes nodded, as if he only now understood. 'It's revenge that drives you, is it?'

'Not revenge,' Thomas answered. 'Justice!'

But at that, Wyckes laughed softly. 'Falconer . . .' He shook his head. 'You are an entertainment, fit for the Revels.'

Then seeing the look in Thomas's eye, his smile faded. 'I've given you fair warning,' he said. 'Keep to your proper duties and no other – if you want to live.'

With a practised gesture, the steward caught up his horse's reins. But as he threw a final, warning look, Thomas spoke.

'I'm called to master Baldwin,' he said. 'As a whitestave, I think he should know all that I know.'

Wyckes stopped in his tracks and turned deliberately towards him. 'Tell him whatever you like,' he said. 'But if you expect him to be grateful, you will be sorely disappointed.'

Then he jerked the reins, and walked his horse away towards the stable.

Fourteen

Thomas did not go to Giles Baldwin.

Caring little what befell him now, he left Sayes Court and walked once again down to Deptford. Wyckes's manner had unnerved him – clearly he had misjudged the man badly. And with Sir Robert gone off somewhere, he felt an emptiness inside. Whatever he tried to do seemed to go amiss. Now he was caught up in matters that both astounded and chilled him, and he was at a loss to know which way to move, or whom he could trust. Save perhaps, the plain folk of Deptford, like Rycroft and Lowdy, and the Lovetts . . . Cox, he had trusted, and the man had paid for it with his life. Sick at heart, he walked into the Sea-Hog.

The inn was warm and heaving with bodies; unwashed and unkempt fellows jostled him on all sides. If word had got out of Dick Jukes's arrest, there seemed to be no sign of it. Instead, almost the entire population of the little village appeared bent on celebrating the season by getting drunk.

He pushed his way to the barrels and found the drawer working the spigot. Calling for a mug of strong sack, he was turning away, when a voice hailed him. And here was Ben Mallam, not quite sober but not yet too drunk, forcing his way through the throng.

'Thomas, just the man . . .' The jingler wore his lopsided grin. 'Isn't there a little matter of some money you owe me? Half as much as the nag was worth, if I recall correctly . . .' Then seeing the look on Thomas's face, his smile faded.

'You haven't earned it yet,' Thomas said.

Ben's brow creased. 'Who was it took you to old Sarah's house last night?' He shuddered, and took a pull from his cannikin. 'By the Christ, I can still see Dan Skeeres's body . . . but did I ask questions? No! I kept my mouth shut.'

Thomas made no reply. It occurred to him that he had nothing left to lose, and so he might as well get drunk like everyone else, then worry about what to do on the morrow. Indeed, what was to stop him leaving for Berkshire? Perhaps Sir Robert had done so already. But recalling his last sight of the man, he doubted that.

He faced Mallam, who was shaking his head. 'Still fretting?' the jingler muttered. 'You're a fool to yourself, master Thomas. Come, dig into your purse, and let's drink this place dry. Then there's a couple of trulls I know, would not turn us away no matter what state we arrive in – what d'you say?'

Thomas was staring at the floor. Then it came to him, that there was yet one thing he had intended to do, which might yield some answers. And when he had pieced together all he knew, he would bypass Baldwin and take his testimony to the palace of Greenwich, by himself. If he were turned away, then at least he would have done all that he could . . .

'What do I say?' he repeated, meeting Mallam's gaze. 'I say help me once more, tonight, and I'll pay you in full. The trulls will still be there tomorrow, will they not?'

Mallam let out a gasp. 'Jesu – you try a man to the limits!' he cried. After a moment he lifted his cannikin, drained its contents and thrust it at Thomas. 'Well – whatever it be, you'll buy me a mug in advance, or three – or I'll tell you where you can shove your money!'

Thomas sighed, took the vessel and turned to the drawer.

Late that night, when the London streets had grown quiet, the two men drew near to Lady Imogen's house.

They had entered the city by the Bridge, just as the gates were closing, and passed the time in a low tavern in Dowgate until Thomas judged the time was right. Then with a nervous Ben Mallam in tow, he had led the way by Thames Street

151

and Tower Hill to Woodruff Lane, and its turning into Hart Street.

In the tavern Thomas had taken a decision, and told the jingler enough to frighten him into sobriety. And Ben's first instinct was to say he wanted no part of Thomas's doings. The promise of money was all that held him. And not for the first time, as they moved silently along the deserted street, he cursed Thomas under his breath.

'If they call the watch, I'm gone,' he muttered. 'If I'm taken, I'll say you forced me at dagger-point. And you may take my word, that this is truly the last time I aid you!'

But Thomas merely gestured him to silence, for they were now at the gate of Lady Imogen's house – and it was locked.

Mallam cursed again, but Thomas merely gripped his arm and shoved him. 'Over the wall,' he said. 'It's not too high.'

Thomas climbed it first, and helped Mallam to descend into the garden. Then they crept to the side of the house. Mercifully, no lights showed anywhere. But Thomas remembered the house-keeper, and guessed the place would not be left unoccupied. For that reason he avoided the kitchen door, and steered Mallam towards the front. Then he stopped, crouching beside a window, and turned to the jingler.

'Let's see you earn your payment,' he murmured.

Cursing softly, Mallam stood up and took his poniard from his belt. There was scratching, then a snap as he forced the catch. Thomas looked round quickly, but heard no further noise. Then he clapped Ben on the shoulder, and pushing the window back, climbed through it. The other followed.

It was pitch dark, and they had to feel their way from the room out to the hallway. But both men were light on their feet, and no sound came from any part of the house. Soon they had found the staircase and climbed it. Then there was a short walk along the upper floor, aided by moonlight falling through a window, before Thomas found the stair to the attic and led the way. Behind him he could hear Mallam, tense as a bowstring, breathing hard.

There were two or three chambers on the top floor – but instinctively Thomas knew which had been poor Jane Derrick's. He did not even need to feel for the hatch in the door, or look for the bars on the single window, for as soon as he entered the room, its air enveloped him like a cold mist.

Behind him, Mallam gulped. 'Jesu – I'm getting out of this . . .'

Thomas turned sharply. 'Wait on the landing and keep a watch,' he whispered. 'Only, give me your light.'

Mallam fumbled in his pockets, found the tinder-box and handed it over. Then he vanished.

Thomas struck a flame, looked about him, and drew a sharp breath. For no lingering doubts now remained that everything Mouka had told him was true: he was standing in what had been Jane Derrick's prison cell.

The room was empty, except for a few stale rushes on the floor. But on the walls were vertical scratches, that probably marked the passage of days . . . and they amounted to many months. He moved to the barred window, and saw that it overlooked the next house and part of the street. Small wonder, he thought, that superstitious neighbours had taken Jane's desperate cries for help as the shrieking of some demon . . . for at sight of her terrible, ruined face, what else would they think?

He breathed deeply, summoning his powers of reason. There was no time to dwell on the poor girl's fate, for she was beyond help now. He needed answers.

Seeing the tinder-box would not last, he quickly fashioned a crude torch from rushes, and pulling threads from his jerkin, bound it tightly and lit it. Then he began to go over every part of the walls, which yielded nothing further. Discouraged, he moved to the tiny fireplace and poked up the chimney, but was rewarded only with a dousing of soot. Coughing, he backed away, then heard a muffled oath from the doorway. Mallam had appeared, his face pale in the rush-light.

'What are you about?' the jingler hissed. 'There's naught here – let's get out!'

'Not yet,' Thomas said. 'I haven't searched the floor.'

Mallam cursed again, but stayed crouching in the doorway as Thomas began to crawl on his hands and knees. Starting in the far corner, moving rushes aside, he worked his way carefully across the floor, examining every board. Then, when he was halfway across the room, he drew a sharp breath. For there was a neat opening, the size of a large coin; and it was no knot-hole. Putting his eye to it, he could see nothing – but he was aware at once of a current of air, slightly warmer than that of the room. He sat back, realizing this could be a spy-hole to the room beneath. But that in itself told him little other than that Jane Derrick might have overheard the goings-on below. Fighting disappointment, he moved on without further discovery. Only when he reached the wall beside the doorway, did he begin to admit defeat – whereupon there came a creak from beneath his knee. Lowering the torch, he saw a small section of board had been cut away, seemingly with a knife: what must have been a slow and painstaking job. Feeling round the edges with his fingers he found a notch, and tugged at it. The board came loose at once, revealing an opening at the foot of the wall. He gasped: a recess had been hollowed out . . . and groping inside, his fingers closed upon a tiny packet. Excitedly he drew it forth and saw a paper, folded many times into a tight little square.

So satisfied was he with his discovery, he started when there came a touch on his arm: Mallam had run out of patience.

'I'm going, with or without you,' the jingler said in his ear.

But Thomas turned to him. 'I'm done,' he said, and extinguished the torch.

They got out the way they had come in, without incident, and scaled the wall once again. Then hearing the bellman's cry nearby, the two of them trotted through deserted streets, back to the dingy tavern in Dowgate where Ben was known, and where they were admitted even at this hour. Calling for mulled sack they went to a corner booth, slumped down and at last began to recover their breath. Only now did Ben notice Thomas's appearance, and gave a shout of laughter.

'Jesu – you're black as the king of spades!'

Thomas put his hand to his cheek, and found it covered in soot. And despite himself, and all his troubles, he faced the jingler and smiled. And in a moment he too was laughing, half in elation, half in relief. And he relaxed, letting his laughter flow as Ben did; both realizing that they were still free men, despite a little house-breaking and what might be construed as a small matter of theft.

Thomas felt for the package in his jerkin, and breathed a sigh of content.

In the early morning, as soon as the gates opened, the two of them left the city and walked the few miles downriver to Deptford. On arriving they went to their lodging, where Thomas was able to wash and find a clean shirt and doublet. Then, as Simon Lovett busied himself in the shop, the two of them sat in Alice's kitchen and devoured a hasty breakfast. After Alice had left them Thomas sat back, his eyes bleary with tiredness, and faced Mallam, who looked none the worse for his adventure.

First, Thomas brought out his purse and paid the jingler for his trouble. But instead of going off as he expected, the other remained seated.

'Well,' Ben said, 'don't I get a look at it? I helped you find it, didn't I?'

After a moment Thomas nodded, and drew the paper from his pocket. A fine dust fell as he opened it carefully, seeing that it threatened to crack at the folds. Then when it was fully open, he laid it flat upon the table-top, and peered at the mass of faint, crabbed writing that covered it from the top edge to the bottom.

But Mallam frowned. 'That's not ink,' he muttered. 'It looks like blood . . .'

Thomas gazed at it, and saw that he was right. For what else had poor Jane Derrick to write with, but the fluids of her own body? Despite her terrible plight, he realized with a surge of admiration, the plucky girl had succeeded in leaving a testimony, and had hidden it well. Presumably she had intended to get it out somehow – until she was taken, and killed. Now her message – shakily written, perhaps with the blunted point of a needle, but still legible – would be read. And Thomas felt himself privileged to be the one to hear it.

But as he read, unease stole over him; and thinking on what Mouka had told him, he began at first to entertain doubts about Jane Derrick's sanity. For here was a tale of such boldness, he found it hard to believe. Yet, her account was so lucid . . .

They met three times in the summer, *Jane had written*, and now they meet by the week. Their plot is laid, and they glory in its perfection. I hear my Lady in her chamber below me prate of it to her lover, and it pains me to see how they excite themselves with it, like ravening beasts. Now I pray this letter be passed to the Queen's loyal servants that they act upon it. Believe this, my sworn testimony writ in my own blood:

The Portuguese is their dupe, a simple-minded fool that rants over the hurt done to his countryman Lopez, the Queen's physician. They have promised him rewards and titles which they cannot give, yet he sees it not, he is but their instrument. He will ride to hunting with the Queen's party, as Amyot's servant. At an unguarded moment when the company are dismounted, he will present the Queen with a nosegay, bending his knee to her, speaking sweet words. Then he will take his poniard and stab her through the heart. Upon that, Amyot and his party will cry murder and seize him, pretending loyalty while the Queen breathes her last. Hence d'Avila will pay for his deed, and none shall credit him should he name those that set him to it.

Upon the Queen's death my Lord will declare himself rightful heir, and his party will flock to Whitehall. Plans are laid to hurry forth the bishops, and force them to a coronation. Then when all is done, my Lord's followers may reap their reward.

It shall happen about the third day after Christmas. If there is more, I have not discovered it. My Lady's steward likes not what was done to me, and may aid me. I have only my body to offer him and pray he turns not from my face as all do now save Mouka, who is my only friend. I will tell her where this paper is hid. God grant me strength to endure till then.

Given under my hand in my own blood, 7th day of December 1594.

Jane Derrick.

There was a scrawled signature at the bottom corner. Having read it aloud, Thomas put the paper down and turned to Ben Mallam, whose frown had deepened.

'Lopez . . . he's the cove the Earl of Essex accused of trying to poison the Queen, is he not? Hanged for it, back in the summer . . .'

Thomas nodded, recalling the scandal of earlier that year. Though many believed Doctor Lopez innocent, he was said to have made confession under torture, and had been executed.

The two men were silent for a while. But when Thomas looked to Mallam again, he saw fear in the other's face.

'Jesu, Thomas,' he muttered. 'What will you do?'

Thomas shrugged. 'What can I do, but take this to the royal palace and tell what I know?'

'And you think they'll believe you?' Ben asked in a scathing tone. 'Who'd take your word against a man like Amyot?'

Thomas felt his spirits sinking. 'Baldwin might listen,' he began, then remembered his last conversation with the Clerk of the Green Cloth. And Sir Robert, who at least knew Thomas to be a truthful man, was gone, no one knew where . . . He gazed again at Jane Derrick's letter.

'Third day after Christmas,' Ben muttered. 'And today's the first . . .'

'I can count,' Thomas told him somewhat irritably. Then his brow creased as he began to reason aloud, for his own sake, caring little whether Ben listened or not.

'She was a clever girl, the goldsmith told me. And she pieced all this together, from what she overheard her mistress

157

say in her chamber beneath – and from what she guessed. She told Mouka, who thought she had lost her mind. Why, then, was she killed? For who else knew what she had discovered?'

Then at once he answered his own question: Wyckes.

Before yesterday, he would not have believed the steward a murderer. But after facing him at the mews, he knew what sort of man he was. And now, he found that he believed every word of Jane Derrick's statement. And anger rose in him once again, for the cruel injustice she had suffered.

Jane had made one fatal mistake: she had at some point spoken to Malvyn Wyckes, perhaps pleading with him to let her escape. But as one of the movers in Amyot's and Lady Imogen's scheme, Wyckes had seen at once that she posed a risk. Moreover, she had drawn attention to the house; and hence, she had to be silenced.

Now he thought of Skeeres's tale: of the men who had waited for him by Petty Wales that night. It was but a short walk to there, from Poor Jewry; and by back streets and alleys, two men might easily have carried their bundle unobserved to the riverside . . . his mouth tightened. Jane was already dead – he believed Skeeres in that, for the man was no murderer. So – it seemed Wyckes had killed her; strangled her with his hands, as he had strangled Skeeres. Cox . . .? There might have been witnesses on the strand, so he had had to be swift, hence the use of a poniard. It was all of a piece: Cox too had poked about and tended to be loose-tongued when he drank – which was often enough. His own loquacity had been his undoing.

He looked up, but the moment he met Ben Mallam's eye, the other shook his head.

'Nay, master Thomas,' Ben said with a wry look. 'Ask no more of me, for I've stretched my luck far enough! I thank you for the payment, but it's time I took myself out of Deptford – out of London, for that matter. There's bound to be a nag for sale somewhere, at the right price – and I mean to find it.'

Thomas sighed. 'None could blame you, for wanting to put some distance between yourself and all of this . . .'

Ben stood up. 'I'll find Alice and tell her,' he said, then seeing Thomas's expression, he frowned. 'And you've no need to look so damned pious. She'll likely seek other company after I'm gone – even yours.' He started for the door, then turned briefly.

'I'll stand you a farewell mug at supper-time, in the Sea-Hog. Then I'm gone.'

Thomas watched him go out, then turned back to look once again at Jane Derrick's testimony.

In the afternoon, still uncertain how to proceed, he went with a heavy heart back to Sayes Court, and began to exercise the falcons. The birds, at least, would not be neglected, despite the turmoil of events. Having flown all of them except the Lady Imogen's merlin, he was taking the little bird on his gauntlet when a voice behind startled him. He turned to see Mouka, muffled in her thin cloak, standing watching him.

'I was walking – I saw you exercising your birds,' she said in her soft voice. 'I hear master Baldwin is displeased. He has given orders that you do not leave Sayes Court again, but wait for his return.'

Thomas hesitated, then said: 'Yet, will you walk with me once more, mistress, while I fly this little hawk? For there are things you might wish to hear.'

She nodded, and walked beside him across the fields. She watched while he unhooded the merlin, raised his arm and let it soar.

First he showed her Jane Derrick's paper – but she merely shook her head sadly: she could not read. So as briefly as he was able, he told her what he had discovered. By the time he had finished they had walked more than a mile into open country. They stopped, and Thomas called the little falcon down and hooded it again. He turned to find Mouka standing still and silent, hiding her face from him in a fold of her cloak. Finally she lowered it and looked up at him, her eyes red from weeping.

'I have been afraid of master Wyckes, ever since he came to serve my Lady,' she said. 'Now, if I could, I would kill him with my own hands – my Lady, too!' She faltered. 'How

159

am I to stay and serve her, knowing what she is – and what has been done?'

Thomas had no answer. And after a moment, the two of them began to retrace their steps unwillingly towards Sayes Court.

As the manor came into sight, Mouka stopped and turned to Thomas with a look of desperation.

'What might we do, you or I?' she asked.

He paused, then answered: 'I can but try to lay the whole scheme bare. I will not rest until I have carried the tale to the palace. And I'll not be silenced, as others have been.'

He turned to walk back to the mews, and froze at the sound of hooves. Beside him he heard Mouka give a little cry, which was quickly stifled. He turned quickly to see Lady Imogen herself, riding her small pony rapidly towards them. And from the look on her face there was little doubt what kind of humour she was in.

'Did I give you permission to fly my merlin?' she cried.

She drew her mount to a violent halt, jerking the rein so hard that the animal threw its head back and whinnied in pain. Thomas bit his lip, feeling himself tense from head to foot.

'The bird needed exercise,' he began, then broke off. For Lady Imogen had turned upon Mouka in fury.

'Get you to the house, and wait for me in my chamber,' she snapped. 'I've had a most trying day!'

And Thomas could only watch as Mouka fought to master her emotions. Finally the woman drew a breath, and hurried away towards the house.

There was a moment, before Lady Imogen swung her eyes upon Thomas. Heart thudding, he met her gaze and waited. The silence grew longer, as the two of them eyed each other across an unbridgeable gulf. Thomas steeled himself for another tirade – but it never came. Instead, as if bored by the encounter, the lady tugged sharply at her rein, and the horse stumbled forward. Flecks of foam showed about its mouth.

As she went, Lady Imogen threw a last word at Thomas. 'See her well watered,' she ordered. 'And have a care with that hood. If it goes missing, I'll know who to blame!'

And she was gone, trotting away across the fields. Thomas stood for a moment, and felt the merlin twitch under its hood, as if the bird somehow understood. He let out a long breath, and bore the little falcon back to the mews.

Fifteen

Aware that he was courting at the very least a severe reprimand, Thomas avoided the house and the watchful eyes of Baldwin's steward, and hurried down the path to Deptford as dusk was falling. There was one man he felt he could count on, and that was William Rycroft. The two of them, he reasoned – one a respected constable – were more likely to be taken seriously when they brought Thomas's discovery to the authorities. So it was with rising hope that he saw the light in the man's cottage, and hurried to the door. But when Rycroft himself answered his knock, he looked uncomfortable at seeing Thomas before him.

'You'd best come in,' he said in a low voice. 'But you won't like what I have to tell you.'

With a frown, Thomas entered and stood in the narrow passage while the man closed the door behind them. Then he turned, and said: 'I'm instructed to arrest you.'

'By whom?' Thomas asked, after a moment.

'By master Giles Baldwin.'

There was a pause, before the constable lowered his eyes, and gestured towards the kitchen. 'Let's take a bite of supper, and we'll speak of it.'

They sat at the table and ate the pottage and rye bread mistress Rycroft had put out, before taking herself off. Rycroft's son also made himself scarce. Finally when he had cleared his platter, the constable faced Thomas and told him that a servant had come from Baldwin that afternoon, to instruct him to apprehend Thomas at the first opportunity, and take him to Sayes Court. Thinking back, Thomas realized that the message had likely been delivered as he and Mouka were walking, out of sight of the house. Only by chance had he avoided being seen.

'Well, master . . .' He eyed Rycroft calmly. 'You have me in your power; now what will you do?'

The other was silent for a moment. 'I thought I'd hear what you had to say first,' he replied. 'Somehow, you don't strike me as a dangerous felon.'

Thomas blinked. 'What felony am I accused of?'

'I know not,' Rycroft told him. 'But Baldwin's a white-stave, the Queen's Controller. He has all the authority he needs.'

Thomas hesitated, then said: 'I came here to tell you of a plot I seem to have uncovered.'

Rycroft frowned. 'What kind of plot?'

'To murder the Queen.'

The other man froze, and Thomas went on: 'To my mind, that's an unlikely errand for a felon to be on – wouldn't you say?'

Rycroft kept his eyes on him. 'Mayhap I would.' He drew a deep breath, and added: 'You'd better tell me of it, then.'

So Thomas told him, leaving nothing out. After a while he drew forth Jane Derrick's testimony, and handed it to the constable. When he had finished reading it, the man was speechless. He stared at the empty platter before him, wearing a deep frown.

'And now, another thing troubles me,' Thomas said, realizing he had avoided thinking the matter through until now. 'Why is master Baldwin so keen to keep his eye on me – and why now does he order my arrest?'

At that, Rycroft drew another sharp breath. 'You think he too is involved in this treachery?'

'I no longer know who to trust hereabouts,' Thomas admitted tiredly. 'Though I'd a mind to trust you,' he added, 'and to ask your help in taking the whole matter to the palace, to put before the Queen's own servants.'

'Yet if we did such,' Rycroft countered, 'and this wicked scheme is as you describe it, involving men of the highest station – then how would we know whom to trust, even in the Queen's household?'

Thomas shrugged. 'We can but count upon our instincts. Try to do what is right, and take the consequences.'

There followed a silence, but Thomas was relieved once again at having shared the burden, even with one of such humble station as a village constable. Finally Rycroft eyed him with the same severity Thomas had first seen, when the man yanked Dick Jukes to his feet from the floor of the Sea-Hog. Picking up the cracked paper with its faded writing, he handed it back to Thomas, who stowed it away in his jerkin.

'I believe mistress Derrick's testimony,' he said. 'As I do yours. And you and I will take it to the palace of Greenwich, at once.'

Thomas sat back, and gave a sigh.

They left soon after dark. But instead of going the shortest way over the green, and crossing the Creek by its little footbridge to approach the palace entrance, the constable turned down the narrow lane towards Deptford Strand. When Thomas queried the route, he said: 'I've a mind to go by the riverside, past the *Golden Hind*, and walk to the water-gate. There are fewer guards, and I'm known to the boatmen.'

Thomas signalled his agreement and soon the two of them emerged on to the strand. Most of the ice was gone now, though a chill breeze blew upriver. They passed Monkaster's yard, and heard the ark-builder at his work, even on such a night: the rasp of a saw spoke of his shaping yet another timber. But now, at this of all times, there came a shout from behind them. Both men turned to see the door of the Sea-Hog flung open, and Ben Mallam framed against the light that spilled out.

'Time for that farewell mug, you whoreson cove!' the jingler shouted, beckoning Thomas forward. 'Hurry up now!'

Thomas shook his head. 'I've other business . . .' he began. But Ben left the doorway and came towards him, somewhat tipsily.

'What business is that?' he demanded, then recognized Will Rycroft and stopped, his smile disappearing. 'Ah . . .

164

that sort of business . . .' He eyed both of them, and took a step backwards. 'Then, I believe I'll leave you men to it.'

He turned to go. 'I wish you luck, hawksman,' he said. 'For I fear I'll not see you again.'

Thomas was about to reply . . . but then he heard the crunch of boots on the gravel: several pairs of boots, coming towards him. He turned quickly, hearing Rycroft ask: 'What in God's name is this?'

Out of the gloom, four or five men appeared. And at their head was a diminutive but angry-looking little fellow, whom Thomas recognized all too readily: Peter Sly.

'Jesu – the Tom-tit!'

Even as Ben Mallam blurted the words, Thomas saw that it was too late for flight – or at least, it was for himself and Rycroft. To his dismay, the jingler took one look at the ill-favoured bunch and fled, back into the inn. The door banged shut behind him. Thomas could only curse the man for a coward as he and the constable drew closer together, to meet their peril. For neither of them was in much doubt as to the predicament they were facing.

'Friends of yours, master Thomas?' Rycroft asked quietly.

'Not exactly, master Constable,' Thomas answered in similar vein.

Then the two of them were reaching for the poniards at their belts, backing slowly along the strand as their assailants fanned out before them.

'Who are you, and what do you want here?' Rycroft demanded, though from his tone, he clearly expected little in the way of an answer. 'I'm constable of Deptford – you assault me, you'll pay dear for it.'

But Sly the Tom-tit jeered. Thomas realized it was the first time he had got a proper look at Ben Mallam's old enemy. When he saw the squat nose and the squint in the little man's eyes, he almost felt inclined to laugh.

'You're the ones who'll pay!' Sly threw back in his high-pitched voice. And both Thomas and Rycroft saw the cudgel in his stubby hands. The other men – tavern louts, by the look of them – made no sound. Each bore a wooden billet, and one held forth a poniard. At a word from Peter Sly the group came forward, seemingly eager to finish what they had been paid to do, then get themselves gone.

And this was one fight, Thomas thought briefly, that he was not going to win. As the first man tensed and sprang towards him, he heard a hammering behind, and realized vaguely that he and the constable had backed all the way to Sir Ralph Monkaster's fence. But then he forgot about everything, save self-preservation.

He ducked the man's swing, then banged his balled fist hard into the fellow's face. He faltered long enough for Thomas to deal him a second and third blow, whereupon the man sank to his knees. But even as he whirled about to face his next attacker, Thomas knew that he and Rycroft were hopelessly outnumbered. From the corner of his eye, he saw the constable struggling to fend off two men at once. From the sudden cry of pain that rose, he knew Rycroft had wounded one of them – but then his poniard-hand was pinioned, and a series of bone-chilling thuds spoke of his being cruelly beaten. Soon he was on his knees, gasping for breath.

For his part, Thomas found himself facing three men – or two and a half, he thought wryly, as the Tom-tit ducked under his flailing arms, and cracked him on the legs with his cudgel. Another man caught Thomas on the shoulder, but he tried to ignore the pain, for the third assailant was the one with the dagger. And Thomas's only thought was to disarm him somehow; for if the man was given the chance to use the weapon, he was finished.

He fought hard, aware that he was weakening. He had lost his poniard, and now he was becoming confused . . . he sensed it, as his assailants did. Grunts of pain and the thuds of connecting blows swirled about him, and he was no longer sure from whose lips they came. He was aware of gripping the dagger-wielder's arm, and forcing it back, but someone was cracking him about the upper arms, neck and shoulders. Desperately he tried to duck the swings aimed at his head – until at last one caught him on the ear. And then he was falling, with a rushing sound in his ears. Bizarrely, he thought of the torrent that flowed under

London Bridge at full tide, and wondered if the piers were free of ice now . . .

He fell, aware of the shingle cutting into his knees. There was more shouting now . . . though where it came from was unclear to Thomas. He thought he heard running feet, but the next moment he knew nothing, except that it was very dark . . .

Pain again; he grunted, lying on his back, wondering why he was conscious. Then he realized no one was hitting him any more, and with a faint stirring of relief he got himself on to one elbow, then managed to sit up. Dizzily he looked round – and began to understand.

About half the drinkers in the Sea-Hog had come to his aid. And to his surprise, Ben Mallam was among them.

Panting, the side of his head throbbing, Thomas could only watch as the fight spilled into Ralph Monkaster's yard. The fence had been flattened. Now, etched against the lantern light from behind, men battled in two and threes, lurching to and fro, arms swinging. Some were falling, others wading in. Planks of wood were seized and swung, kicks aimed . . . to one side, he saw the jingler dancing about excitedly, shouting instructions. Trust him to hang back, Thomas thought wryly . . . then he blinked as a small figure detached itself from the mass of heaving bodies, and ran towards him. Peter Sly had managed to duck through someone's legs, and was bent on making his escape.

But even as Thomas tried to stand, and fell back weakly, he saw another figure appear suddenly from behind, and seize the little man by the collar. Sly shrieked and swung round, waving his cudgel, but the heavy-set man merely grabbed his arm and twisted it. Sly screamed with pain and dropped the weapon. And only now, did Thomas recognize his assailant: Simon Lovett.

But this man was not the bumbling ships' chandler he knew: he was a stranger. His good eye blazing, face streaked with blood, the man picked up the writhing Tom-tit like a child and shook him. Then he set him down, gripped him about the neck, and squeezed . . . and Thomas called out, surprising himself by the hoarseness of his voice.

'Simon . . . think what you do!'

But he was ignored. And in that moment, Thomas saw the real Simon Lovett: the grizzled, hardened seaman who had sailed with Drake, and fought many terrible battles . . . and he knew without doubt that the man was bent on killing.

Somehow, Thomas got to his feet. Ignoring the noises behind him, which were diminishing now, he staggered towards the pair: Sly twitching and gurgling, on his knees now, his face purple; Lovett bending low, his big gnarled hands squeezing, tighter and tighter . . . even as Thomas shouted again he saw Sly go limp, and his eyes close. Then Thomas was grabbing Simon Lovett about the shoulders, trying feebly to pull him away.

With a roar Lovett whirled round savagely, letting go of his victim, and raised a fist. Then he saw Thomas . . . and checked himself. For a moment the two men eyed each other, both breathless and sweating – Lovett wild and bloodied, Thomas fighting pain, struggling against the exhaustion which threatened to pull him back into unconsciousness . . .

Then, mercifully, it was over. Thomas staggered, and Simon Lovett caught him. Gently he laid him down beside Ralph Monkaster's broken gate, then leaned over him and spoke.

'By the Christ, I would have killed you . . .'

Thomas swallowed. 'I believe you,' he croaked. His eyes wandered to the prone figure of Peter Sly, lying a few feet away. Following his gaze Lovett looked round briefly, grunted, and turned back to Thomas. 'Why did you want to save this runt?' he asked. ''Twas him that started it all, was it not?'

But Thomas looked about in alarm. 'Rycroft,' he muttered, 'what's happened to him?'

Lovett straightened, recovering his breath, and wiped his face with his sleeve. 'Down,' he said. 'That's all I know . . .' Then he stiffened. Thomas looked, and saw Ben Mallam emerging from the group who now stood about the yard, talking quietly among themselves. Sly's men had been dealt with, that much was obvious. But at what cost, Thomas had

168

yet to learn . . . bleary-eyed, he looked up as the jingler approached. And to his amazement, Ben was wearing his lopsided grin.

'Thought I'd left you in the lurch, didn't you?' he asked, and bent to peer down at Thomas. 'Well you're wrong – took me a minute or two to summon aid, that's all . . .' His grin faded. 'It's a nasty bump you've got, hawksman . . .'

Then abruptly he grew aware of Simon Lovett, standing very still. And as Ben turned towards him, an uneasy look spread across his features. 'Simon – are you hurt?' He met Lovett's gaze, then lowered his eyes and put a hand nervously to his chin. 'Some scrap we got into, was it not?' he said, with an attempt at levity.

Simon eyed him. 'Most of us did,' he replied. 'Only it seems you escaped without a scratch. Then you've always had the luck of the devil, master Ben – is't not so?'

Ben blinked, and Thomas saw what was about to happen. But even if he had had time to call out, he knew it would be to no avail. For Simon Lovett's huge fist came up from nowhere, and connected sharply with Ben Mallam's nose. There was a thud and Ben staggered, to sit down heavily on the gravel, a look of astonishment on his face.

'You'll be moving out tonight, will you not?' Simon stood over him, hands on hips.

After a moment the jingler nodded dumbly, then looked down as drops of blood ran from his nose, staining his jerkin.

Thomas sighed, and got slowly to his feet once again. And this time, he managed to stay upright. He was about to go looking for Rycroft, when there came a cry. Alice Lovett, a shawl flung hastily about her shoulders, hurried up out of the darkness. She stopped abruptly on seeing Ben Mallam, still seated on the shingle. Then slowly she turned to gaze upon her husband.

'Lord, Simon . . .' she muttered. 'What have you done now?'

Lovett said nothing. But Alice came towards him, and reaching up, dabbed at his face with the edge of her shawl. There was a moment . . . and then Ben Mallam could only watch, as Alice took her husband's arm tenderly. And without looking back the two of them walked away, towards their home.

Thomas offered his hand. And finally Mallam took it, allowing himself to be pulled upright. Then he walked to the prone figure of Peter Sly, and gave him a gentle kick. The Tom-tit opened his eyes, and struggled to sit up. Then he groaned and put his head in his hands.

Other men were gathering around now. They filed out of Monkaster's yard, many bearing cuts and bruises, but Rycroft was not among them. In some alarm, Thomas began easing his way through them, passing along the bulk of the half-built ark . . . some of its timbers, he saw, had been torn away for use as weapons. One or two of the Deptford men spoke to Thomas, asking him what was the cause of the coil, but he made no reply. With rising unease, he began to call Will Rycroft's name . . . then to his relief there came answer at last. Beside Monkaster's outhouse, where not many days ago the body of Lorel Cox had lain, Rycroft sat with his back to the wall. And kneeling beside him, was a shaky Sir Ralph Monkaster.

'Thank heaven . . .' Thomas hurried forward and dropped to his knee beside Monkaster, who started in alarm.

'This man needs doctoring!' the ark-builder cried. 'There's been mayhem and savagery, and blood spilled in my house!' Then he took a better look at Thomas, and saw his condition.

'You too are hurt . . .' The man's white beard bobbed in the lantern-light. 'What in God's name was all this madness about?!'

But Thomas peered at Rycroft, saw the blood about his head; his jerkin too was soaked with it. He had been stabbed in two or three places, and badly beaten. Turning to Monkaster, Thomas said: 'This is a brave man – and he could die for loss of blood. Is there no surgeon here?'

The ark-builder hesitated, and an odd look came over his features. But then to Thomas's relief, Rycroft opened one eye. 'Sir Ralph was one, master Finbow,' he said softly. 'Did you not know it? One of the best ship's surgeons in the navy . . .'

170

Thomas turned in surprise, and met Monkaster's eye. 'I did not know . . .' he began, then frowned slightly as the ark-builder made a quick, dismissive gesture.

'That was in another life,' he said. 'Before I found the secret, and my true vocation!'

There was a moment, then Rycroft groaned, and closed his eyes again.

'Will you not help him, sir?' Thomas asked. But Monkaster flinched at the look in his eyes. He opened his mouth, then closed it. He seemed to be fighting some inner battle with himself.

'Other men are hurt, too,' Thomas persisted, looking hard at the man. 'They need your skills – will you forsake everything, for the building of your ark?'

Still Monkaster hesitated. Then at last, he gave a long sigh, and nodded. 'Send someone to me,' he said quietly. 'I will instruct him where to find my case of instruments . . .'

With a nod Thomas rose, and went to do the man's bidding.

Beside Monkaster's flattened fence, he was relieved to see that some sort of order was now being restored. Lanterns had been brought, and some of those injured in the fight were being tended by folk from the village. In fact, quite a crowd was gathering. Having sent a boy to assist Sir Ralph, Thomas walked painfully on to the strand, and found Ben Mallam – who was still standing grimly over Peter Sly. As Thomas approached the jingler looked round and said in a triumphant tone: 'The whoreson javel's lost this time!'

But as both of them glanced down at Sly, the little man opened his eyes. 'That's what you think, Mallam!' he cried, and managed a sickly grin. 'Who d'you think spiked your precious Galloway for you?!'

'You!' Ben froze, and stared down at him in fury. 'I knew it . . . I've a mind to finish you while I can!'

'You wouldn't dare, in front of witnesses!' the other shot back. Both men were gazing at each other now with a pure, bright hatred.

'As long as I've breath in me, you'll have to look over your shoulder, Mallam,' Sly snarled. 'You and I aren't done yet!'

171

But Thomas had stepped forward, and to the Tom-tit's surprise, grabbed him sharply by the collar. 'You killed the horse?' he breathed. 'Who else did you spike?'

Sly flinched. 'No one . . . let go of me!'

'Cox, the player,' Thomas cried. 'Did you kill him?'

'I never heard of him!' Sly shouted. 'There was none here save the crazy old man . . . I waited till he'd gone into the house, then did what I came to do and got out!'

Thomas peered into the man's eyes, but saw nothing to make him disbelieve his answer. After a moment he let go of him and stepped back, breathing hard.

But then Sly turned his head quickly, and Ben Mallam turned his. Both had heard, as Thomas now did, the tramp of heavy boots . . . and they seemed to be walking in time.

People looked round, falling back in alarm. For from the direction of the palace, a small troop of guards in helmets and cuirasses appeared, marching rapidly with halberds at their shoulders. And to Thomas's surprise, leading them was Baldwin's steward, Nicholas Capper.

'Thomas Finbow!' The man saw him at once, and pointed. And as Thomas started, soldiers hurried to surround him. He heard the shriek of steel, as swords were drawn.

'Master steward . . .?' Thomas stared in disbelief as Capper thrust himself forward, his face taut with anger.

'You're arrested for affray, by orders of the Clerk of the Green Cloth!' he cried, seemingly unaware of how absurd his words sounded. He gestured to two of the guards, who stepped to either side of Thomas and seized his arms.

Then he was marched away along the strand, stumbling on the gravel. And the folk of Deptford, Ben Mallam among them, could only watch, as he disappeared into the gloom.

Sixteen

He awoke from a troubled slumber, with a pungent smell in his nostrils that almost made him retch. He was aware of having dreamed fitfully, and having woken in darkness before drifting off to sleep again. Now daylight stabbed at his eyes . . . he blinked, feeling the soreness in his limbs as he struggled to rise. Finally he sat up, and saw that he was lying on a pallet, fully clothed, and half-covered with a horse blanket. Gingerly he put a hand to his throbbing right ear – and found a bandage about his head. He looked round, but did not recognize his surroundings: he was in a small room, roughly plastered, with a door, a single window and a low roof. Then he saw the wooden churns, and a row of earthenware jugs, and knew at once what the smell was: he had been put in the dairy.

He lay still for a moment, then cocked his ear as a familiar squealing rose from somewhere outside: of course – he was at Sayes Court, and Bridget was feeding the pigs. He opened his mouth to shout, but only a croak emerged. Glancing round, he saw a pitcher of water had been placed at his side. In a moment he had raised it and drunk thirstily. Then he got stiffly to his feet.

He walked across the floor of beaten earth, and tried the door. He was not surprised to find it locked. Now the events of the last night flooded back . . . and quickly he fumbled in the pockets of his jerkin. When his hand closed upon the folded paper bearing Jane Derrick's testimony, he breathed a sigh of relief.

He remembered being marched through the lanes, by torchlight. He must have been half-conscious by the time they had reached here: he recalled strong arms supporting him, and voices . . . then he started, remembering something else: *the third day after Christmas . . .*

Now he had to fight a rising panic. Today was surely the second day . . . he had time yet, he told himself quickly, to deliver his message. Rycroft . . .? He frowned. The last he had seen of Rycroft, the constable was in no shape to do anything. Hence, unless the man had confided in someone, Thomas was the only one who knew of the Queen's peril . . . In sudden anger, he banged upon the door, but its heavy timbers held firm. Moving to the window, he peered out and saw that it faced east, to the fields behind the manor. Unsurprisingly, there was no one in sight. He shouted, and shouted again. But his only reward was a chorus of grunts and squeals from the pig-pen.

'Bridget!' he called, and rapped on the window. But the glass was thick; and even if he broke it, he saw the casement was too small to admit his tall frame. Looking round, he wondered if this place had been used as a lock-up before; it was certainly secure enough. Mastering his frustration he returned to the pallet, sat down with his back to the wall of roughcast and tried to think. And now, one fact stood before him with crystal clarity: Baldwin had to be a part of the plan to murder the Queen.

He shook his head, berating himself for his failure to see it. He had misjudged the man from the start . . . why else were Amyot and the Lady Imogen staying here as his guests, within walking distance of the Queen's palace of Greenwich? And there was Wyckes, who seemed to have the run of the place, to come and go where he would. He recalled his chance sighting in Woodruff Lane of the steward, together with Amyot and the fellow whom he now assumed to be d'Avila: the plotters' 'instrument'.

A weight seemed to press upon him; if only he had acted sooner . . .

He banged his fist angrily upon the floor, as other things became clear. He had been watched, more closely than he realized. How else would Capper and the guards have known when and where to lay hands upon him? He drew breath suddenly: was it not odd, that Peter Sly and his rogues had also known where he was?

He caught up the pitcher again, swallowed another mouthful, then dashed the rest of its contents over his face. The ice-cold water revived him somewhat, and he began poking about the bare little room. Somehow he must get out, and make his way to the palace. Nothing else mattered now . . .

He halted, standing in the middle of the room. At least his hurts had been tended, he thought, and his head bandaged . . . briefly, he wondered why they had bothered to do that. And more, he now wondered – what did Baldwin intend to do with him? Would he be sent off to London, to Newgate or one of the other terrible prisons . . . he shook his head. Surely they could have taken him there already? A darker notion formed, which made him take a deep breath, staring at the row of jugs without seeing them. More likely, when the time was right he would simply be killed; as Skeeres had been, and Cox . . . because quite simply, they had known too much.

Well, he thought, *I will put up what resistance I can; why should they have it easy?*

He sat down again, conserving his strength, staring at the door. Whoever came through it, he would be ready for them.

But he was not ready.

He had dozed . . . he awoke with a start, not knowing what hour it was. Then he heard the bolt being drawn, and ignoring the pain in his limbs, got quickly to his feet. The door was pulled back, and a slight figure came hesitantly into the room. Thomas drew breath in surprise.

'Mistress Mouka . . .'

The young woman stopped when she saw him. She was carrying something covered with a cloth. She drew the covering back, to show a bowl of porridge with a hunk of bread soaking in it.

'I have been allowed to bring you this,' she said. Then her eyes moved, and Thomas saw the two guards standing just outside the door, watching him closely.

'I thank you,' he said. Mouka nodded, then bent to place the bowl on the floor. She straightened, meeting his eyes, but all he saw was the same look of resignation that she had worn when they first spoke, at hawking upon Shooter's Hill.

He moistened his lips, aware of the guards' eyes upon him. This might be his only opportunity . . .

'Do you know how the constable fares, mistress?' he asked. 'He was badly injured last night . . .'

She shook her head. But as she turned to go Thomas stepped closer, making her flinch. 'Ben Mallam, the jingler,' he said in a hoarse whisper. 'Please get word to him, in Deptford – tell him where I am . . .'

'Stop!'

He looked up sharply, as one of the guards stepped through the doorway, levelling his halberd. Thomas glanced at Mouka: to his dismay, she seemed not to have heard him. Without looking back, she walked past the guard and disappeared through the door. With a hard look at Thomas, the guard followed, slamming it behind him. Then the bolt was rammed home, and Thomas could only walk back to his pallet and throw himself down, to stare at the floor.

For hours he shivered on his pallet, wrapped in the rough horse blanket. He had eaten the bread and porridge, and quickly fallen asleep. When he awoke it was dark once again, and he cursed aloud: had the food been laced with something to send him into unconsciousness? The thirst he now felt seemed to confirm his suspicion. Angrily he got up, and forced himself to walk repeatedly around the dark room. He beat his arms together, fighting the cold which seeped through his dirty clothing. Only once did he bother to go to the window, for there was nothing to see there but the stars.

This was his worst time; for another day had passed, and he had done nothing. He had been through every possible plan: make a tunnel, dig through the walls, find something to force the door . . . but each time he raised his hopes, he seemed to hear the guards walking round the little dairy, stamping their feet against the cold. Once there had been voices, but he could not hear what was said. Finally he flung himself down again, and drew his knees up to his chest. There was still a day, he reasoned, but with increasing desperation. The third day after Christmas . . . they had allowed

Mouka to bring him food once. Surely they would do so again? When that happened he must act – seize one of the soldiers if he could, and take his weapon from him. If he died in the attempt, at least he would have tried. Anything was better than this confinement . . .

Dawn was coming; he saw a faint greyness stealing across the room. He had grown used to the stale smell of butter, as he had become sick of looking at the churns and the jugs. He rubbed his hands and blew upon them, waiting for the birdsong that would herald the new day . . .

A sound; distant, and barely audible. He tensed . . . then quickly he stood up. And at once, from somewhere outside there came a blood-curdling shriek, followed by another.

There was a muttered oath from just outside the door, then footfalls, and at once Thomas darted forward and pressed his ear to it. He frowned, scarcely able to believe it: the guards were running! He heard their voices growing fainter . . .

A terrible moment passed, seemingly an eternity, though he realized later that it was less than a minute. Then came the rasp of the bolt being drawn back . . . he half-crouched as the door flew open – then gasped. For there was Ben Mallam with a stick in his hand, and a very scared expression on his face.

'Out, you whoreson fool,' the jingler cried. 'Run!'

Thomas ran.

With Mallam close behind him he ran from the dairy, past the pig-sty and across the deserted kitchen yard. It was early dawn, and mercifully no one was about yet. In seconds, he had reached the stables and flung open the doors. The horses stamped uneasily in their stalls, as Thomas and Ben hurried in and halted, staring about them in the gloom.

'What was that scream?' Thomas asked, catching his breath.

'An old skill I picked up,' Mallam answered. 'Never mind that – they'll soon know it was a trick. Get yourself horsed, and quickly!'

To Thomas's relief, the black gelding from Petbury was in the end stall, shifting its feet nervously. Unhurriedly he walked forward, speaking quietly to the animal as he untied it. Seizing a bridle from a peg, he quickly slipped it over the horse's head, then led it to the doorway.

Mallam was crouching by the yard wall, still clutching his stick, which would have been little use if it came to a fight. He turned quickly as Thomas brought the gelding out.

'I owe you, master Ben,' Thomas said gratefully. 'Was it mistress Mouka who got word to you?'

Mallam shrugged. 'She gave no name . . . but if you mean a pretty dark-skinned maid, that's the one.' He gave a low whistle. 'What I'd give, to know her better . . .'

There was no time to saddle the horse. Thomas led it on to the cobbles, then said: 'If you'll climb up behind me, we'll make ourselves scarce.'

But Mallam shook his head. 'Are you mad?' he cried. 'If I'm caught, it's the Clink or the Counter for me at the least – and with my luck I'll never come out again! You ride on, hawksman. And if I'm questioned I know naught of you, nor how you got free.'

Thomas hesitated, then swung himself on to the horse's bare back. He eased it forward with his heels, to the yard entrance. And here, the two men parted.

'You've done a greater service than I can ever repay,' Thomas said, and reached down to offer his hand. Ben took it briefly, but made no reply. The next moment he was sprinting away towards the trees that lined the road; then he was gone.

Thomas shook the reins, easing the gelding from a trot to a canter. Soon he had crossed the deserted highway, and Sayes Court was falling away behind him. Then he was racing through open country, feeling the breeze in his face; seldom, he realized, had he felt so glad to be free.

He galloped a few miles south-east, skirting Shooter's Hill, seeking a place to hide for an hour or two. Beyond that he had no other plan than to ride to Greenwich Palace and demand to be admitted. Though his appearance alone, he realized, would likely cause suspicion . . . and now, as he rode, his nagging doubts quickly grew into real fears.

Capper had come to apprehend him under Baldwin's orders, backed by a troop of the Queen's guards. Hence, surely word would be spread of an escaped prisoner answering to Thomas's description? They were likely sending men out already, to search the area . . . the only reception he would get if he reappeared, would be arrest and a speedy incarceration.

Fighting his fear, he steered the horse into a tangled thicket of hawthorn and beech, ignoring the branches that tore at his face and clothing. But the animal slowed, then reared as Thomas tried to urge it forward. Berating himself, he drew rein and allowed it to halt, clouds of steam blowing from its nostrils. Then he dismounted to stand beside it, patting its neck and soothing it with soft words.

He looked quickly about and saw that he was well-hidden, for the moment at least. Then breathing hard, he sat down on a fallen tree with the reins in his hands, and dared to take stock of his position.

If time were not so precious, he could have waited until nightfall, then got himself back to Deptford – perhaps to Rycroft's house. The constable alone understood the situation, and would get word to the palace somehow. Then a notion struck Thomas: two nights had passed since his arrest . . . surely Rycroft would have acted by now? Even if he were unable to rise from a sick-bed, he would have sent some message. So perhaps Thomas's mission was superfluous, after all . . . in which case, he reasoned, what was to stop him riding away, and taking his chances?

The next moment he sagged, cursing himself for a fool; there were many things to stop him. He had no way of knowing Rycroft's condition: the man could be dead, or delirious, and in no shape to send word to anyone. Besides, what proof had he? Once again, Thomas put his hand inside his jerkin and felt the reassuring edge of Jane Derrick's paper. He alone had written evidence to show, for the daring plot against the Queen's life . . .

But then, new fears rose. Even with Jane's testimony, who would believe him? They could say it was a forgery – the whole thing was preposterous! A humble falconer, arrested

179

after a riverside brawl – who would take his word about anything, let alone an accusation that some of the Queen's own circle were bent on murdering her? Giles Baldwin would speak harshly of him – and he only needed to recall Amyot's face, to guess what that worthy would say. Even his master Sir Robert, Thomas thought unhappily, must now be discredited; he had forsaken the Queen's company and simply ridden away, no one knew where . . .

He sat up, taking long breaths. Despite everything he must act, and soon. The matter was too grave for him to consider his own position. The Queen was in peril, and that was enough. He glanced at the sky: a pale sun was rising at last, above the tree-tops. He would wait an hour, and no more . . . He found himself breaking into a grim smile, for he realized that he had no idea at what time the Queen rose from her bed. Some of the nobles he knew rarely appeared before dinner-time . . . what then should he do? March up to the palace gates, and demand entry to Her Majesty's private chamber?

He stood up, and tugging at the reins, led the horse gently out of the thicket into open woodland. Then he walked it down a slope, until he found a tiny stream where the animal could drink. Thomas too drank, scooping water up in his hands, then dashing a little over his face. Then he made some rudimentary attempts to improve his appearance. Unwinding the bandage from his head, he was relieved to find there was little blood upon it. His ear was bruised and sore from the cudgel-blow it had received, but at least it was intact. Wadding the bandage and dipping it in the stream, he used it to bathe himself and clean his clothing as best he could. Then once again, he set himself to waiting. Finally, when he judged the morning was advanced enough, he remounted and pointed the gelding northwards, in the direction of the Queen's palace.

There were a few folk on the highway, wood-gatherers perhaps, but fortunately they paid Thomas little mind. Only too aware of the odd figure he must cut, being somewhat ragged in appearance, and without saddle or trappings, nevertheless he was able to cover the miles without being challenged. Once he heard hooves, and his pulse quickened: a party of riders seemed to be moving, somewhere to the east of him. But he saw no one, and finally he passed by Shooter's Hill with some relief. Then as the ground dipped gently, he rode clear of the trees and halted. Deptford was in the distance, smoke rising from its chimneys; and to his right, loomed the towers of Placentia. Drawing a long breath he shook the reins, and urged the gelding towards it.

The palace was vast: almost the size of a small village. In the centre was a huddle of many-sided turrets, while on the far side buildings stretched along the river. The whole place was walled about on its landward side, with a gateway in the centre. And now as he drew close, Thomas's fears rose: for there were guards, of course . . . several of them, the polished steel of their cuirasses gleaming in the winter sunlight. Beyond the palace the Thames sparkled, free now of the ice that had clogged it.

As he walked the horse forward, Thomas formed a resolve: boldness was his only stratagem. If he looked the least bit furtive or even timid, he was lost. He saw no other course than to arrive as a humble but concerned citizen, bearing vital news which touched upon the Queen's safety. Surely that was enough?

A dozen yards from the gates he stopped, dismounted, and led the horse forward. At his approach there was a stir from the guards who were standing about; somewhat idly, he thought. He counted four of them . . . and now, he frowned. For the gates were wide open, and in the courtyard beyond folk seemed to be passing to and fro in an unconcerned fashion . . .

His suspicions crystallized abruptly into a terrible doubt: was the Queen gone? He looked up, and saw to his relief the royal standard fluttering from the tallest turret. But the next moment he was on the alert, as two guards levelled their halberds at him. Tall, heavily-bearded men in the royal livery, they showed no emotion. Now was the moment. Thomas drew a breath, and spoke.

'Forgive my hasty arrival, masters,' he said in a clear voice. 'But I bear a message for the Queen's Council, which must be heard at once!'

181

There was a pause, before the guard on the left snorted. 'Who the devil are you, fellow?'

Thomas gave his name and station, mentioning Sir Robert's name. Then he waited.

The guards glanced at one another, then the same man answered him. 'Give me your message, and I'll take it to the Lord Chamberlain.'

Thomas shook his head. 'I must take it myself.'

But that would not do. The four men bunched together, facing him with stern expressions. 'If you're Sir Robert's man,' another asked, 'where's the proof of it? Come to that,' he added with a frown, 'where's your saddle?'

Thomas spread his hands. 'I came in haste,' he said. 'The tidings could not wait . . .'

But their suspicions were aroused now. With difficulty, Thomas concealed his alarm as they began to fan out before him. His right hand gripped the gelding's rein tightly.

'You'd better come with us,' another guard said. 'Once inside, you can tell your tale to the Keeper of the Keys . . .'

Thomas's heart was thudding. 'I pray you will hear me,' he began; then he checked himself, cursing silently. Of course he was not believed – how could he have thought otherwise? Who would not be suspicious of one who looked as he did? With mounting desperation, he gazed from one grim-faced soldier to another.

'I swear I'm a loyal subject of the Queen,' he said quickly. 'I bring word of a plot newly discovered, which threatens her very life . . .'

But to his dismay, the soldiers laughed.

'Then you're somewhat late!' the first guard told him. 'For the Queen is out hawking. You must be the only one hereabouts who didn't know it!'

Thomas froze . . . and even as the guards took a step forward, he heard the distant blast of a hunting horn, from somewhere behind him – and understood. He had skirted Shooter's Hill on its west side – while the royal party were passing by on the east! The hoof-beats . . . what other body of riders would be abroad, in the royal hunting grounds?

Now, he saw they would seize him. Without further hesitation he grabbed the horse's neck and leaped on to its back. Then as the guards shouted and ran forward, he dug his heels into the animal's flanks, turned it and rode away as fast as he could.

Seventeen

The sun was in his eyes. Cursing it under his breath, Thomas crossed the Kent Highway and galloped southwards without looking back. All his efforts, he thought bitterly, seemed to have been in vain; he might as well have stayed in the dairy at Sayes Court and awaited his fate. Now for all he knew, the wicked deed was already done . . . bile rose in his throat, and he fought it, struggling to keep himself upright on the gelding's back. This was not a time to get himself thrown.

Shooter's Hill rose to his right. He cocked his ear for the sound of the hunting horn, but heard nothing. His mind in turmoil, he flattened himself along the horse's sleek neck, squinting ahead. Trees loomed in his path, and he could only trust to the animal's skill as it plunged among them, veering from side to side. Branches whipped past, brushing the top of his head. Mercifully the trees soon thinned and he emerged on heathland, feeling the ground rise beneath him. Then the sun's rays smote him again, almost blinding him.

He must slow down, he told himself. At this speed, with neither saddle nor stirrup, he could easily fall off, whereupon he would very likely break his neck. He struggled to draw rein – but to his alarm, the gelding did not respond. For some reason the horse seemed bent upon putting as much distance between itself and Greenwich Palace as it could. Nor can I blame you, Thomas thought, struggling to control the animal. By degrees, speaking low in its ear and tugging at intervals upon the rein, he slowed it; then with a frantic jerk of its head the horse stopped at last, and stood stamping and blowing. Breathlessly Thomas leaned forward, patting its neck until it quietened. Then he sat upright, and tried to take his bearings.

The country was oddly silent. He listened, but there came no sound of hooves, nor had he heard a horn-blast since his frantic flight from the palace. Now, came a moment of near-panic: had he missed the royal party entirely, passing them in the woods? His spirits sinking, he peered about in all directions, and saw nothing . . .

Until he looked overhead.

Squinting into the sun, he shaded his eyes . . . and saw two familiar shapes, high above, floating easily upon the air currents. And his heart leaped: the Queen was at hawking, the guards had said – and so she was! Now, from two or three hundred yards away, he heard the bark of hunting dogs. And at once he urged the gelding forward, easing it into a canter.

There was a low ridge in front of him – and now he saw dead bracken, crushed flat by the passing of horses. He rode up to the crest, then slowed, peering ahead – and almost shouted with relief. Below him was a body of riders, bunched together. Even from this distance, the sunlight glittered on silk and jewels . . . the Queen's Court, he guessed, wore their best attire when they accompanied their Sovereign. And as he watched, one man raised an arm, allowing his falcon to soar from the gauntlet. It mounted to a great height, and the party moved slowly forward, following their birds.

With a sigh of relief, Thomas began to descend the slope. But then he whirled about, fancying he heard a noise. He looked, but there was no one. On both sides of him the ground sloped away to woodland. He peered into the trees, but saw no movement of any kind. So, setting his face to the riders below, he increased his speed. Soon they would hear him, whereupon once again he would have some explaining to do. He could only pray that this time, someone would be prepared to listen to him.

He descended the gentle slope, and now the royal party were barely a hundred yards away. He saw men in hunting clothes, with feathered hats, some bearing falcons on their wrists. There were ladies, too, sitting side-saddle. One that caught his eye was a tiny figure, mounted on a small pony, and at once he tensed: Lady Imogen. Then he heard hoof-beats.

There was a shout – but it came not from the hunting party. In fact, one man in the rear turned around to look in Thomas's direction. But Thomas's head snapped to his right – and his heart gave a jolt: several armed men were riding swiftly towards him out of the trees. To his surprise, at their head was Baldwin's steward, Nicholas Capper, and he looked a very angry man indeed.

'Stop!' Capper shouted, and spurred his mount forward at an angle, to cut Thomas off. Thomas shook the reins and dug his heels into the gelding's flanks, but the animal was too slow to respond. In seconds, the soldiers had galloped up and surrounded him.

He drew rein, breathing hard. And all he could think of was to sit upright and cry, at the top of his voice, 'The Queen is in danger! Guard the Queen!'

He reeled as Capper reached out and struck him hard across the face. At the same time another man grabbed the gelding's bridle. The horse reared in alarm – and the next moment Thomas was slipping from its back, arms flailing, to land in a heap on the ground. He scrambled to his feet . . . and knew that it was too late; for the guards had dismounted quickly, and were forming a circle about him. Now he recognized two of them as his jailers, from outside the Sayes Court dairy; and each looked as angry as Capper did.

The steward got down from his horse, and strode furiously towards Thomas. 'Stand still!' he cried. 'And be silent!'

He raised his hand as if he would strike Thomas again, out of sheer rage. He was red-faced and sweating, hair awry, as if he had ridden hard through the woods and lost his hat in the process. Quickly, however, he mastered himself, and gestured to two of the soldiers to seize Thomas's arms, which they did only too eagerly.

And now, Thomas's spirits sank; for he had failed. He let out a sigh, and forced himself to face Capper.

'You're my prisoner!' the steward snapped. 'And if you

try to resist further I'll knock the daylights out of you – do you understand?'

Thomas made no reply.

'Do you understand?' Capper shouted again, leaning closer.

But then his face clouded, and he looked round quickly, as did the others. For a tall man had detached himself from the royal party – who to Thomas's dismay had moved further off, out of earshot – and was riding at a leisurely pace up the slope towards them. And now Thomas froze, as he recognized Sir John Amyot.

Capper turned to greet the knight, and made his bow, forcing a sickly smile. 'Sir John,' he murmured. 'I trust you're having good sport today . . .'

Amyot halted, and stared down at the group. 'What the devil's going on here?' he asked.

'Naught that need concern you, sir – or any of Her Majesty's company,' Capper answered quickly. 'This man escaped arrest, but he is now recaptured. With your leave, we'll take him away at once.'

But Amyot looked uneasy . . . as well he might, Thomas thought. For his plans might now be thwarted . . . with a shred of hope, he looked Amyot grimly in the eye. But he could read nothing in the man's cold stare.

'Sir Robert's falconer, under arrest?' Amyot was frowning. 'What has he done?'

'He was taken after a brawl, Sir John, at the tavern in Deptford,' Capper replied smoothly. With his smile still intact he added: 'He's a rogue, sir, who consorts with known fugitives. My master wishes him brought back to Sayes Court at once, to answer for himself.'

There was a silence. Thomas's thoughts were racing: but now, to his immense frustration, he could only keep silent. Had any other member of the royal party ridden over to see what the commotion was, he would have thrown caution aside and blurted out the whole tale. But of all people, it had to be Amyot . . .

Slowly Amyot began to relax, and the man's habitual, sardonic smile appeared. He glanced fleetingly at Thomas, as if he were a stranger, then faced Capper again.

'Then you'd best remove him, master steward,' he said dryly. 'Perhaps the fellow takes after his master, who from what I've heard now skulks in the countryside, forsaking the company of his peers . . .' He threw a look of contempt at Thomas. ''Twas always said, Sir Robert could not even control his own servants!'

Then without further word, the knight wheeled his mount and trotted away, back towards the hunting party.

Thomas, along with Capper and the soldiers, watched him rejoin the group. And suddenly, Thomas's heart jolted. For now he noticed the slim, erect figure in the centre, riding a tall grey horse, wearing a russet gown and hat . . . and Sir Robert's words, spoken what now seemed weeks ago, came back to him: *a jewel . . . the centre-piece of a setting of lesser jewels . . .* and so indeed it appeared, for without any noticeable effort, she was the focus of attention. And as he watched, Amyot rode up alongside her, and doffed his hat with an elaborate gesture, to the Queen.

The Queen was yet unharmed! Surely, Thomas reasoned desperately, there was still hope . . . but now Capper turned to him, and wagged a gloved finger in his face.

'If you utter another sound, Finbow,' he breathed, 'we'll have no choice but to silence you, the quickest way.' He glanced at the nearest soldier, who whipped a poniard out and pressed it against Thomas's throat. Then at a word from Capper, the little group began to move, back towards the tree-line from which they had emerged, steering Thomas between them.

For some reason they did not remount, but led their horses downhill, into the trees. Thomas risked a backward glance, but the royal party were now out of sight. Overhead, the falcons still soared . . . then the next moment he was manhandled roughly, and had to look to the front before he stumbled.

The trees thickened about them. Thomas breathed steadily, fighting panic. There was yet hope, he repeated to himself. He could try and make a break, run for all he was worth towards the Queen's party . . . he might at least get close enough to be heard . . . a notion occurred, and

188

he seized upon it. True, Lady Imogen and Amyot were there – presumably Wyckes, too – but could he be certain this was the moment they had chosen to implement their plan? *About the third day after Christmas* . . . Jane Derrick's words rose in his mind. He screwed his eyes shut, tamping down his fears. How could she have been certain? They might have changed their plan . . . the Queen went hunting and hawking often, perhaps every day when she was in the country . . .

He stumbled over a tree-root, but the guards hauled him upright, gripping him tightly. Behind, two were leading the horses, including his own gelding . . . but one man still held the poniard, making sure Thomas saw it. It struck him that Capper, who was striding ahead, seemed more concerned that Thomas would call out than anything else . . .

Then cold fear hit him, dashing his hopes: they wanted the plan to succeed! If Baldwin was a part of it, likely Capper was too . . . but then, why had he looked so ill-at-ease when Amyot rode up? To Thomas, it had looked as if he were eager to get rid of the man . . .

His mouth was dry. He swallowed, thinking fast . . . he could trust no one, and he had to do something. If there was a chance, any chance at all, he must take it. But now there were sounds ahead, among the trees . . . he peered forward, and drew breath sharply.

A larger body of soldiers, grim-faced and silent, stood close together, holding their horses' bridles. At the forefront was Giles Baldwin, in riding clothes, wearing a sword. And a few yards away, stood none other than Lady Imogen's steward, Malvyn Wyckes.

As Thomas was brought forward, the two men gazed dispassionately at him. At a gesture from Baldwin, the guards released him and walked away to gather the reins of their own horses. There was some taking of positions, but not a word was said. The troop had a purposeful look about them – and, Thomas now realized, an air of intense expectation. His mind whirling he faced Baldwin, who raised an eyebrow, and finally addressed him.

'Falconer,' he murmured, with a slow shake of his head.

'You will soon discover how close you came to ruining everything. What am I going to do with you?'

Thomas had no words. No longer caring what befell him, he met Baldwin's gaze coldly. From the corner of his eye he saw Capper taking up his own horse's reins, and turning the mount to face the way he had come.

Then suddenly, Thomas found his voice. 'You may do what you like, sir,' he said. 'But you will have to kill me too, for I will not let my mouth be stopped!'

'Kill you too?' Baldwin frowned. 'Who else are you referring to?'

Thomas did not answer. Baldwin seemed about to repeat his question, when Wyckes stepped closer to him and murmured something. At this Baldwin nodded, and turning to Capper and the other men, raised his hand. And at once, every man got himself mounted. There was a jangling of harness, and the soft blowing of the horses.

Baldwin turned to Thomas. 'You had better get horsed too, falconer,' he said. 'But I'll have your word that you will remain in the rear, and make no sound. Otherwise . . .' He gestured briefly to one of the guards, who eased his horse forward. 'Otherwise,' Baldwin continued in a matter-of-fact tone, 'we'll have no choice but to shoot you.'

Thomas looked . . . and saw beside each man's saddle a stout leather scabbard, from which the stock of a caliver protruded. With a practised movement, the one designated to watch Thomas drew the firearm out, and levelled it at him.

Moving deliberately, Thomas walked to the gelding and took the rein from the man who held it. Then, with his eye on Baldwin, he swung himself once again on to the animal's back. As he did so, the muffled sound of hooves made him look round. Another rider, armed like the rest, appeared through the trees and halted before Baldwin. The two exchanged words briefly, then Baldwin turned to the others, raised his arm again and gave a signal.

They moved forward, and Thomas, glancing from side to side, could only ease the gelding into a trot and follow.

It was a matter of minutes, though to him it seemed an age.

The trees thinned, and riding bunched together, the party emerged upon the long, south-facing slope where Thomas had been captured. The sun was in their faces, but they did not check their pace. Stirrup to stirrup, they turned downhill and began picking up speed. Thomas, in the rear, drew a sharp breath as he saw Giles Baldwin loosen his sword in its scabbard. And now, in the distance, he saw a slow-moving body of riders, and knew it was the Queen's party.

So, it was really happening . . . Dumbly he realized that until now, he had only half-believed it. But here at last was the reality: the most terrible of conspiracies, given form not in some bed-chamber, or dark corner of one of the Queen's palaces – but in the starkness of a bright winter's day, before a host of people. Its daring took his breath away.

But of course, he realized, there had to be witnesses: nobles and stewards and waiting-women, to confirm that the Queen had truly been killed, otherwise the Claimant's case would be weakened. And now, he saw what an air of theatre it all had; and at once he recalled Lorel Cox, who thought everything was play-acting – until he tried to play a spy, and paid for it with his life.

The royal party were fully in view now – and Thomas started. For now he saw the horses were stationary; the company had dismounted. Perhaps the Queen was tired, he thought dully, and she wished to walk, or to rest . . .

Baldwin's men rode quietly towards the rear of the group, but no one seemed to notice them. Now Thomas saw Amyot, on foot, talking with two of the gentlemen. Other men wandered about, some holding their horses or drinking from flasks, others still with falcons on their wrists. And now, he saw the Queen plainly. She was surprisingly tall, standing very erect, smiling as she conversed easily with her ladies. In fact there was a holiday air about all of the company – but then, why should there not be? Because it was a holiday – the Christmas Revels were not yet done. Thomas heard their voices, and their cheerful laughter . . . He looked down, and saw he was gripping the rein so tightly his knuckles showed white. Desperately he glanced about, seeking a chance, no matter how slim. The notion that, as it now appeared, he too was to be a witness to the most dreadful act of treason he could imagine, chilled his heart.

Then he saw the assassin.

He had almost forgotten d'Avila, the squat Portuguese . . . their *instrument* . . . the poor dupe who was to do the terrible deed, and then pay for it. He had not noticed such a fellow among the royal group . . . but he saw him now, with crystal clarity. And so did everyone else, for the stocky figure, in a somewhat garish hunting suit, appeared from somewhere among the party, smiling broadly, and approached the Queen.

Thomas tensed himself, preparing to spring from the horse; but his guard was ready. Something pressed sharply against his side, and glancing down, he saw the dull barrel of the caliver.

'You wouldn't . . .' The words came feebly from his mouth, as he raised his eyes to meet the guard's. But the man's gaunt, expressionless face brooked no argument. He merely tightened his finger on the trigger, and looked Thomas unflinchingly in the eye. The weapon was primed; he smelled a faint whiff of sulphur from the match.

Feeling only an emptiness, Thomas forced himself to turn his head, and watch the little tableau played out.

D'Avila had an odd, bird-like gait. The long pheasant's feather that stuck from his hunting cap only added to the resemblance, as he strode towards the Queen from behind. Then the man darted around Her Majesty to stand before her, and quickly fell upon his knee. Even from this distance, Thomas saw the little nosegay of bright flowers that he held, and wondered for a second where he had obtained them in mid-winter . . .

Now people stopped talking and watched as the Queen, in relaxed manner, put out her hand to accept the token. From this distance Thomas could not hear the words that passed between them – but he heard the laughter, and guessed the assassin had some little speech prepared. He glanced towards the unmistakeable figure of Lady Imogen, standing nearby. Amyot was further off: the innocent bystander, hand on hip, in what now appeared to Thomas a pose of deliberate casualness.

His mouth was so dry, he coughed, knowing he must shout at all costs. But even the guard tensed now, as Thomas saw to his horror the Queen take the gift from d'Avila and put it to her nose. He opened his mouth to call out . . . he saw the Portuguese stiffen, and put his hand to his belt . . . then came a deafening blast from a hunting horn. And at once, there was mayhem.

A great cry went up – and only now did Thomas see that some of the royal party had eased themselves into position, close to the Queen. Only now, did he wonder why few seemed to have paid any mind, as Baldwin's men rode up to the edges of the party . . . and only now, did he understand! For there came a shout from nearby – and it was voiced by the steward, Nicholas Capper.

'Treason! Seize that man, in the Queen's name!'

And even as the poniard glittered in D'Avila's hand, men sprang forward, fell upon him and threw him to the ground. There were screams from some of the Queen's young ladies – and a general surge towards the Sovereign. But now, Thomas saw that it was but to protect her.

And suddenly, he found himself unguarded. The man who a moment ago had been ready to shoot him, had spurred his horse forward and leaped from the saddle, to join his fellows.

Almost dizzy with relief, Thomas watched as the confused mass of people and horses resolved itself into some sort of order. And now, he too was free to dismount! With growing elation he jumped to the ground, to hurry forward and see the plotters caught; as, he now knew, they were doomed to be all along . . . he shook his head in disbelief at the outcome of it all, and gazed at the scene.

Lady Imogen was shrieking and writhing like a lizard, held fast between two guards. And then – as if free at last from a cruel mistress – her little pony reared and bucked, pulled its rein from the man who was holding it, and bolted for the trees. No one tried to pursue it. Instead all eyes were upon the Lady as she spat out her hatred, railing at everyone

– especially at Amyot. Finally a guard placed a gag about her mouth and drew it tight, stifling her cries, to the relief of all.

And here was Amyot, white with fear and rage, being seized like a common criminal, and forced to his knees at sword-point. Here too was d'Avila, bursting into tears as he was dragged to his feet, his arms quickly bound by two burly guards. And now at last, Thomas understood Giles Baldwin's part in it all . . . and he could only watch in dumb admiration, as the Clerk of the Green Cloth, the Queen's loyal Controller, bent his knee to Elizabeth, speaking softly to her.

But if the Queen was afraid, she did not show it. And Thomas could but smile, as he saw her extend her fingers for Baldwin to kiss. Then she bade him stand and face her, to receive her grateful thanks.

And now, no one paid any attention to Thomas. He could walk away, he realized – he could even ride away, for the black gelding stood unattended, where he had left it. As he watched, the animal lowered its head to see if there was anything on the ground worth eating. It made him want to laugh with relief.

But he did not leave; for he knew there were yet things he should do. And now perhaps he would get the answers he had sought, these past days . . . he frowned suddenly, and thought of Sir Robert. What now would become of him? And how much did he know . . .?

He shook his head. He had known the knight most of his life. And whatever else he had done, Thomas knew the man would have had no part of this scheme. He sighed: Sir Robert was a dupe, that was all – like the hapless assassin.

He started, looking away to his left. There was one who could provide answers, standing alone on the fringe of the group, observing everything. Until now, Thomas had all but forgotten about Malvyn Wyckes . . . he shook his head. He had misjudged the man entirely: he was no part of this conspiracy after all. No one had seized Wyckes; in fact Baldwin, Capper and the rest studiously avoided looking in his direction.

And Skeeres's words came back to Thomas: *one of their best projectors* . . . he almost gasped. Wyckes was the prime mover, who had played the succession plotters along to the last; even to the point where the dagger was drawn . . .

And all the while, he was working for the Crown.

Eighteen

By midday, on Baldwin's instructions, Thomas was back at Sayes Court. Having washed himself hastily, he went to the falcons' mews and busied himself tending the birds. And here, for the first time after that eventful morning, he was able to gather his thoughts into some sort of order.

With others, he had stood on the heath and watched Amyot, d'Avila and the Lady Imogen taken away under close guard. He recalled the look of hatred on Lady Imogen's face, and had breathed a sigh of relief that at last, Sir Robert was free of her grasp. He had also watched the Queen's party recover their falcons and ride swiftly away, back to Greenwich. Then, unsure of what to do, he had waited until Nicholas Capper approached him and told him he should return to his duties, and wait to be called. The man's manner had altered considerably, since he had ridden furiously out of the trees to seize Thomas. He even offered a gruff apology for having struck him – and for imprisoning him, too.

'Yet you understand now why I had to do so, do you not?' the man demanded. 'You might have spoiled the whole projection!'

Thomas had nodded briefly, and walked away.

But his last act had been to take Jane Derrick's paper from his jerkin and hand it to one of the guards, saying it was for master Baldwin's eyes only. The man took it, and promised to convey it at once.

Now, having snatched a bite of dinner in the kitchen, where gossip was rife about the thrilling events of that day, Thomas took the falcons out one at a time and exercised them. He flew the Lady Imogen's little merlin too, and wondered what would now become of the bird. Moreover, not for the first time, he wondered what would happen to him, too.

The afternoon waned, and dusk was falling before he was summoned at last – but not to the main house. For want of something to occupy himself, he was in the stable giving the gelding a rub down after its exertions, when one of the grooms appeared. Master Baldwin had returned, the man said, and would speak with him alone, at the mews.

So Thomas took a lantern and walked back to the mews, seeing the lights of Deptford glowing in the distance. He sighed; there would be no welcome for him now in the Sea-Hog. Cox was dead, and Mallam was no doubt long gone; he wondered if he would ever see him again. Then he remembered Rycroft: he would not leave without finding out how the constable fared.

There were footsteps, and he turned to see Giles Baldwin rounding the wall of the stable yard. The man saw the lantern and walked quickly forward, whereupon Thomas made his bow, and waited.

'Falconer!' Baldwin's tone was warm. Thomas met his eye, and saw that despite the man's obvious tiredness, a burden seemed to have been lifted from his shoulders. He even managed a thin smile.

'You should know,' Baldwin began, 'that I have received a good deal of intelligence about you and your activities, these past days.' His smile faded. 'You do see why I had to have you detained?'

After a moment Thomas nodded. 'I confess I was puzzled, sir,' he remarked, 'at how your steward knew just where to find me, that night . . .'

Baldwin gave him a wry look. 'There are times,' he replied, 'when it is necessary to use desperate measures – and even desperate men.'

Thomas started. 'Men like Peter Sly?' Now he saw it, and frowned. 'You paid him to pick a fight with me, so that I would be arrested for affray?'

Baldwin shrugged, and Thomas let out a sigh. 'Had I known what was being planned from the outset,' he said, 'I would have left well alone!'

At that, Baldwin raised an eyebrow. 'What is it that you think was being planned?' he asked.

Thomas thought of Cox, and their conversation some time ago in the Sea-Hog. 'That a certain Lord,' he answered, 'who believes he has a right to the throne, had set in motion a chain of events to remove the obstacle to his succession – that is, our Queen, whereupon—'

'Enough!' Baldwin held up a warning hand, and his brow furrowed. 'I did not intend that you should lay forth the whole matter, from its very beginning!' he said. Then almost as an afterthought, he added: 'In any event, this Lord, whom neither of us will name, was arrested but a few hours ago and conveyed to the Tower.' He looked away for a moment before meeting Thomas's eye once more.

'I see now that I acted too hastily, in setting you on the road to uncovering the killer of that poor girl . . .' He winced. 'I have read her testimony. After you told me what befell her, I was filled with horror. And I swear to you, I had no idea until then that she was Lady Imogen's woman. And what was done to her, was done without my sanction!'

He looked away and sighed. 'I had much on my mind, falconer. I should have guessed that you would piece things together – but had I known you would uncover all, when we first spoke of the body found here on the shore, I would have warned you off much sooner.' He sighed again. 'I merely wanted the matter tidily despatched.'

Thomas said nothing, and Baldwin's manner grew brisk. 'Surely you understand,' he said, 'that no chances could be taken when the Queen's life was at stake? Anyone – *anyone* who threatened the success of the enterprise was expendable. Hence . . .' He hesitated briefly, then: 'Hence, in these matters the Crown's agent has a free hand, to act as he thinks fit.'

Thomas still made no reply. He thought not only of Jane, and of Cox, but of the desperate fight in Monkaster's yard, and the plain men of Deptford who had been hurt – especially William Rycroft. His mouth tightened.

'Even to doing murder, sir?' he asked.

But at that, Baldwin merely shrugged. 'I've already told

you more than I should,' he said. 'For you have acted bravely, and from the best motives, to uncover what you could. Yet I would ask you now to forget all that you have seen. Go back to Petbury, is my advice, and await Sir Robert's return – if he has not gone home already, that is.' Baldwin was frowning again. 'For sooner or later, he must face up to what he has done, and make some amends.'

Thomas drew a sharp breath; one further matter had become clear to him. 'You invited him here so you might keep an eye on him!' he said abruptly. 'You saw his infatuation, and how Lady Imogen meant to snare him—'

'Falconer!' Baldwin held up a hand again. 'Let us not speak of that. Suffice it to say that I always had the best interests of Sir Robert in mind. He's a decent man, and a loyal knight of the shires, even if he lacks . . .' The man fumbled for the right word, whereupon Thomas came to his aid.

'Perception?' he said dryly.

'Indeed . . .' Baldwin gave a wan smile. 'Perception. And I say to you now, what I said to you once before: I believe Sir Robert will reinstate you as his falconer. In fact, I will see that he does.'

Thomas managed a nod. A dozen questions still begged to be uttered, but he now saw that Baldwin wished to be gone. So keeping a respectful tone, he said: 'With your permission, sir, I'll spend my last night in Deptford, and take my leave tomorrow.' He paused. 'I would dearly like to see my wife and daughter again.'

'Of course.' Baldwin nodded quickly, then as if he had only now remembered, fumbled at his belt.

'You must be rewarded for what you have done – and for the pains you have endured,' he said, and held out a purse.

Thomas hesitated. 'You have already paid me for the days I've served here,' he began – then broke off as the other shook his head.

'You misunderstand,' he replied. 'This payment comes not from me, but from the Royal Treasury.' He made a wry face. 'There was much heated consultation this afternoon, at the Queen's Council. All was sifted and examined, and re-sifted

and re-examined . . . and even the small part that my temporary falconer played in our little pageant was not overlooked.' He indicated the purse. 'Your reward comes from
the Queen, with her blessing.'

And at that Thomas could only take the purse and watch
as Baldwin turned and strode away towards the house.

Then it was that another question rose to his mind: what
now would become of Mouka?

Having seen the falcons settled for the night, he went to the
kitchens for a welcome supper. And though Bridget and others
plied him with questions, he merely shook his head and
pleaded weariness. Finally they left him alone at the table,
to ponder on events.

Though Baldwin had told him little, he now saw the grand
design, and how he had unwittingly been caught up in it. It
almost took his breath away. His mind drifted back eight
years, to 1586, and the uncovering of the plot by the Queen
of Scots, to seize the English throne. Elizabeth's crafty secretary, Sir Francis Walsingham, had known of the plan from
the start – had even encouraged it. He intercepted messages
that passed between Mary Stuart and her conspirators, copied
them, then allowed them to continue as if nothing had
happened. And all the while, the net was closing about the
plotters: as it had been, Thomas saw, around Lord Beauchamp
and his followers. Sir Robert Cecil, another crafty man, had
laid his plans well. Blissfully ignorant of the fact that their little
circle had been infiltrated by a bogus steward, Beauchamp's
friend Amyot, his lover Lady Imogen and their hapless
instrument d'Avila had been permitted to play their game to
the last turn. And Giles Baldwin had been there to perform the
final act: the unmasking of the conspirators, and their
triumphant arrest.

He shook his head, staring at his empty platter. Finally he
rose, intending to walk to the strand and pass his last night
at the Lovetts'. He would ask after Rycroft, and perhaps take
his farewell of Sir Ralph. He still wondered at the change
in the ark-builder's manner when his old surgeon's skills
were suddenly in demand.

But unknown to Thomas, another encounter awaited him before he walked down to Deptford.

Later, he would reflect on the fact that if he had not decided to look in and see the gelding settled for the night, he would never have seen Malvyn Wyckes again. But as he stepped from the chill night air into the warmth of the stables, he was aware at once of another's presence. He looked round – and saw Wyckes, in the act of tightening the girth of his horse. The animal was bridled, with a pack tied across the saddle.

As Thomas's eyes fell upon him, Wyckes stiffened. Then quickly he looked away, and made a show of checking the horse's trappings. In a moment he would have put a foot in the stirrup, had Thomas not taken a step towards him.

He turned sharply, and met Thomas's eye.

'Master steward . . .' Thomas gazed evenly at him. 'I thought you'd left already.' When Wyckes made no reply he added: 'I would like to put a few questions to you—'

But the other interrupted him harshly. 'And you will not!' he snapped. 'Now stand aside, and let me take my horse out.'

Thomas did not move. 'Not yet,' he answered. 'First, tell me why you killed Jane Derrick.'

Wyckes drew a sharp breath. 'Have a care, Finbow,' he said quietly. 'You know not who you deal with.'

'I think I do,' Thomas countered, with rising anger. 'You're one of the Council's best projectors – at least, that was what Dan Skeeres called you. You killed him too, didn't you? As you killed Lorel Cox – a player, who was no threat to anyone . . .'

'No threat?' Wyckes's tone was scathing. 'You know naught of it – as you know naught of me, Finbow. I have my work, and I'll not be judged by you!'

'Your work!' Thomas struggled to master his feelings. 'I know why you killed Skeeres: he was a rogue for hire, without conscience or scruples – he was a threat to your enterprise, and he paid the price. Even Cox – though I'll never forgive you for it, I can see why you wanted him silenced. But does your *work* include the killing of a defenceless girl, who had suffered untold hurts already – locking her up like a beast until she'd all but lost her reason—'

'I don't have to listen to this!' Wyckes's voice was ice-cold. Taking up his horse's reins, he was about to lead the animal forward. But still Thomas barred his way.

'I want to hear you admit it,' he said, matching the other man's tone. 'There's no one else present, and I'll never speak of it to anyone. But I need to know why you took that poor, ruined girl, and wrung the life from her—'

Then he broke off, for Wyckes had put a hand to his back with uncanny speed, whipped out a poniard, and thrust it towards him.

'You didn't heed me the last time I warned you,' the man said softly, 'and you seem bent on not listening now. So for the last time, move aside – or take the consequences.'

But Thomas remained calm, ignoring the dagger's point only inches from his face. 'Jane trusted you,' he said. 'Even though you served the mistress who had treated her so cruelly – even though you had become her jailer, her last hopes rested upon you. She would speak to you, she said, for she believed you liked not what was done to her. And all she had to offer you was her body, when she told you what she had discovered—'

'Where did you get this?' Wyckes snapped. And to Thomas's surprise he wavered, a hint of doubt in his eyes. 'Where?!' he repeated.

'I went there,' Thomas told him. 'To the room at the top of the house in Poor Jewry, where she was held all those months . . .'

'You went there . . .' Wyckes stared at him. 'And found what?'

'A letter,' Thomas answered. 'Well hidden. Written in her own blood, for that was all she had. It told all that she had learned . . . though what she didn't know, and could not know, was that you were the Crown's instrument, charged with bringing the matter to its desired end. Entrapment – is that not what you call it?'

Wyckes made no answer. Something had shaken the man, though Thomas knew not what it was. For a moment the two gazed at each other, then to Thomas's surprise Wyckes lowered the poniard, and put it away.

'It seems you know enough already,' he said in a tired voice. 'Piece it together at your will . . . I'm but a servant of the Crown, as you say. It matters not that you know . . .' He smiled suddenly. 'You don't think Wyckes is my real name, do you?'

Now Thomas too wavered, and the other man gave a harsh laugh. 'Falconer . . .' He shook his head. 'Lorel Cox and his fellows, the whole Lord Chamberlain's Company of Players, would be hard pressed to match the skills I and a few others have. If he gave a poor performance, the worst that could befall him was being thrown out of work. If I failed in mine, I'd likely fetch up on the rack with my limbs torn out – or in the river with my throat cut!'

Now, the man's mouth had a bitter twist to it. 'You think the death of one wretched creature like the goldsmith's daughter preys on my conscience?' he cried. 'I've watched kings and queens breathe their last . . .' He looked away suddenly. A bleak expression, together with a great weariness, had settled upon him. His face was grey in the dim light of the stable.

'Naught to offer but her body,' he said, so quietly that Thomas could barely hear. 'Much good that did her – as did the telling of what she knew!' He looked away. 'She was clever; too clever, and that was her undoing. She had to be removed – that is all.' He looked up at Thomas, who had no words left. 'Let me pass,' he said, in a tone that suggested he cared little whether Thomas did so or not.

And at last, Thomas stood aside. Whereupon the man he had known as Malvyn Wyckes, the killer of Jane Derrick and the others, tugged at the reins and led his big roan horse across the flagstones.

And now the cold injustice of it all made the bile rise in Thomas's throat. For not only would this man never be brought to book for his wicked deeds – he would be rewarded for them! And afterwards, a loyal servant of the Queen, he would merely move on to his next assignment, under a different name.

He watched as the other shoved the door open and drew the horse outside, letting in a gust of cold air. Hooves clattered briefly on the cobbles; then quickly they receded into the night.

Soon after, Thomas left the stable and walked by the moon's light down to Deptford Green, to the house of William Rycroft. His knock was answered, and to his relief he learned that the constable was not only alive but recovering from his wounds. He had received treatment from Sir Ralph Monkaster, but now he needed rest. So, facing the doughty mistress Rycroft, a stout woman with a commanding eye, Thomas begged her to convey his goodwill, and said he would call again on the morrow before he left Sayes Court.

But to his surprise, the woman stayed him. 'Will you not remain another day in Deptford, master Finbow?' she asked. 'For on the morning after, the poor girl that was washed up on the strand will be buried – here, at St Nicholas.' She pointed over Thomas's shoulder, across the green, and added: 'I believe Will would wish you to be there – as would others.' Her expression softened. 'With all that's happened you're become the talk of the village, did ye not know?'

Thomas murmured an embarrassed reply, and took himself off.

He walked down to the strand, and stood for a moment watching the river slipping by; an outgoing tide. He glanced round, but no longer did the steamed-up windows of the Sea-Hog beckon him. Thrusting his hands into his jerkin, he trudged the remaining yards to the ships' chandler's, and went in.

There was no one in the shop, but he heard voices from the rear and walked through to the kitchen, unsure of what kind of welcome he might receive. But at once there was a stir, as Alice and Simon looked up from the table to greet him. And it lifted his heart somewhat to see them in good cheer.

'Mallam's gone – in a hurry too,' Alice told him, and poured out mulled ale. 'Never so much as a farewell – even left his best shirt and hose behind.'

Thomas nodded, wondering if he should offer some explanation for the jingler's sudden departure. But he knew he had no words for it. In fact, he wished for nothing now, except an undisturbed night's sleep.

But he sat and drank with the couple, even joining in with their reminiscence of the great fight at Monkaster's yard, realizing that the tale would be told in Deptford for years to come. He asked after Sir Ralph, and was pleased to hear how the ark-builder had toiled through the rest of that night, tending the injured men. He had even allowed his house to be used as a makeshift hospital, for those that were too weak to walk. As for Peter Sly the Tom-tit, it seemed he had disappeared in the confusion, soon after Thomas had been arrested.

And now Simon fixed Thomas with his good eye, and said: 'Listen to us prate! For we have not asked how you fared, master Thomas, when that ruffling steward took you off . . .' He hesitated. 'Some thought you'd been taken to London – clapped up in Newgate, or some such place . . .'

So Thomas gave the two of them a very brief account of his arrest, ending it by saying that all was well now – the misunderstanding was cleared up, and he was at liberty to leave for home.

'So we are to lose both our lodgers,' Alice murmured. But as she turned to Simon, a smile grew. 'Well then, we must set to with a will, my duck, and find new customers – is't not so?' To Thomas, she said: 'I've brought Simon to his senses, made him see he's a poor hand at shop-keeping. So we're opening up a lodging-house for sailors! Will ye wish us well in it, master Thomas?'

Thomas smiled, and raised his mug to them both. 'I do,' he said. Then he caught the sly look in Alice's eye, and sighed.

He had the feeling that in time, for one reason or another, mistress Lovett's house would be the talk of every vessel on the high seas.

Nineteen

The next morning Thomas rose early, feeling better than he had done for a long while. He had slept well, and the pain of his hurts had lessened. After a bite of breakfast, he took leave of Simon and Alice Lovett and walked to Sayes Court. It was the last time he would tend the birds, and he intended to ask Giles Baldwin whether he would engage a falconer to take over the work. But he had only been at the mews a short while when one of the grooms appeared from the yard and hailed him. Leaving his tasks, Thomas walked over – and received news that both relieved and worried him, in equal measure: late the previous night, Sir Robert Vicary had returned to Sayes Court.

With mixed feelings he went back to his work, telling himself that Sir Robert would summon him if he had anything to say. But try as he might, he could not put the matter to the back of his mind. Finally he gave in to his desire to confront his former master, and went to the house.

He walked through the kitchens without looking about him, and made his way to the main stairway. Then he ascended to the chamber where Sir Robert had stayed, and where he had dismissed Thomas so harshly from his service. Already, it seemed an age ago.

After a moment's hesitation he knocked on the heavy door, and received no answer. He knocked again, and was on the point of turning away when there came a muffled voice from within. Summoning all his nerve, he entered.

Sir Robert was not in the bed, which was undisturbed. Thomas's eyes scanned the dimly-lit room, noticing the heavy curtains were drawn . . . then he stiffened. Fully clothed, the knight was seated on a chest by the wall, staring at the floor. Nor did he look up as Thomas stepped into the room.

'Your pardon, sir . . .' Thomas said uneasily. 'I'm much relieved to see you returned . . .'

'Are you, truly?' At last the knight looked round, and Thomas drew a sharp breath. Never had he seen such tiredness in Sir Robert; he looked as though he had not slept in days.

'Truly,' Thomas echoed, taking a pace forward. 'All who know you, have been concerned for you . . .' Then he broke off, as the man turned away and put his head in his hands. There was a silence before he looked up again and said: 'I've been an utter fool, have I not?'

Thomas hesitated, then answered: 'I cannot deny it, sir – not if I'm honest.'

'Nay – who could?' Slowly Sir Robert got to his feet, and moving like a man twenty years older, crossed the room and tugged at a curtain. Daylight flooded in, making him blink. Turning to Thomas he said: 'I talked with master Baldwin, for what felt like half the night. He's told me everything.'

Thomas nodded, and waited.

'Today I'm summoned to the palace,' Sir Robert went on, frowning to himself. He wore his flame-coloured breeches still, and stood in his stockinged feet. From the look of the clothes, they had not been changed since he had ridden away on Christmas Day.

'After I've given an account of myself,' he added, 'and faced the Queen's displeasure . . .' He winced at the thought. 'After that, Thomas . . . I will make ready to return to Petbury in the morning. Will you . . .?' He broke off, and there was a look of such abject misery upon the man's face that all Thomas's resentment melted away.

'Will I return with you as your falconer, you mean?' he said. When Sir Robert gave the briefest of nods, Thomas managed a wry smile. 'Of course, sir. I wonder that you would think otherwise.'

But as the knight showed his relief, a thought struck Thomas. 'Might I beg a condition, however?' he asked. 'That we delay leaving until later in the day? There's a burial in the village that I would like to attend.'

After a moment, Sir Robert nodded. And emboldened, Thomas added another condition. 'And might we also make a short detour on our homeward journey, to Wantage, and recall Simon to your service?'

Sir Robert let out a sigh. 'Ask what you will,' he muttered. 'I'll deny you nothing.'

So with a surge of relief, Thomas made his bow. 'Then I will keep myself busy, sir,' he said, 'until we leave . . .'

But Sir Robert put a hand nervously to his unkempt beard. 'Thomas . . .' He forced himself to meet Thomas's eye, and went on: 'Thomas, you have been my rock these weeks, while I have been adrift like a . . .' The knight made a vague gesture, and abandoned his seafaring comparisons. 'She would have thrown me aside, the moment her hopes were realized!' he said abruptly. 'You know whom I speak of.'

Thomas made no reply.

'I was clay in her hands,' Sir Robert went on unhappily, 'to be moulded as she wished! Yet spend what I would, it was never enough to satisfy her tastes . . .'

Thomas concealed his embarrassment. 'Sir Robert,' he began awkwardly, 'I pray you not to berate yourself. All men stray at times . . .'

'Indeed! Yet I was warned, and took no heed of it . . .' Sir Robert sagged suddenly, and looked as if he would slump to the floor. But as Thomas started forward, the knight made a dismissive gesture.

'After today, I can never show my face at Court again,' he said in a dull voice. 'Already I'm mocked – they'll make ballads about me. A country clod of a knight, who should've stayed at home in distant Berkshire, and looked to his dogs and his hawks!'

When Thomas said nothing, he went on: 'I was angry, when I returned last night, to learn how my loyalty had been in doubt. Had it not been for master Baldwin, I could be cooling my heels in the Tower at this moment . . .' He broke off. 'Now, I see how it looked. And I give thanks, for I have had a very lucky escape.'

He looked up. 'I'll not stray again, Thomas.' Then he

brightened suddenly. 'And I am in haste now, to have sight of my first grandson!'

And at that Thomas made his bow, and left the room with a lighter heart than he had had in weeks.

The rest of the day was his own. Yet so restless was he to return home, that it passed unbearably slowly. He tried to busy himself, packing his few belongings and spending time at the mews. Then in the afternoon one of the grooms came to him, and said he had been told by Giles Baldwin to take over the care of the falcons. So Thomas occupied himself in giving the man what instructions he could. At dusk they parted, and Thomas was on the point of walking to Deptford, when a voice startled him. He turned to see the slender figure of Mouka approaching him with her familiar small steps.

He was relieved, having intended to seek out the girl before he left, for he had seen nothing of her since the arrest of Lady Imogen and the others. Now he grew sombre, seeing her sad expression, unchanged from the very first. He murmured a greeting, but Mouka came forward quickly. And now he saw a look of urgency in her eyes.

'They told me you will leave tomorrow,' she said. Then before he could reply she added: 'Please – take me with you!'

Thomas blinked. 'I doubt if that's possible, mistress . . .'

'You must!' Mouka put out a hand, and scarcely knowing what he did, Thomas took it.

'Master Baldwin is kind,' she said in her soft, lilting voice. 'He says I may remain here until he finds a place for me in London, yet I cannot stay there. The city is foul and filled with noise – I loathe it!'

Thomas had nothing to say. He could only stare into Mouka's dark eyes while she tightened her grip on his hand.

Finally he said: 'I will do what I can . . .'

And at that, Mouka nodded, and the tension eased from her face. With a final squeeze of his hand, she turned and hurried back to the house.

*　*　*

The burial of Jane Derrick took place the following day, as mistress Rycroft had said it would. But on that grey morning, few folk gathered in the little churchyard to see the young woman's remains laid to rest. Thomas stood at the graveside beside Lowdy Garth. And a current of understanding passed between the old man and Thomas, each recalling the moment they had stood together on the freezing shore, at the spot where the body had fetched up. And now Lowdy seemed content, as he watched the simple casket lowered into the earth.

To Thomas's satisfaction, William Rycroft was also well enough to attend. Though he looked pale, with his arm in a sling, the constable greeted Thomas warmly, and they exchanged a few words. Mistress Rycroft was not there; instead the constable's son accompanied him, lending an arm for his father to lean on. And there was another boy, too, whom Thomas did not know; then when he saw the lad walk to Lowdy's side, he understood. The finders of Jane Derrick's body, who had stood guard over her on the shoreline that cold day, had come together again to see her buried.

The service was brief, and the white-haired parson shivered as he intoned the final words, eager to be gone. As he hurried away, the sexton came forward with his spade to throw the earth in – but the mourners did not leave. And Thomas stood among them, looking down, aware that each was busy with their own thoughts of the murdered girl. And he was content, to think that if Jane Derrick had not received full justice, then at least she was at peace.

He was turning to go – then looked round, for the matter was not quite done. All eyes were on Simon Lovett as he hurried into the churchyard, aware that he was come late. But quickly, almost furtively, the big man put a hand in his jerkin and drew out something that glittered. And meeting his gaze, Thomas gave him a little smile of understanding. Along with the rest, he watched as Simon cast Jane Derrick's necklace into the grave. It landed on the coffin with a clatter, which made the sexton blink. Then as the mourners moved away he shrugged, sank his spade into the pile of soft earth, and began to shovel it. Thomas looked back long enough to see the necklace disappear under the soil, before he too turned to go.

A short while later, he led the black gelding out of the Sayes Court stables. Sir Robert's fine new Neapolitan steed, none the worse for its recent wanderings, was already saddled. Thomas had made his farewells to Bridget and the servants, as he had to the Deptford folk: Rycroft and the Lovetts, even Sir Ralph. But in the last he was saddened, for the ark-builder seemed to have forgotten all that passed between them, as they crouched over the injured Rycroft on that bloody night of violence. His surgeon's skills, it seemed, also belonged to the past. Nothing filled his thoughts now, save that he must finish his self-appointed task.

'I did not tell you my secret, did I?' Sir Ralph had said, peering at Thomas with his bright little eyes. When Thomas merely shook his head, he gave a shout of laughter and added: 'And I never shall! Once the deluge comes, it matters not – for none shall be left to hear it!'

And Thomas had murmured his farewell and left the yard, hearing the man's hammering begin again. But Lowdy was there to help him, and Thomas saw now that he would never tell Sir Ralph the truth. His ark would not sail, but it mattered little, for Thomas read it in Lowdy's expression: the vessel would never be finished.

Now he waited until Sir Robert appeared, accompanied by Giles Baldwin and his steward, who was as stiff-necked as ever. The farewells were brief and somewhat formal, Sir Robert meeting Baldwin's eye with difficulty. But Thomas was on edge, casting one eye towards the house as Sir Robert prepared to get himself mounted. Then at last he was relieved to see Mouka appear in her cloak, carrying her few possessions in a small bundle. As she walked forward to stand beside Thomas, he turned to face Sir Robert.

'Sir,' he began, 'you said yesterday that I might ask what I would, and you would deny me nothing.'

Sir Robert froze, then stared from Thomas to Mouka and back. Baldwin, Capper and the grooms did not react.

'And what I would ask,' Thomas went on hurriedly, 'is not for myself . . .' He caught Baldwin's eye, and took encouragement from the man's expression. 'Not for myself,' Thomas repeated, 'but for mistress Mouka, who has suffered much, and needs a home . . . a place where folk are valued for their hard work. I merely thought – if master Baldwin were kind enough to agree – that she could come with us, to Petbury.'

When Sir Robert still made no reply, he added: ''Twould make it a fine Christmas for Lady Margaret, sir. She has been adamant that she wishes for a waiting-woman – one who knows when to speak, and when to keep her own counsel.'

There was a silence. Sir Robert bristled, then in embarrassment looked at Baldwin, who said at once: 'An excellent notion, sir. I am sure Mouka will be a great asset to your household. She is as quick-witted as she is wise and honest. And such qualities are to be prized above gold in this age – are they not?'

Sir Robert winced, then lowered his eyes. Finally he turned to Thomas with a helpless expression. 'But . . . how will she travel?' he asked lamely – whereupon at a gesture from Thomas, one of the grooms hurried into the stable. There was a stamping of hooves, and the man led a brown mare out on to the cobbles. The horse bore a side-saddle.

Sir Robert threw a wry look at Baldwin, who merely stared back. 'I smell a conspiracy,' Sir Robert said.

Then he sighed, and turning to Mouka, gestured to her to come forward. With a quick movement the young woman made her curtsey, then lifting her head, gave Sir Robert a grateful smile. And at that, he melted.

'See now – we've delayed long enough!' the knight muttered, and cleared his throat noisily. Stepping on to the mounting block, he swung himself into his saddle and gripped the reins.

And now it merely remained for Thomas to help Mouka climb upon her horse, then get himself mounted. And at last, with a clattering of hooves, the three of them rode out of the yard and into the lane.

Only Thomas looked back, to see Baldwin standing alone, watching them leave. Then with a brief wave of his hand, the Clerk of the Green Cloth walked away to his duties.

But there was one farewell Thomas had yet to make; though it was not one he had expected.

The day was fair, with a light breeze from the west. Thomas felt it on his face and his heart lifted, to be heading homewards at last. The little party turned out of the lane and on to the London Highway, and soon the rooftops of Sayes Court were lost to sight. All traces of the earlier snowfalls were now gone. Bare trees lined the road: elm, beech and oaks . . . Thomas's gaze wandered southwards, towards open country: then he started and gripped the rein tightly, uncertain of what he had seen. Another tiny movement caught his eye – and now he knew he was not mistaken. A figure had darted out from behind a tree, signalled to him, and disappeared again.

Sir Robert was ahead, his eyes on the road. Mouka rode in silence behind Thomas. Now he turned and bade her draw alongside. 'Stay close to Sir Robert,' he said quietly. 'There's someone I will speak with.'

The girl nodded, and Thomas urged his mount forward, to draw abreast of his master.

'Sir, if you please . . .'

Sir Robert turned sharply.

'I would like a few minutes, to ride into the trees there,' Thomas said. 'I'll catch you up anon.'

The other frowned. 'What is it?' he enquired. Then seeing Thomas was lost for a reply, he sighed.

'Nay – tell me not!' he growled. 'You're a closed book to me these days, Thomas. Were I not certain of your good nature, I'd have sent you packing long ago!'

Thomas suppressed a smile. 'You did so not long since, sir,' he reminded Sir Robert, who looked away.

'Conduct your business, and be quick about it,' the knight ordered, and shook the reins, easing his horse to a faster pace. Behind him, Mouka struggled to catch up.

But Thomas wheeled the gelding and rode swiftly off into

213

the trees. He looked about, but could see nothing. Then, when he had gone perhaps a hundred yards, there came a whistle from behind him. He drew rein and looked round – to see Ben Mallam standing there, wearing his lopsided grin.

'At last,' the jingler said, and walked forward. 'I thought I'd missed you . . . I'll have you know I've waited by this whoreson highway since sunrise. I know every bump in it now – any longer, my ears would've frozen off!'

Thomas dismounted and led the gelding towards him. Then he halted, and for a moment the two men gazed at each other. To Thomas's surprise, Mallam was looking none the worse for his recent adventures.

'I didn't expect to see you again,' Thomas said. 'Where in heaven's name have you been?'

The other grimaced. 'To Hades and back,' he said. But there was a gleam in his eye that made Thomas raise his brows.

'Let me guess,' he said. 'Your luck's truly turned, at last?'

Mallam nodded. 'That it has, master hawksman. And if you want the proof, I'll show it you!'

And beckoning Thomas to follow him, he turned and walked off, deeper into the trees. Intrigued, Thomas led the gelding down a slope, towards a clump of small beeches. He saw movement . . . and the next moment he stopped in his tracks.

Mallam had darted among the saplings, and reappeared with a long rope in his hands. Now a small grey shape came into view . . . and Thomas stiffened in amazement: the Lady Imogen's pony.

Ben was almost hopping about with excitement. ''Twas the same morning I freed you from the dairy,' he said. 'After you took off I headed for the woods . . . I tell you plain, I was a scared man, Thomas. Wasn't sure which way to run . . . thought I'd hide out here until nightfall, then make my way to Redriff . . .'

He reached out to rub the pony's neck. The animal appeared docile – which was a surprise to Thomas, for he remembered only too well his last sight of it, as it bolted from its mistress. He shook his head in disbelief at the turn of events.

'Anyway . . .' Mallam was grinning again. 'There I am, skulking like a knave, cold and hungry – when I hear hooves. And would you believe: this trim little jade gallops out of the trees, saddled and bridled but sans rider – straight into my path!'

Thomas was smiling now. 'I believe it,' he said.

'Well – but know you not what it is?' Mallam asked excitedly. 'A thoroughbred jennet in her prime, fed on the finest grain by the looks of her – not a mark upon her! Worth fifty nobles, if she's worth a penny!'

Thomas smiled at him. 'Mayhap there's justice after all,' he said. 'Your reward for what you did that day, master Ben. And I would add my heartfelt thanks, to your good fortune.'

'Consider the debt cleared,' Mallam said, with a magnanimous wave of his hand. He paused: 'And would you believe – since yesterday, the pain in my arm's gone?' As proof he raised it above his head with a smile. Thomas could only grin back.

Taking up the pony's rein Ben drew it forward, to stand close to the gelding. His grin fading, he looked the big sleek Petbury horse over. 'That's a fine mount,' he murmured. 'What do you think he's worth?'

Thomas shook his head, and threw him a wry smile. 'I must be on my way,' he said.

Mallam nodded. 'I too.' He leaned forward to take Thomas's outstretched hand. Their fists closed about each other's in a tight grip.

'Look for me in the spring,' Ben Mallam said. 'I've a mind to be at the horse fair in Wantage. We'll take a mug, and talk of our luck.'

Thomas put his foot to the stirrup, and climbed into the saddle. 'Let's do that,' he said.

Then with a wave, he urged the gelding to a canter, and rode off towards the Great West Highway.

Ben Mallam watched until he had disappeared. Then he sighed, and led his fine new pony away through the trees.